ABOUT THE A

Catherine Deveney is a multi-award-winning journalist, feature writer and novelist. For many years she worked at *Scotland on Sunday*'s *Spectrum* Magazine, conducting in-depth interviews with a wide range of subjects from Adele to Alex Salmond, Donald Trump to Deborah Mitford, serial killers to cyclists. In 2010 she made the leap to fiction, with *Ties that Bind*, followed by *Kiss the Bullet* and *Dead Secret*. Her acclaimed novels are marked by their in-depth, realistic portrayals of characters in extreme or unusual psychological states.

THE CHRYSALIS

CATHERINE DEVENEY

Published in Great Britain in 2016 by
Old Street Publishing Ltd
Yowlestone House, Devon EX16 8LN
www.oldstreetpublishing.co.uk

Paperback Original ISBN: 978-1-910400-44-9

Ebook ISBN: 978-1-910400-45-6

10 9 8 7 6 5 4 3 2 1

A CIP catalogue record for this title is available from the
British Library.

Typeset by JaM

Printed and bound by CPI Group (UK) Ltd, Croydon, CR0 4YY

For Patrick with love

CHAPTER ONE

Marianne

The night Patrice Moreau died felt like the last night of summer in Saint Estelle, the first sharp hint of autumn cutting through those lazy evenings of heat we thought would never end. I remember shivering slightly, though not only with the cold, as I stood in the shadows of the alleyway that ran from the Rue de Chèvre to the cul-de-sac where Bar Patrice stood. It was a Wednesday, the night before the bins were emptied, and the air still smelled warm and rank, the metal bins so full that the rubbish dribbled lazily, half in and half out, from open lids. In the half-light, I knocked against one and grabbed out frantically for the lid to stop it falling, but it clattered noisily onto the street and I froze.

"Merde!" I muttered. "Shit!"

I moved back against the wall and looked up to the first floor apartment above the bar. The light were full on and I saw a figure – Patrice - move to the window and glance down briefly into the street. A woman with long blonde hair moved in behind him and he smiled as she turned him round towards her. She was facing me; I saw her face quite clearly. Patrice ran his fingers down her cheek, a gesture so sensual and tender that my heart jammed with the pain of it. Then he turned back to the window and closed the wooden shutters, and only fragments of light escaped out into the street, leaving me in the darkness.

It was the end of more than summer.

A cat shot past me in the lane, upon me before I heard it, and my jangled nerves made me jump at the movement. Then I crossed the road briskly to the bar. It was almost deserted in the front bar that night but I felt the eyes of the old men swivel appraisingly as I walked in. Old goats. I hated Bar Patrice with its dismal, dust-covered orange lights and worn, scuffed tables. They are not fastidious the French. And I hated Henri, who served there, with his coarse, thick lips and his eyes like dried raisins.

"Gitânes," I said abruptly. I had stopped saying please or thank you to Henri long ago. I slapped the money down on the counter so that he would not notice the tremble in my hand, then tore the cellophane off the packet on the spot. One of the old goats stood up to light my cigarette.

"Merci," I muttered, without glance or gratitude. I could hear the dull thump of music and glanced up at the doors near the back of the bar, before looking at Henri who was watching me silently.

"Je cherche Raymond."

Henri said nothing but nodded briefly towards the back door. The clock on the peeling wall above the door said 11.16. I threw the cigarettes into my bag and walked up, barely hesitating as I turned the handle. A soft rumble of noise opened up with the door and I closed it behind me, seeing the old goats eyeing me curiously through the open doorway as I turned.

The room beyond was dimly lit, with no windows and only flickering candles and votive lights, floating in bowls of water with scattered flower petals. My eyes narrowed, trying to acclimatise to the darkness, and I became increasingly aware of the shape of pillars and the silhouette of bodies looming towards me. I hoped Patrice had come downstairs but there was no sign of him. No sign of the blonde woman. No sign of Raymond either.

"Marianne!" For a moment, above the music, I could not tell where the sound came from. "MARIANNE!"

Then I saw that it was Jasmine who called, walking unsteadily towards me, arms outstretched.

She was an exquisite creature, Jasmine, delicately boned with long dark hair and kohl-rimmed eyes so wide open they looked incapable of closing. She wore a black and white, Mary Quant-style, geometric shift dress that stopped mid-thigh, and her legs were slim and shapely.

Only when you looked more keenly at Jasmine did you notice that her shoulders were broader than you might expect, her hands bigger. Her skin was not creamy but white as lilies and something about the unnatural pallor of it, the association in my mind with funeral flowers, made me a little uneasy round her. And of course there was our history.

"Marianne," she said softly, stroking my back much too intimately for me to be comfortable. I shifted slightly.

"Have you seen Raymond?"

Jasmine shrugged and waved her hand.

"Somewhere. He disappeared."

I could smell the alcohol from her, see the sleepy, sexy haze it produced in her eyes.

"Never mind him," she said, linking her arm through mine and wrapping herself around me. "Come and have a drink."

I did not know why I had this effect on Jasmine. It was not something I was used to. I have never been what you would call a beautiful woman. My life has not been oiled by good looks and so I found other ways to get what I wanted. Women like me have to fight for everything. My face was always too odd, eccentric even, to be pretty; my broad, mobile gash of mouth almost too wide for my face. As for my eyes, I suppose they were nice enough in their way - dark and lively, I am told - but too small and deep set to be truly attractive.

There was a time, a brief blossoming, when youth was on my side and lit my face kindly, gave a creamy lustre to my skin and a distinctive, quirky beauty to my lopsided looks. I grew into myself. It lasted perhaps ten years, in my late teens and twenties, the most powerful period of my life. That was when I met Raymond. But age somehow happened quickly, re-arranging my cheekbones almost overnight into a strangely angular assortment of peaks, while my cheeks collapsed into squashed hillocks. I had to become cleverer to get what I wanted. Or keep it.

At this time, when Jasmine accosted me on the dance floor, I was perhaps in my thirties. I was already past the winter of my blossoming, yet she was still drawn to me for reasons I could not fathom. For some reason, I intrigued her. Anyway, this night she swayed slightly against me, murmuring close to my ear, and trying to encourage me to dance with her. I felt the old claustrophobic fear of the place settle round me and my eyes darted round, still hoping to see Raymond emerge from a dark corner... yet somehow knowing I would not.

The seductive wail of a saxophone had drawn several bizarre couples onto the tiny dance floor. Right in the middle was Mel and his partner. Mel was a raging queen from Essex, usually referred to as Melanie, who had a purple feather boa wrapped around his scrawny neck and clung with what was, quite honestly, distasteful fervour to a butch Frenchman with Popeye biceps.

Then, on the left corner by the pillar, was the Parisian manager of a bank in town, a fat, slug-like creature who dressed in stockings, suspenders and the kind of short skirt that the sixties had tried to make acceptable but never could. Or perhaps I simply disapproved of miniskirts because I was jealous that my legs were not like Jasmine's. Nor were the bank manager's, come to that. I was relieved now that midi and maxi lengths had become fashionable, choosing to hide myself beneath their flowing lines. In any case, the bank manager I speak of was middle-class trash, a man who perspired a lot and left his trail of slime over a bored looking youth with a special overdraft arrangement. How I hated Bar Patrice and its sordid little secrets.

In my anger, I shrugged Jasmine off when she tried coaxing me forward and she stumbled in surprise. Jasmine looked at me reproachfully. We had history together, though not as much as she would have liked. For a while, Raymond had tried to assuage his own guilt by pushing me towards her. In a desperate search for liberation from my feelings for him, I kissed her once. She was James then, not Jasmine, and the rough stubble of unshaven cheek had irritated my skin. James was a good-looking man, but Jasmine was an even more beautiful woman. Her average height as a man became strikingly tall and willowy when she switched gender, and she developed a presence that her masculinity had simply swallowed up. But I was not interested in James and was even less so in Jasmine. I was heterosexual but that was not the reason; the reason was that I was never interested in anyone but Raymond. Never could be.

"I am still the same person," Jasmine said bitterly, as I walked away. "The same person," she yelled suddenly at my back, and her voice held deep pain and a hint of despair. She thought I hated her. She did not understand how much I feared her.

Bar Patrice, as I saw it, was a refuge for misfits and deviants. (You should not, by the way, assume 'deviant' to be a term of disapproval. These people did, literally, deviate from the norm and as a lawyer, I am comfortable using analytical terminology. It is true I did not like most of them, but I like to use language correctly.) They were not all beautiful as Raymond was. Men dressed – badly on the whole – as women; women dressed as men; transvestites, transsexuals, gays, lesbians, bisexuals… Their proclivities were different but they herded together in their sense of otherness. It was a place of safety for lonely and confused people who were liable to come out of an ordinary bar with a glass embedded in their skull. To Raymond, visiting Bar Patrice felt safe and secure. For him, it was like coming home.

The front bar was ordinary enough. Entrance to the back room, to the secret heart of Patrice's underworld, was carefully selected. Raymond and I had been popping into the front bar for some time before Patrice spoke to him. I had gone to the farmer's market to buy some bread and cheeses for a light lunch and arranged with Raymond to meet him at Patrice's for an espresso. When I came in, I noticed immediately that there was something very intimate about the way he and Patrice were sitting, their heads almost touching. Patrice was murmuring something in a low voice and smiling at Raymond like he was the only person in the world. Such a thing was never going to escape my attention.

Patrice had fewer boundaries than any other person I have ever met. There was an amoral quality to him. He was certainly very handsome - in that French kind of way. A soupçon too much oil, if you ask me. His smile had something of the hungry crocodile about it, but I could see that Raymond was very taken with him. Raymond tended to like masculine men. Men with broad shoulders and some metaphorical dirt in their fingernails. Patrice, on the other hand, liked butch men and queens, straight women and dykes. Anyone, in other words. But he did not like me. The feeling was mutual.

As I approached the table, Patrice stood up immediately and took his farewells.

"Madame," he said politely, inclining his head towards me before disappearing through the back.

Hard to believe but it grew - all of it - from there.

Chapter Two

Patrice Moreau died like a pig with its throat slit. His blood seeped from him, dripping through the floor of his apartment onto the ceiling of Bar Patrice, forming a mysterious dark, damp circle. Forensic evidence suggested he died sometime between midnight and 2am. His door had been left wide open with no sign of forced entry. It was mid-morning the next day before Henri noticed and went to investigate the damp patch. According to what I heard, moments after he disappeared there was the loud thump of a door slamming on the floor above, the sound of Henri's heavy footsteps running on the stairs, and then he burst back into the bar, white-faced and shaking. I almost wish I'd been there to see the implacable Henri shaken from the certainties of his narrow little existence.

Raymond and I stayed away from Bar Patrice for the next few days, an uneasy silence growing between us that never completely disappeared in the years that followed. We had our own flat in town, a light, airy, first floor apartment above a boulangerie and pâtisserie that scented our apartment with heady wafts of warm dough and caramelised sugar, baked apple and cinnamon, and rich, dark Belgian chocolate. I bought our bread there, and cakes, and sometimes for a treat, little cellophane twists of dark chocolate truffles tied with pink or lilac ribbon. I like things to be nice.

The apartment was beautiful. It was so warm in the south that our windows were always open during the day, the light voile curtains fluttering over polished golden floorboards, patterned by shadows and shafts of wavering sunlight. If it had been anywhere else, I would have loved it unconditionally. But part of me hated that place to which Raymond gravitated like a homing pigeon. One week in spring, two in late summer, and a week in autumn, without fail - and whatever other impromptu trips we could manage. This place was the price I paid for keeping Raymond. It was a high price.

Everyone in town was shocked at Patrice's death. Things went quiet, though there was plenty of hushed whispering. No comings and goings from the bar. At first, locals had drifted in ghoulishly, on the pretext of offering sympathy to Patrice's wife and family, and also to Henri, but really straining to see the mark on the ceiling. The entrance to Patrice's flat was quite separate from the bar, so the gendarmes had no objection to the bar staying open – frankly they were a little slack in a small town like ours – but after two days, Henri simply closed up and the shutters remained firmly locked.

Raymond and I did not address the issues much. The atmosphere was strained.

"Where were you that night?" I said eventually, after a full day of near silence.

Raymond looked at me incredulously.

"Where?"

"Yes, where?"

He turned from me.

"You know where I was."

9

Yes but earlier. I was looking for you."

"Looking?"

"I am always looking for you."

He crossed to the window and I watched him from behind as he leaned against the frame and watched the movement in the street below.

"You never said you were going but I knew," I persisted.

"If you know where I was, why did you ask?"

"I wanted to know if you would lie."

Raymond did not reply.

"Why didn't you say where you were going? You know I can't stand it when you sneak around."

There was an almost imperceptible movement of Raymond's shoulders, a tiny slump. I could tell he was upset. I can always tell.

"I know it makes you unhappy," he said. "*I* make you unhappy."

"You are all I've got."

A horn blared through the open window from the street, then a torrent of angry French drifted upwards. I crossed the room to stand beside Raymond and look down on the scene below: some altercation over a parked car that was blocking the street. They are so dramatic, the French, with their huffing and puffing and grand gestures. I turned, impatiently. I prefer things on a smaller, more British scale.

"The gendarmes are making inquiries, door to door," Raymond said. He glanced round at me. "They will come here."

"I saw Patrice."

Raymond blinked.

"The night he died. I saw him at the window. I was outside the bar."

I held Raymond's eyes as he watched me silently.

"He was with a woman. A woman with long blonde hair. Perhaps I should say…"

I could hear the ticking of the kitchen clock through the open door.

"A woman," he said.

"Yes, a woman."

"You should tell the police," he said finally. "Tell them what you saw."

He walked to the kitchen and I heard the rush of water in the kettle.

"Yes," I said, though he was no longer in the room. "I will tell them."

Raymond and I sat a little stiffly, side by side, when the Gendarmes arrived. We were not familiar with their ways because they were not like our police. Not thorough, not painstaking. Without our eagle eye for detail. One of them actually smoked in our house, in uniform. Even as a smoker myself, I found that unprofessional. I would not blow smoke over any of my clients. But I simply smiled and ingratiatingly offered them coffee and a Gitâne - which of course, they accepted.

To them, we were simply foreigners and therefore of little use. What could we know about local goings-on? The French are so intolerant of anyone who does not speak their language. Non, they shrugged when I asked if they spoke English. They did not. In fact I understood more of what they asked than I let on; my French is not that bad. "Pardon," I said politely, over and over, when I did not want to answer, "Je ne comprends pas." It was too difficult for them to communicate, so they drank their espresso and smoked their cigarettes and were content to take a little rest from the grind in the pleasant apartment of the English holidaymakers.

One thing, I said, eventually, in halting French. I saw Patrice Moreau very briefly the night he died. I had gone to the bar to buy cigarettes – obviously, I said nothing about looking for Raymond – and I had seen Patrice at the window. They listened with casual interest as I stumbled through the faltering explanation.

"A blonde woman," I said, looking at Raymond as if searching for his help with the French words. "How do they say?" I looked questioningly at the gendarme who seemed to be in charge, a long-faced man with an unhealthy grey pallor to his complexion. "Une femme blonde?" I said questioningly.

The policeman raised his eyes in slight surprise but showed little more emotion than that at this possibly crucial snippet.

"Quelle heure?" he said.

I shrugged. "Onze… ou onze heures et demie?"

"What colour is Moreau's wife's hair?" I heard him ask his companion in French.

The other shrugged.

"I don't know just now. She dyes it different colours, I think. It was blonde once but it might be auburn now."

"Trying to keep up with his desire for change!"

"One is never enough."

"Certainly not for Moreau!"

They both smiled wryly, scribbled some notes carelessly, but seemed little concerned, unfurling themselves from the depths of my sofa soon after, and leaving. Raymond moved behind the curtains and looked out as they walked down the road to their car. I watched him from my seat, thinking how beautiful he was as a man compared to how I was as a woman. Thick black hair and broad shoulders and soft dark eyes that could express so many delicate nuances. I knew how anguished he felt inside, how turbulent these days had been for him. How much he grieved inside. I looked at him, standing there in that perfect light against fluttering voile and knew how broken he was, and how much I loved him. I would do anything for him.

For the next two days, I waited impatiently for our flights home, roaming the flat, putting things in order. I could not wait to be gone, but even in the present circumstances I think Raymond was sad as we locked up the apartment. He always left part of himself behind in this little town when we went home. He always said he was most truly himself here. This time, as he locked the door he must have feared that it was for the last time, that we would never unlock it again.

We had not told the gendarmes we were going. Why should we? They didn't ask les Anglais about their plans. We took a taxi in the early morning, trundling down cobbled back streets in the rising light of a new day. At the airport, we walked past a news stand. Raymond turned slightly as we went by. "LA FEMME BLONDE," it said, and his eyes met mine briefly.

I felt my heart beat faster as the aeroplane engines throbbed on the runway. Now, now, now, I thought. Take off. Fly away. Raymond's eyes were closed beside me, consumed by the loss of leaving, but I peered through the window, a last glimpse of the south of France. When I think back, it is the light I remember most, the watercolour light of a sweat-drenched landscape, an insipid sky running into hard, baked earth. The plane lurched forward suddenly, quickly building up speed, the subdued colours rolling into one another through the window, burnt orange and terracotta, cream and grey blue. Faster and faster. Then the nose of the plane lifted, and my heart lifted with it, and suddenly I was weightless, floating, the plane tilting, rising steeply into a sky that seemed to shimmer with heat haze. I looked sideways and Raymond's eyes were closed still, his head tilted back. I might have thought he slept, were it not for a single tear that trickled from the corner of his eye and ran unabated into his hairline.

We were gone, gone, gone, and never coming back. And we would never be the same again.

CHAPTER THREE

It is all so real when I recall those events in the south of France. As if it happened yesterday. I live for memories now. I cannot create new ones of any value so I run the mental videotapes of old ones. I am young. Raymond is by my side. I do not try to block out the terrible events of Saint Estelle. How could I? They shaped my life. But at least it WAS a life. It was never dull as it is now.

The view from my window is of the care home's back garden. It is a big, bay window, and most days I sit my chair in the light, the soft English light, and look out at the pink rhododendron bush in the corner, and the green woodland beyond, the rich greenery of trees filling the horizon. So green and lush compared to the south of France.

Sometimes, I play my music as I sit, let it fill the space between me and the past. "A cigarette that bears a lipstick's traces…" How I would love a Gitâne again! The events of yesterday are a little hazy but the events of long ago are crystal clear. "An airline ticket to romantic places…" My fingers tap on the chair. The heat, the dust, the passion I felt.

It was the early autumn of 1968 when we left France that last time, a remarkable year for us but also for France - and indeed,

15

the rest of the world. It was the year Kennedy was assassinated, and Martin Luther King. The year of riots in Peking and Mexico and Chicago and Berlin and Warsaw and Prague. That spring, before we arrived for the summer, had seen the heady days of student riots in Paris with barricades all over the Left Bank. Upturned cars, wheels spinning to the sky, were strewn across the roads, stranded like beetles that had been tossed on their backs.

It was a cultural revolution that heralded the end of the de Gaulle era, the finale of thirty years of booming post-war prosperity in France, but it was not the politics that excited Raymond as he listened eagerly to reports about the rebellion, while the blossom rained down from the cherry trees in our small and very English village that May. The village I have somehow always returned to, despite the fact that sometimes I felt claustrophobic within its benign confines and found myself longing for distant horizons.

No, it was because 1968 was the year after the San Francisco flower power revolution and young Parisians were challenging the conservative status quo – as indeed they did all over Europe and America – to demand increasing sexual freedom. Students wanted the right to have partners sleep over in halls of residence and it was that spirit of liberalism that so excited Raymond. That summer, he could not wait to get to France. He watched, mesmerised, as 8 million French workers joined the students in rebellion, creating the biggest industrial unrest in French history. The old certainties of society as we knew it were crumbling and Raymond wanted to stand in the rubble. But six weeks later, long before we even left for our summer break in Saint Estelle, it was all over. The workers had returned to the factories and the students were on holiday. The effects, though, lasted longer. Much longer.

How many years have passed since then? Thirty? Forty? More? However long it is, I can conjure those times, those emotions, inside me at will. They never abate completely. I live them over and over, swapping today's reality for yesterday's. I turn them down at times, like a volume switch, but the melody is there in the background, always.

Outside, some of the pink blooms from the rhododendron bush have fallen to the grass. The summer is flying past. The time of year we would have begun planning our trip, booking our flights. "These foolish things remind me of you."

"A wee cup of tea, Marie?" The trolley trundles into the room.

My name is Marianne.

"A wee cup of tea, pet?"

I do not look at her, but shake my head. They do not expect me to speak. They shout, as though I am deaf or senile. I let them think it. It suits me. They leave me to my own thoughts which is the way I prefer it.

"Not want one, Marianne?"

I turn in the direction of the voice and smile as Zac bends down at the side of my chair.

Zac is my favourite nurse, the only one in here I have any time for. He lives in a small town close to here, the town where my law practice used to be, but his mother, he has told me, is French, with a mixture of French and Spanish blood on her side of the family. With his dark hair and eyes, Zac has inherited more of the Spanish look of his maternal grandmother than the French side.

Our mutual interest in France has led to many conversations between us over the last couple of years about French ways and customs. Zac's French is, like mine, good rather than perfect but we amuse ourselves sometimes by holding conversations over what we laughingly call café au lait - cheap instant granules from the cash-and-carry mixed with powdered milk that ends up look-ing like dirty water from the washing up bowl - and speaking in French so that nobody else understands.

"Pâtisserie?" Zac will say, handing me a dry digestive.

"Merci, monsieur," I reply graciously.

It is our secret world.

The plane touches down in light, grey rain after we leave the south of France that last time. There is a feeling in me of reach-ing a place of safety, the other side of the barrier. I like the feel-ing of the rain because it is *here* - not *there* - and my spirits lift a little. Raymond sits silently in the taxi, brooding. A light has gone out in him that I know will never switch on again. If I am honest, I am glad of that. It makes him more docile. Before, he was like a bird fluttering against the wire cage. I was too scared ever to leave the door open. Now he will sit on the perch and swing, per-haps mournfully but at least without actively trying to escape. He will content himself to ring the cage bell, and watch his reflec-tion in the mirror, and splash a little in the water bath. And I will feed him and water him and stroke his feathers and admire him.

Such beautiful coloured feathers.

"I will look after you," I say, when we reach the house.

"I do not want to speak about it. Not ever."

"We won't."

It is a pact. Our pact.

"The police will not come here." I hold him, feel the smooth, muscular line of his back beneath his shirt. He is strong, Raymond. But there is something else, a flutter of emotion that ripples through his body. I rub my hands gently up and down his back, soothing him.

"There is no need to feel fear," I whisper. "I will not let them get to you."

Zac has taken my hand. I look down at his young fingers curling round my old hand and wonder how one turns into the other, when it was that my veins first began to stand out so prominently. Zac's hands are soft, the blood pulsing strong and warm. He must be early twenties, certainly no more than 25. My skin is thin, tears like paper, as though it is not strong enough anymore to contain what bursts from beneath. I hold his hand in mine and look out at the swaying branches of the trees.

"What do you think, Marie?" says the woman. "There's some biscuits too."

There *are* some biscuits, she means. Ignoramus. She is shouting. I glance briefly at her sorry assortment of pink wafers and digestives and turn back to the window without answering. That scent in the apartment stairway. Remember? Young legs that took the stairs two at a time. Running from Raymond, laughing. Cardboard boxes and paper ribbon. Tarte au citron, sweet and tangy, crumbling pastry rich with butter. Éclairs chocolat. Croissant aux amandes oozing warm marzipan. My mouth waters at the memory. Zac squeezes my fingers gently then lets go. I look down at my hands. Ordinary hands that did ordinary things. That's the thing about life. Being ordinary does not prevent you from being caught up in extraordinary things.

"I will come back when I can," Zac says.

"You are wasting your time with her," the other one mutters, pushing the trolley from the room. It is all the insight you can expect from a woman who peddles pink wafers for a living.

I dream of Raymond still. His lips on mine. The smell of his hair, the taste of his skin, the heat of us together when we first met. The sight of bottles of French aftershave glowing amber on the glass shelf above the sink in the bathroom, the scent lingering in the air after he had showered there in the morning. It is a mistake to think old age and passion are mutually exclusive. Sometimes I wake and reach for him automatically, hungrily, as if he is still here, as eager for him as I was when I was 30. My hand reaches out to touch the warmth of him and I feel only the cold sheet, and I remember. And then I ache.

When we returned from France, he shut himself away for hours on end in his art studio. I would stand outside, wondering whether to interrupt him, hearing the music from the radio drifting into the hall. 'Hey Jude' dominated the chart for months that autumn and I listened to McCartney's nasal whine on the other side of the door.

"The minute you let her under your skin,

Then you begin, to make it better."

I never heard any movement from inside, though sometimes I heard Raymond sing softly.

"Remember to let her into your heart,

Then you can start, to make it better."

I had the strong feeling that he was not painting, but simply escaping.

Let me in, I'd think, standing alone in the hall. Let me in.

"Pardon?"

Oh. I have said it aloud, not just in my memory. "Let me in." I look up into Zac's dark eyes.

"Pardon?" he repeats.

I wave my hand. Nothing.

"There is to be a sing-song downstairs. A group of musicians. Would you like to come down?"

20

"No, I would not," I say crossly.

Zac smiles.

"Sure?"

"Very."

"A walk then?"

"Yes, a walk."

"In a little while."

"Why not now?"

Zac smiles.

"So impatient!" he scolds gently. "I need to take some of the others downstairs before I can escape outside for a few minutes. When they're having the sing-song."

I say nothing. A breeze is stirring the pink rhododendrons, rippling through the blooms, the petals raining down softly on the lawn.

Zac's hand pats my shoulder.

"We will escape together," he whispers, and though I do not respond, I smile a little inside.

———

What is it about Zac?

I do not know, I told myself for the first year that I knew him, while all the while my brain screamed, "You do, you do!" The instinct about him was there from the start but I only acknowledged it gradually.

He fastens my scarf carefully around my neck, a soft, lilac cashmere with a hint of creamy check.

"It is so soft," he says, "such a pretty colour."

"You always notice colours, textures," I say. "Unusual in a man."

He blushes.

"You have a good eye for clothes."

"My father doesn't think so!" Zac smiles lightly.

"You remind me of someone," I say, watching his face closely. Zac's features are very feminine, full of delicate arches and graceful precision.

"Do I?"

He is not really paying attention. Old people's words, like children's, are to be humoured rather than engaged with. I won't say any more.

His hands still for a moment, as if he understands that I have retreated.

"Who?" he says.

"Who, what?" I retort, as if I do not understand.

Zac does not challenge my moods. He wheels my chair to the outer doors which spring open as we approach. The air is not cold exactly, but it rushes towards me, and after the suffocating heat of the home, it feels fresh. It finds the gaps at my neck and I pull the scarf tighter and fasten the top button of my jacket clumsily. Zac pushes my chair down the path to the bench by the rhododendron bushes.

"Do you want to stand?" he says. "A few steps?"

I nod.

He takes my arm and hauls me up, his youthful strength easily overcoming my infirmity. How I envy him.

"I've got you," he says.

I lean on him, tottering slowly for a few steps before finding my balance. He is surprisingly strong. I look around.

"Escape," I say.

He looks at me, almost as an equal this time, and grins.

"Escape," he agrees. He inclines his head towards the bench. "Shall we?"

I nod.

"So who do I remind you of?" he asks as he helps me lower myself gingerly onto the bench.

"Raymond. My husband." Zac has black hair and soft dark eyes, just like Raymond had.

"Oh that's nice, Marianne. Thank you. I know how much Raymond meant to you."

Zac's black swept fringe is falling into one of his eyes a little. These modern haircuts. Very arty. Androgynous. But very annoying, I would think, to have your hair constantly falling into your eyes like that.

"How do you get those on?" I ask, pointing to his feet.

"My shoes?"

"No, the jeans. The holes don't look big enough to get your feet through."

He laughs.

"They are called skinny jeans, Marianne."

"Skinny all right," I say. I look up at him. "Lanky long legs."

We both smile.

"Raymond used to wear shoes with pointed toes like that."

"Is that why I remind you of him?"

"Oh no."

My answer is so definite, so piercing, that I can see it unnerves him. He doesn't want to ask.

"You have a girlfriend?"

"Yes."

"Hm."

"What do you mean, 'hm'?"

Zac does not look at me.

"What's her name?"

"Abbie."

"What does she look like?"

He shrugs.

"Pretty."

"Yes, she would be."

Zac says nothing.

"Blonde?"

"Yes."

I laugh softly. Trophy femininity.

"Blue eyes?"

"Yes."

Zac bends down to the path and picks up a pink bloom that has been blown from the bushes.

"Are you happy?"

I can feel his discomfort.

"Yes! Well, sometimes. Who is happy all the time?" he says, pulling the petals from the bloom and dropping them onto the path.

He refuses to look at me.

Raymond would have said the same.

"Why do I remind you of your husband, then?" he says. "If it's not the shoes…"

"You transmit something."

Zac's face infuses suddenly with colour, pink as the rhododendron blossoms.

"What?"

"I don't know. But I recognise it."

He glances sharply at me.

"You have eyes like an eagle," he says, almost accusingly.

He is not talking to me like an old lady now. I feel a rush of satisfaction, as if for a moment I really have escaped.

"Are you frightened of me?"

"Should I be?"

"Probably."

"Why?"

"Because I know you better than you know yourself."

Zac exhales audibly, as if he's been winded.

"I doubt it," he says, trying to retain control.

"It's the consolation of old age," I say. "Don't grudge me it."

Another gust of wind, cooler this time, ripples over us and I shiver.

"Let's go in," I say. "But keep me away from the bloody crow's choir."

Chapter Four

Zac

Zac stares into the dark, eyes wide open. He cannot sleep. Sometimes, it gets this way when he cannot stop memories, feelings, sensations bombarding him. A good day is when he falls asleep instantly, preferably before Abbie has come to bed. He turns from his back onto his side and Abbie stirs, flipping over in her sleep and curling into his back. He listens intently but her breathing steadies. The duvet feels suffocating and he uses his toes to lift it gently back and create a draught over himself. Like the breeze in the garden today. He closes his eyes trying to rid himself of the way the old woman looked at him. The way she saw through him. It always feels like Marianne sees through him.

The dress. He sees the dress again. He hates this memory, but loves it too. He gets the same kick of adrenaline every time, a rush of excitement and fear. Sometimes just the memory makes him tremble and a wave of heat breaks over him. A narrow escape. A liberation. A death. A birth. An awakening.

Silk. It was peach silk. His sister Elicia was to be a bridesmaid and the dress hung on the outside door of her wardrobe because it was too long for the inside; the hem would get crushed inside. It had a plastic covering over it and when he first unzipped it, top to bottom, it was only to run his hand over the cool softness of it. He imagined, then, what it would feel like to wear such soft fabric next to your skin.

It wasn't deliberate. Not really. The door to Elicia's room had been half open. He passed by, saw the light hitting the dress so that the colour looked alive, luminous. The house was empty save for him and he hesitated out there on the landing. The floor-boards creaked. His senses were so heightened, so alive with possibilities, that the creak made him jump. He laughed nervously at himself, pushed open the door a little more. Peach, silk, light, softness… it was seductive. He stood for a full minute trying to work out what this was that he was feeling.

He had taken a step into the room. The noise of the zip on the protective cover seemed loud in the stillness. Only a few inches at first, just enough to access the shoulder of it, run his fingers over the fabric. The neckline was studded with small creamy flowers with peachy inner petals. He wanted, instead, to run his fingers over the full length of the satin skirt so he ran the zip right to the bottom. What would it be like to wear such a thing next to your skin, he wondered. The thought that he might find out, that he might lift out the dress and try it on, was suppressed at first. It was a betrayal to creep into Alicia's room this way, he thought shamefacedly.

But perhaps she wouldn't mind, he thought then. He tried out that thought, examining it. Certainly she would mind her fifteen year old brother wearing a girl's dress. Everybody minds that. But in terms of him, Zac, wearing something of hers… no, that she would not mind, he thought. They were close, after all. It made the betrayal seem less. There was only one aspect to it then. The idea that as a boy, he should not wear a girl's dress. And she would never know that, would she?

His heart was hammering as he carefully lifted the dress out, held it up against himself to look in the wardrobe mirror. The peach colour was flattering even for a boy, he realised. It lit his face, made his skin seem creamier and brighter. But what would the silk feel like if he put it on properly? He had slipped his jeans and tee-shirt off, kicking them over towards the door. The petticoat of the dress rustled coolly under the silk as he removed it from the cover. God, what if he marked it? If the zip got stuck? For a moment he imagined the shame of being caught and hesitated, but he had come too far. He stepped into the skirt quickly before he could change his mind and pulled the bodice up to his shoulders. It wrinkled over his flat chest but he did not dare try to zip it.

He looked in the mirror. It felt wonderful the way the full skirt hung, swung, moved with him. His eyes were on the dress until he suddenly caught sight of his face, black eyes shining back at him, lit from within. He almost didn't recognise himself. A little gasp of a laugh exploded from deep inside him. What would it be like to wear high heels with this dress, to walk regally, to feel eyes on you? His feet were too big to wear Elicia's shoes. But he walked in front of the mirror on his tiptoes, felt the sway of the fabric. He swirled round, as if dancing, felt a burst of happiness explode inside him, the way sherbet explodes on your tongue, sweet and sharp and tingling, full of fizz.

There was a lipstick on the dressing table. He lifted it, opened it, gazed at it. It was a burnt orange colour and in a sudden rush before he changed his mind, he painted the outline of his lips, a little shakily, before placing it carefully back in the exact spot from which he'd lifted it. The pearlised texture felt strange on his lips and he ran his tongue over them. It was extraordinary the way the lipstick made him feel. On the one hand it felt a little alien and uncomfortable, heavy and sticky like jam, and yet, on the other it made him feel provocative, smouldering. He narrowed his eyes as he looked in the mirror, softening his outline, trying to see only a female form looking back. He realised suddenly how alive he felt and he swirled away from the mirror in a sudden surge of euphoria.

Mid swirl, Zac froze suddenly. The crunch of wheels on gravel. Shit. Heart thumping, he dived to the side of the window and squinted out, pulling his arms out of the bodice of the dress as he did so. His parents and Elicia were home. He ran to the bed, falling against it in his haste to step out of the dress. A car door slammed. Footsteps on the path. Fingers trembling, he pulled the dress over the hanger and did up the zip. There was a key in the lock now, voices. Shit, shit, shit! The dress was twisting in the plastic cover.

"Zac?"

The voice rose up the stairwell.

Zac clunked the hanger over the wardrobe door in panic and ran to the door sweeping up his jeans and tee shirt in his hand.

"Zac? Are you home?"

Clutching his clothes, Zac ran towards the bathroom.

"I'll be down in a minute," he shouted, and slammed the door of the bathroom behind him. He leant his back against the door and breathed deeply.

He heard footsteps running on the stairs. Elicia. She went into her room but quickly came out again.

"Hey Zac!"

His heart thumped.

"What?"

"Result. Persuaded the old dears to bring in a takeaway."

"Nice one, sis."

"And the Brit Awards are starting in five minutes. Hurry up!"

"Cool."

Zac sat on the edge of the bath and put his face in his hands, suddenly overwhelmed. What was that all about? So close. He would never do it again. Never. What had made him do such a crazy thing in the first place? He stepped into his jeans, put on his tee-shirt and as he unlocked the door, turned to check in the mirror.

"Shit!" he said aloud and pulled the lock back quickly.

He had forgotten the lipstick. His lips looked grotesque to him now, like a drag queen's. He was foolish, ugly.

"C'mon Zac!" shouted Elicia, disappearing downstairs again.

He heard the thump as she jumped the bottom few stairs. Elicia always made the house alive with her noise and her energy. She made the veneer of normality that hid their dysfunction seem thicker, more cushioned. The thought surprised him as soon as it came into his head. Dysfunction? Were they really a dysfunctional family? From the outside they looked pretty normal, successful even. Two parents who owned their own home and weren't divorced. A father who was a policeman and a coach for the local boys' football team, and a mother who devoted herself to her family. Then there was Elicia, who was pretty and lively. Everyone loved her. Wasn't that 'normal'?

So what *was* their family's dysfunction? Zac asked himself. Well of course it was him. Zac was the reason his father mooched morosely through life, silent and surly, spilling beads of disappointment or disapproval constantly as he went. That, in turn, was the reason his mother was in a permanent spiral of anxiety which annoyed his father more. Conchetta's desire to make everyone happy, instead of simply her husband, made his father feel unsupported. His father, he suspected, wanted her to take a hard line with their son, 'stamp out' Zac's silly, 'soft' ways.

Zac grabbed a piece of toilet paper and scrubbed at his lips in disgust, so hard it hurt. Turning on the tap, he threw cold water over his face before chucking the paper into the toilet. The water rushed, and he watched the orange stained tissue swirl into the vortex before disappearing. He had to make sure it had really gone and he stood staring into the toilet, overcome by a sudden rush of deep self-loathing.

—◦—

Zac turned his face into the pillow at the memory. Of course, he had done it again but that first time was sharpest in his memory. There was always a trigger. The next time, it had been his mother's tights in the washing basket, sheer evening tights with a light sheen. There was invariably something sensuous as well as sensual about these secret episodes, something to do with light and colour and texture, the feeling on his skin and then the feeling in his soul when he looked in the mirror. A simultaneous experience of fear and of peace. He could look in the mirror and see a strange hybrid creature looking back at him with scarlet lips, and dark manly hairs sticking through sheer stockings on his legs, and he would feel ugly and beautiful at the same time. But the most important thing was that he felt more strongly himself, more closely 'Zac,' than at any other time in his life.

The pattern was always the same. Temptation, resistance, submission, euphoria, guilt, self-loathing. Temptation, resistance, submission, euphoria, guilt, self-loathing. Round and round and round…

In her sleep, Abbie wrapped her leg round him and it felt like a chain. He longed to disentangle himself. In every way, really. To be free. To be Zac again. It was building into a pressure that he felt would one day explode inside him. He had tried to put it behind him, to tell himself that those old experiences were just normal, adolescent experimentation. They were in the past. But he found himself running his hands over Abbie's things when she wasn't there. He turned in bed to look at her face. Even scrubbed of make-up, she was lovely. Short, ditzy blonde curls. A pert little nose and full, cupid's bow mouth. Her long lashes quivered momentarily and then her eyelids opened.

"Hello," she said, smiling sleepily. "Are you watching me?"

"Go back to sleep," murmured Zac, and he reached out a finger and closed her eyelids gently, like blinds. He leant forward and kissed her head and her breathing quickly steadied into a sleeping pattern.

He cared about her, he really did.

Face the truth, a voice inside his head urged.

He closed his eyes as if closing them would make the voice stop.

Face it.

He ran a finger down her cheek. Her skin was so soft, childlike almost. He loved her but he suspected not in the way he should. It felt almost like the way he loved Elicia. That wasn't enough. Not enough for him and not enough for Abbie. He looked at her face in repose and felt a stab of guilt. Abbie was a way of conforming, of pretending that everything was all right. That HE was all right. But he wasn't. And she couldn't make him all right.

He was just using her.

He remembered his father's reaction when he first brought her home. His shock. The glimmer of relief that perhaps his son with the silly, floppy hair and the gentle manner was a chip off the old block after all. It had all been worth it for that look. Then there was the way his father had looked at Abbie. She had walked over to shake hands with Conchetta and he caught a fleeting glance from his father at her retreating figure. A flick of the eyes. My God, his father was watching his girlfriend's ass! Zac felt torn between discomfort and amusement. He hoped Conchetta hadn't noticed.

"Do you want a beer?" his father had asked and a bubble of laughter rose in Zac's throat. His father never offered him beer. The grudging respect in the tone held the promise of something he had looked for all his life but which had never quite arrived: acceptance if not approval. It had once seemed unachievable but perhaps he could be a proper man after all. Strange, Zac mused, how he didn't need to *like* his father to want his approval.

Conchetta loved him unreservedly. He had no doubt of that. He didn't even need to try. But that look that his father had given him when he saw Abbie, that thin, delicate thread of *something,* felt so very hard to give up.

CHAPTER FIVE

Marianne

Raymond was quiet for a long time after we returned from France. There was no outlet for him anymore, I understood that. I was foolishly glad that Saint Estelle was behind us – as if no outlet meant 'it' would not come out. How stupid I was!

Raymond returned to the school where he taught art but this time, he did not have his French trip to look forward to in the autumn break, as he would normally have had.

"You can do this?" I asked him one day. I did not even have to explain what "this" was.

He shrugged.

"I have no choice."

"I can be enough for you?"

He smiled, a little sadly I thought, and opened his arms to me. I walked into them and buried my head in his shoulder.

He did not say yes, though. He did not say, "Yes Marianne, you can be enough."

"Everything that has happened," he murmured against my head. "It is my fault."

I did not contradict him, not least because I knew that the guilt he felt tied him to me. As long as he felt it, he would remain in his cage.

After a few months, I talked to him about selling our flat in France. I made the mistake of doing it in his studio when he was working.

"No," he said flatly.

"Raymond, we cannot go back there."

"For God's sake Marianne, I know that!" he said, and he lashed out with his closed fist so violently that he swept everything from his desk: tubes of paint and brushes and pencils and notepads. A final paper fluttered down in the ensuing silence. His venom shocked me. Fury was so out of character.

"Don't you think I know that?" he repeated quietly, bitterly. "Don't you?"

I looked at the debris on the floor.

"I'm sorry," he muttered.

"We all get angry," I said.

His eyes flashed darkly at me.

"Yes."

"What is the point of keeping the flat?" I asked.

He leant his head forward into his hands, fingers gripping his dark hair. I sensed that the anger and despair were caused by me rather than simply the situation.

"I am not ready," he said.

He would never be ready, I realised. I knew he felt as if selling the flat would be selling himself. It would be acknowledging that life was over, that Patrice was gone, that he would never find peace. There were moments, and this was one, when I fully glimpsed the torment that Raymond endured.

I think for many years, there was a fantasy inside his head. He did not know how it was going to happen but he thought eventually there was going to be a moment of transformation, that he would emerge finally from the chrysalis and become this beautiful winged creature. Leaving France, never going back, was like admitting that he would always be an ugly, hairy caterpillar.

"Besides," Raymond had added, suddenly lifting his head from the desk. "We cannot draw attention to ourselves by selling up quickly."

He tried to put a practical spin on it, but I knew. For many years afterwards, he dealt with arrangements for the flat, not secretly exactly, but never bothering me with the details. I think perhaps he hired someone – I suspected Jasmine - to go in once or twice a year. The place had been locked up the day we left, the shutters closed over and the rooms left in sombre darkness. When I thought of it, I imagined dust falling through the silent interior like debris through space. A pregnant pause in its history while it waited for someone to come in and throw open the shutters again, and let light spill onto its wooden floors.

The key to the flat was in my jewellery box for many years. Still is. We never sold it. Strangely, I think of the flat more now than ever. Sometimes, when I look in the box for a string of pearls, or a pair of earrings, my fingers stumble upon the hard key at the bottom and I finger it for a moment and imagine. It was Raymond's escape then and sometimes, I imagine it to be mine now. I pretend that I leave this place and go to the flat again, stopping at the pâtisserie on my way upstairs. A box with lilac ribbon. The way I imagine it, I am me again, able to walk up the stairs unaided. I fix myself some lunch, a little plate with smooth pâté and crusty bread and rocket salad with tomatoes, glistening with olive oil. I sit and eat, with the windows open, in shimmering light. It is all pretence, of course. But I have always been very good at pretending.

I sense that in some way, Zac and I are both trapped. Perhaps that is another reason I feel drawn to him. He is tired today. I sit by the window in the lounge but I watch him as he gives out the afternoon medication. What else is there to do? He is patient and gentle as usual but I sense his tension. His skin has a greyish pallor and there are dark circles round his beautiful, inky eyes. Our eyes accidentally meet and he smiles wanly but I flick my eyes away as if I was not deliberately looking.

"What's wrong?" I say when he reaches me.

"Wrong? Nothing's wrong, Marianne. Why should there be?"

"Hm," I say.

Zac turns to the trolley.

"And you can take those away with you," I tell him. "I'm not having them."

"Come on, Marianne," he coaxes. "You know they have been prescribed for you."

I don't even look at him. I prefer to say nothing than to argue.

"I'll put them on here," he says, placing them on the small table beside me, "and perhaps when I come back in a little while..."

"Some things aren't fixed by tablets," I say.

"No," he says, shortly.

His hand trembles as he tries to screw the top back on the bottle.

"How is Abbie?

Zac turns from the trolley

"You remember her name!"

I almost want to laugh.

"You disappoint me, Zac."

"Why?"

"You believe them."

"Believe who?"

"Them." I wave my hand dismissively over my shoulder.

He looks at me intently for a moment, as if deciding whether to speak. Then does.

"Shona said that you could not remember what you had for breakfast on Thursday, a couple of hours after you'd had it."

"Oh Shona! What does Shona know?"

Zac looks uncomfortable at my disdain.

"It was an indifferent breakfast," I continue.

"I see."

"Why would I want to remember a watery poached egg on soggy toast?"

"So you did remember!"

"Well…" I turn my chair from him and move it closer to the window. "Perhaps that was Wednesday."

I have my back to him but I can tell Zac is staring at the back of my head, wondering. Then I hear the trolley trundle onwards. Outside, the pink blooms have begun to brown at the edges.

———

Six months later, the French police paid us a visit. I couldn't believe it but it was almost a relief when we heard they were coming and the long awaited dread became a reality rather than a nebulous fear. The case of Patrice Moreau did not hit the headlines in Britain so nobody was any the wiser about our involvement. Naturally, Raymond did not want to go into long-winded explanations with his Headmaster, a dull geographer in an earth-brown suit who was hardly his greatest fan in any case, and so he simply took a day off sick. I, who had more control over my hours, made sure to come straight from the office and deliberately arrived at the house a few minutes after they did. Subtle messages are important. They could wait for me.

I was dressed in a dark suit with a long line jacket that hid the disproportionate width of my hips quite successfully, a creamy blouse with a tie neck, and high heeled court shoes. A marcasite brooch that Raymond had given me, a peacock with open feathers, was pinned to the lapel of my jacket. I was every inch the professional woman.

Raymond was sitting in an uneasy silence in the sitting room with two French officers perched on my sofa when I arrived. I sailed into the room and put a pile of legal folders down casually on the table. I saw their eyes flick to the embossed name on the front of the folders. ANDERSON, BROWN, AND BATES, LAWYERS.

"Sorry to keep you," I said briskly. "How can we help?"

They had made sure, this time, to send English speakers, at least. There was one who did more of the talking than the other, a middle-aged, square-jawed man with a tight, military haircut and cold eyes. Jacques Charpentier, he said his name was. He introduced his partner, Emile Pascal, a young man who looked to be in his twenties.

More information, Charpentier said, had come to light about Bar Patrice. They understood that Patrice Moreau had some "unusual clientele" who visited the back room of the bar. They were trying to get as much information about these people and that back room as possible and it had been suggested that perhaps we were part of Patrice's "special circle." A private club, almost.

Damn Henri Duval, I thought.

"We were holidaymakers in the town," I said. "Hardly part of his special circle."

Raymond kept quiet during this exchange and Charpentier glanced at him.

"Monsieur?"

Raymond shrugged.

"We knew Patrice," he said. "We visited once or twice."

"How close were you?" asked Charpentier bluntly.

"To Patrice?" I answered for him.

Charpentier stared at me.

"Were you lovers?"

"Certainly not!"

I have no idea why he did not ask Raymond the same question directly. And I have no idea how Raymond would have answered if he had. I simply embraced the jewel of luck that life threw in my direction.

"Patrice had so many lovers…" I said. "I would not have lowered myself to be one of the long line." I could see Raymond was not pleased by my reply. He gives too much away, I thought.

"But the back room of the bar, it was…" Charpentier broke off and had a short, sharp exchange in French with his partner. "It was a club for sex? A meeting for swingers?"

I smiled at the stilted English but Raymond was angry. Patrice's was never just about sex for Raymond.

"No," Raymond said shortly. "It was not a sex club."

"So why did you go there?"

I answered before Raymond could.

"As I said, we were on holiday. It was a different world. We were invited." I shrugged. "We were curious."

Charpentier's partner, who had said little up to now, looked up from taking notes. His English was much more accented than Charpentier's, more difficult to understand.

"But you were not there one holiday only," he said. "You have apartment there?"

"That is correct."

"How long ago did you buy the apartment?" Charpentier cut in.

"Four years."

"And you knew Patrice Moreau how long?"

"Three years."

"Can you tell us any names?" he asked. "Of people you met, of Moreau's lovers?"

"Not really," I replied. "We were there – but not often enough. We did not know anybody well enough to remember names."

It was my intention to give a little information: to give none would look suspicious. But not enough to cast suspicion on ourselves. We had to look like bit-part actors in this drama.

"No, wait a minute," I said turning to Raymond. "There was one - what was the name again Raymond - long dark hair, pale skin…."

Raymond looked at me neutrally.

"Jasmine," I said, as if it had only just occurred to me. "Jasmine Labelle."

Charpentier muttered something in French that I did not catch. His partner grunted.

The blonde woman, Charpentier said, the one that I had spotted at Patrice's window. Had I seen her before? I shook my head.

We circled for another half hour. They had obviously decided Moreau's death was a crime of passion – in that they were not wrong – and were intent on finding out all the possible combinations of relationships that had gone on in the back bar in the hope of finding a motive and a suspect. No, we did not have any French lovers who were part of the Bar Patrice scene. No, we did not know anyone who had a grudge against Patrice, or a reason to kill him. No, there was no other information that we had not given.

Charpentier was getting frustrated but lawyers know how to deal with the police. I know how they work and I kept calm.

"You left without telling us."

I looked him straight in the eye. I have watched the furtive behaviour of enough suspects to know you must maintain direct eye gaze.

"Why would we tell you we were leaving? We stuck to our plans. Are you saying we were suspects, Monsieur Charpentier? Because certainly, nobody suggested such a thing at the time."

Charpentier said nothing but glanced down and began writing in his notebook.

"When do you expect to be back in France?" he demanded finally.

"I don't," I said. "Not surprisingly, Patrice's death has shocked us. The area is quite spoiled for us. I think it will be quite some time before we venture back."

"We may need you to come back," he said.

"Are you talking extradition, Monsieur Charpentier?" I asked coolly.

It was a risk, I knew, but he looked taken aback.

"Not at this stage, no," he said, "but…"

"In that case," I interrupted, "I don't think you will see us back for some time."

I smiled and stood up.

"But forgive me. I am forgetting my manners. Can I fix you gentlemen some coffee?" I felt their eyes burning into my back as I walked to the door. "You have come such a long way to see us. Is this the first time you have been in England?"

Whatever evidence they had, they did not have enough. We did not see them again. And Patrice was, after all, in the eyes of the conventional, a misfit, a pervert, a man few claimed or mourned for. Nobody – other than his family of course – was clamouring for his killer to be caught. He had put Saint Estelle on the map in a way its inhabitants did not want and they were happy to forget. Things were different back then. But perhaps Monsieur Charpentier and his companion would have taken some satisfaction if they had known how destructive their visit was to Raymond and me. How many heart-stopping times over the years that we jumped at a sharp knock at the door, an official envelope through the post, or the persistent ring of the telephone.

CHAPTER SIX

Zac

It has been nine months, Zac thinks, fingering Abbie's lace shirt. Almost a year. He has come close a few times but never succumbed. For the first couple of months, he was so relieved at the prospect of being normal, that he barely thought about it. Back then, he thought the euphoria that came from finally conforming would last forever. Abbie was a defence against a life he did not want. A life where he would always be on the outside, ridiculed and despised and shunned. He'd had a taste of that at school. The whispered comments when he'd walked by, the suppressed sniggers. Gay boy. Poof. Shirt lifter. Inaccurate but the closest schoolboys could get to what was "wrong" with Zac. Then Abbie, pretty as a poppet, had come along and he had grabbed hold and clung to her as if she were a life buoy.

She was due in from work soon. But there was still time, he thought. No, there wasn't, another voice in his head shot back immediately. Yes, yes, yes, there was. He pulled his shirt over his head and slipped his arms into the shirt. He wondered what it would look like with proper underwear underneath and he opened the drawer on the side of the dressing table. It felt like lancing a boil when he slipped his arms through the bra straps, and then fastened up the shirt buttons. The inexplicable thing was that from that very first time that he had slipped Elicia's dress on, there had always been an incredible feeling of peace underneath the more urgent emotion, which was a fear of discovery.

Until he stood up and looked in the mirror. It wasn't right. He didn't look right. He looked in aguish at his own reflection, his tall, flat-chested masculine body that so distressed him, with its lumps and bumps in all the wrong places. He looked ungainly in the lace shirt and there was chest hair visible in the v of the neckline.

"You are ridiculous," he said aloud to his reflection. He sat down at the dressing table and felt a surge of anger and sadness. He picked up a lipstick and plastered it over his mouth furiously. Clown, he thought. You are a clown.

The lipstick spread over the edges of his mouth and he threw it down before grabbing an eye pencil and drawing a grotesque thick outline round his eyes. There were tears spilling even as he attempted to apply the mascara, and the salty rivers ran black and bitter on his cheeks. His nose filled with mucous and he didn't stop to wipe it as a drop formed at the end of his nose. He deserved to look ugly.

"You are disgusting!" he whispered.

When the door banged, he did not move. Why wasn't he moving? He was pushing the self-destruct button, he realised. He wanted to be found. It would be a relief. There was time, still, to run, to hide. God knows he had done it before. He stayed where he was but reached for a tissue from the box on the dressing table and scrubbed the angrily applied lipstick from his mouth.

"Zac?"

Abbie's voice floated upstairs, just as Elicia's had done years ago. Still he did not move. He took another tissue and wiped the worst of the liner from his eyes but it smudged into grey blotches underneath. He pulled another tissue from the box and wet it with his tongue. His heart hammered as he waited. A thought crossed his mind. If Abbie accepted him, loved him even now, would it be enough to make him love her back? Properly love her? Acceptance was such an enormous thing.

"Zac?" The door pushed open. "There you -"

Abbie stopped dead. There was a part of him that noted, with surprisingly impassive interest, that the first emotion on her face was not anger or outrage, but fear. Terror even. It matched his own.

She gave a little nervous laugh, as if to reassure herself that this was not as it seemed; it was some joke.

"What are you... Zac?"

Her voice spiralled upwards.

Tears were cascading now, washing down Zac's face.

"I'm sorry, Abbie," he whispered.

"What is it Zac?" she moved forward to him, put her hand tentatively on his back. Her first instinct was to protect him, he thinks. He waits for the disgust to kick in. "Zac...?" Her voice was shrill, desperate for reassurance. "What are you doing?"

"I can't help it."

She knelt down beside him.

"Can't help what?"

"This." He looked down at himself. "This."

He felt her hand stiffen on his back. He realised she was looking for an explanation. She wanted him to laugh and say he was just fooling around, going to a fancy dress party, anything rational. His seriousness was frightening her. She wanted him to smile. She wanted him to say anything as long as it wasn't the truth.

"Why are you wearing this, Zac? Why are you dressed like…?"

"Like a drag queen?"

She looked at him in a way he didn't recognise, and he knew in that moment that some element of her sexual attraction to him had just died. You couldn't control that. Zac knew that better than most. She was still kneeling beside him and he looked at the plump cushions of her lips and thought, without any hint of desire, how perfect they were. There was something intensely feminine about Abbie, not just in the way she looked but in her sexual preferences. There was little doubt in Zac's mind that while she liked his carefully styled appearance, it was the masculine beneath that she was physically attracted to. Take that away and she might still care emotionally, but the sexual chemistry would be gone. There was no element of androgyny with Abbie.

"Why have…"

"I don't know."

He couldn't look at her.

"Zac…"

"I don't *know!*"

She looked at him with such vulnerability that she seemed to him like a child and he grabbed hold of her wrist.

"Abbie, I'm sorry. This is just something I feel compelled to do sometimes. It's just… it's not anything to be frightened of. It's part of me. Honestly it just makes me feel…"

"You've done this before?"

"I…"

"This isn't… you've been doing this all the time we've…" she said, her finely plucked eyebrows rising into an inverted 'V' of indignation. She wrenched her wrist free of him. The terror had gone suddenly, changing as rapidly as drifting clouds into an emotion of a quite different shape.

"No! No, I haven't!"

Abbie looked at him coldly.

"You look ridiculous."

Zac flinched inside. She wanted to lash out, to hurt him as she was hurting, but wasn't she just confirming what he had had told himself?

She stood up but Zac didn't move. He wanted her to hold him more than he'd ever wanted her to hold him before, but he knew she wouldn't. He was sore with the need to be touched. Abbie walked to the door.

"Abbie, I swear I haven't done this while we have been together."

"You're lying."

"Abbie…"

"What?"

He could hardly hear her voice it was so quiet. He almost wished she would shout or scream or even cry. This was so much more silent, and so much worse, than he had imagined. At the door, she turned and looked at him as if she was simply looking straight through him.

He shook his head. Nothing. There was nothing.

She closed the door quietly.

———

Zac stood outside the kitchen, listening to the sudden rush of the kettle. His face was scrubbed clean now and he was dressed in his own clothes. He reached out for the door handle but his hand hovered for a minute before retreating back to his side. He couldn't go in. A familiar, cramping pain twisted in his abdomen. Just caused by stress, his doctor had said dismissively over the years. Try not to get stressed. Zac's hand snaked out again. He couldn't stay out here forever. He had to face her. Tentatively, he opened the door.

Abbie didn't even look at him.

"Do you want tea?" she asked. Her voice was flat and small.

He had diminished her, he thought, and the realisation seared him. Abby knew where her power lay: it was in the way she looked. Zac was responsible for making her feel less desirable, less confident in her femininity. Sometimes, his own life had felt like a process of getting smaller and smaller until he feared there would be nothing left. He didn't want to do that to anybody else.

"Do you want tea?" she repeated.

"No. Thanks."

He pulled out a chair at the kitchen table and sat down. A half emptied bag of shopping was spread over the top. A carton of milk. A jar of Thai curry paste. A small bunch of cheap supermarket daffodils, still in their cellophane; a bar of chocolate. Friday night treats.

Abbie reached for the milk and opened the fridge.

"Are you… are you gay, Zac?"

She was rooting in the fridge, pretending to rearrange it but he could sense that she was holding her breath.

He shook his head.

Labels, he thought. What good were labels? Gay boy. Poof.

"No," he said. Even as he said the word, he knew it was misleading and felt a kind of despair. But what was he supposed to say?

Her relief was overwhelming. Zac could feel it filling the room. It gave her the confidence to ask the question she really wanted to ask. The one she wanted to ask the minute she saw him dressed in her shirt. She closed the fridge door and looked at him directly for the first time.

"Is it me… you don't fancy me?"

"No, Abbie. Honestly, it isn't about you."

She came and sat down on the chair next to him.

"Zac, is this… is it just some weird sexual thing? Some experiment?"

A feeling of hopelessness seized Zac. There were no words.

Abbie tried to laugh.

"Something you want to do together?"

He understood the question. She felt excluded. The hurtful thing for her was imagining a whole facet of his sexuality that didn't include her. She was pushing her own boundaries, trying to find what she could be part of, what she could tolerate. He felt strangely moved by her desperation. But this wasn't something he wanted to "do together". It was expressing who he was.

Women wanted to be the excluders, not the excluded, Zac thought, watching her. Ever since he had been a child, he had gravitated towards female company. He had liked the less physically robust nature of their interaction, the constant verbalising of what was going on in their heads, the less combative nature of their imaginations. They were more constantly creative in their play than the boys he hung around with, but their make-believe was based on a kind of reality; they were more likely to pretend to own homes and drive cars and have children who gave them no end of anxiety than they were to imagine they were astronauts invading another planet, or that a shoal of sharks was about to engulf them and turn the sea red with blood.

But they could be just as cruel as boys. Zac was different from the other boys and though neither they – nor he for that matter – could identify exactly what his "otherness" was, they certainly knew it was there. Girls were more tolerant of that otherness but never quite allowed him into their inner circle. He remembered once sitting with some of Elicia's friends when one suggested they play 'my favourite'.

"You start, Elicia."

"My favourite colour is orange because it makes me feel happy and it reminds me of ice lollies on warm days," said Elicia.

"My favourite tea is pizza and chips because I love dipping the hot chips into the melted cheese!" said her friend Rachel.

"Mm!" said Elicia.

"My favourite ice cream flavour is mint chocolate chip because... just because it is!" said Wendy.

They all giggled.

Zac was enchanted by the game, knew exactly what he wanted to say.

"Can I go next?" he asked.

Three pairs of eyes swivelled towards him. They waited expectantly.

"My favourite cloth is -"

"Favourite what?" said Rachel.

"Cloth," repeated Zac. "Material."

Rachel looked at Elicia who shrugged.

"My favourite cloth," said Zac, "is silk because it is soft and lovely on your skin and feels like someone is stroking you and my mum has a pale pink nightdress that is made of silk and it's really pretty and I like when she cuddles me when she's wearing it."

There was silence for a second before all three girls erupted suddenly into laughter, bending their heads together and clutching each other's arms.

"Zac, you're weird!" said Rachel.

"Shut up!" said Elicia, though Zac wasn't sure if this was addressed to him or to Rachel.

"Weird!" said Wendy.

"For a boy!" added Rachel.

Zac blushed pink to his ears. What had he said? He had played the game, hadn't he? What had he said that none of them would?

Elicia said nothing, suddenly aware of the depth of Zac's discomfort and torn in her loyalties.

"Let's go play on the swing," said Rachel, jumping up, and Wendy immediately raced her across the field.

Elicia hesitated.

"Coming Zac?" she said.

He shook his head. Elicia looked at the retreating figures of her friends.

"Wait for me," she shouted, before taking off after them across the park.

Zac suddenly became aware of Abbie talking.

"So you've done it before…" she was saying, a statement rather than a question.

He nodded.

"How long? What age?"

"Fifteen."

"Oh my God!"

Zac reached across the table and took her hand. She did not move but he could feel her resistance, her desire to pull away from him. She left her hand resting in his for a minute then shifted awkwardly and stood up.

"I'll make the tea."

She didn't want to make tea, Zac thought watching her. She just couldn't bear to have him touch her.

Abbie lifted the kettle then put it back down again without pouring,

"It's like I never knew you," she said, keeping her back to him.

How could she possibly know him, Zac thought. He didn't even know himself.

Chapter Seven

Marianne

It is hard to describe the extent of my contempt for Shona. She has no depth of understanding, no incisive capacity for analysis; she is just a squelching mass of emotional impulses and misplaced empathy. There is something pallid about her: the thin, straw-like hair and watery blue eyes, the skin that has the grainy, grey tone of a cadaver. Plain women like me have a respect either for the beauty we can't have, or for the acuteness of mind that we have had to develop. Shona has neither. I have no interest in Shona.

She comes after breakfast, her leather sandals squeaking on the floor as she walks towards me with that inane smile she has.

"Hello Marianne," she says, pulling a chair up beside me.

I glance up at her but say nothing.

"How are we today?" she says.

I have no idea how YOU are, I think to myself.

"Marianne?" she says, patting my hand gently as though I haven't heard her.

"Nurse! Nurse! Help me!"

Annie's plaintive wail seems to fill the lounge. Shona turns.

"What's wrong, Annie?"

"Nurse! Nurse! Help me…" Annie seems locked into the wailing, unaware that Shona has even spoken. She is slumped into the corner of a settee as if she has no backbone to keep her upright, a tiny heap of bones with pleading eyes.

"You're all right now, Annie," Shona says, lifting the old lady's hand from the arm of the chair and clasping it. "What's the matter?"

Annie looks at her fearfully.

"Help me," she says.

I look at Annie. All that is left of her is a heap of bones and a series of almost electrical impulses that make her shout out. Out in the hall, the board that links the call buttons in residents' room buzz and buzz, lights flashing. That noise. All day that board buzzes until some days it feels like it's buzzing inside me, that there's a bee trapped inside my brain. Buzz, buzz.

Shona glances out, then back at Annie.

"You're fine, Annie. You're safe here."

"I want to go home," says Annie. "Can you take me to my mum's house?"

"You're safe here, pet," says Shona in that voice that makes me want to shoot her. I watch as she lifts a hand to Annie's shock of thin white hair and gently pats it down.

Buzz. Buzz. Buzz.

"Do you know what we've got for lunch today?" Shona asks Annie, in a conspiratorial tone.

Annie looks up at her, almost hopefully, shaking her head.

"Roast pork!" whispers Shona delightedly. "Apple sauce!
Pureed kack.

A ghost of a smile twitches on Annie's lips and her eyes do not leave Shona's face.

"And pudding!" says Shona. "What's your favourite pudding?"

"Ice cream," says Annie.

"Well," says Shona, "You're going to be a very happy girl today, aren't you Annie? There's ice cream for pudding today!"

Annie smiles.

Buzz. Buzz. Buzz. I can see the lights flashing through the open door at regular intervals, like lights on a Christmas tree.

"All right Annie?" she says. Annie says nothing but slumps further into the cushion as Shona drops her hand and walks to the door.

"Marie! Can you get the buzzers on the first floor, please?"

"Sorry, Marianne." Shona sits back down beside me. "Our wee chat got interrupted, didn't it?"

"You were the only one saying anything," I mutter.

"Quite right, Marianne. Quite right, pet. It's your turn now, isn't it?"

I look across at Annie whose eyes are drooping, her head falling forward.

"I was thinking we could have a wee chat about the old days," says Shona. "It's always nice talking about the past, isn't it?"

"My long term memory is fine, thank you." I tell her sharply.

"Of course it is, Marianne. I just thought it would be nice to have a chat. I bet you've got lots of interesting stories inside that head of yours."

If only she knew. Perhaps I should tell her. That would be interesting.

"What did you work at, Marianne?"

A nurse pops her head in the door.

"Shona, Mr Peters has another bladder infection. I've asked Dr Martin to call."

"Okay, thanks Marie."

"I was a lawyer."

"Goodness me, Marianne!" Shona's almost transparent pupils widen as she turns back to me. "You WERE a clever girl, weren't you? But then we knew that. Very clever."

Shona knew that already. She's trying to give me affirmation all over again. I don't know why she thinks I would care about her affirmation. I could buy and sell her.

"Help! Help! Nurse…"

Annie begins to call instinctively, before her eyes are even properly open. Then, almost as soon as they are open, they begin to close again.

"You're fine, Annie," Shona calls. We both watch as she drifts back to sleep.

"And what about your husband, Marianne? What did he do?"

"Raymond."

"Yes Raymond."

Raymond. Raymond. I miss you.

"Marianne? What did Raymond do?"

"Art teacher."

"How interesting!"

"Oh yes, Raymond was interesting."

Annie has begun to dribble as she dozes and I close my eyes to block her and Shona out.

"Tell me about him."

"He was very beautiful."

"Handsome," says Shona gently. "We say handsome for a man, don't we?"

"No we do not!"

Shona flinches slightly.

"Raymond was beautiful."

Shona blinks, trying to smile.

"Did he take you dancing?"

I could almost laugh. I seem so old to her that she thinks Raymond and I are of a generation that went waltzing. If she could only see inside my head to Patrice's: the dusty, seedy, half-lit sprawl of it… The seductive wail of the saxophone shimmering from the tiny stage. The river of red wine and the faint whiff of bitter orange from the open Cointreau bottle, a shimmer of cannabis smoke above the tables, musky and pungent. Jasmine leaning against the pillar in a tight black dress, her lips slashed with vermillion red, a feather boa coiled around her neck like a snake. Jasmine's femininity as a man had been so suppressed that when she transitioned, she turned the dial up full.

"We went to clubs, yes."

"What did you wear, Marianne?"

Wear? What did I wear? Why would she ask me such a thing? I ignore her.

"Do you remember?"

"Yes, I remember."

"I'm sure you had some lovely frocks."

Frocks!

"Raymond wore black," I say. "It suited him. Black jeans, black shirt." He was so slender. "Black hair."

"Oh very dramatic," says Shona. "I wish I could have seen him! I do like a man in black."

Perhaps it was the way she said 'I', the almost subliminal positioning of herself next to Raymond that angers me so. She is trying to flatter, of course, but she would not belong in the same room as Raymond. Or perhaps it is the way she makes him sound like any man in black.

"Raymond was not like other men."

"He was very special to you, Marianne," she says soothingly. "I know that. You must miss him terribly. Tell me about his job. His art."

"I have told you that my memory does not need to be tested."

"We're just having a chat, aren't we?" She pats my hand. "It's very interesting for me. Did Raymond paint at home?"

"Yes."

"What did he paint? Still life? Or landscapes?"

I don't answer.

"Or maybe portraits? Did he ever paint you?"

"Yes."

"Oh how wonderful! What did it feel like to be the muse of a painter?"

She looks genuinely intrigued. Nobody would ever paint Shona.

I do not want to talk about that portrait. Raymond's painting of me was crueller than a bad photograph. He caught me in a way I could not catch myself in any mirror. We all prepare ourselves when we look in a mirror, make subconscious compensations for what we are about to see there that we do not like. Besides, we always see ourselves from the same head-on angle. But this was me without any time for compensation: I was confronted by my true self.

When he had finally let me look at it, Raymond watched my face intently, a hopeful smile on his face. But as he witnessed my reaction, the smile disappeared.

"You don't like it?" he said, his face tight with disappointment.

How could I like it? The thin-lipped gash of a mouth dominated my face while the strangely shaped hillocks of my cheeks made me wince. There was nothing feminine about me. It is true he had captured the vivacity of my eyes, but they were small in comparison to my other features. Almost piggy. I knew that Raymond loved me in some way, but when I looked at that painting, I also knew he did not love me physically. He had painted me exactly as I was, without the subtle ameliorations that love would

58

have wrought. This was how he saw me. This was how I was. A plain woman with an oddly shaped face and grey skin.

"You don't like it," Raymond repeated, a little stiffly.

"It's wonderful," I said, which, if one looked only objectively at the painting, was true. But I could not look objectively because I was the subject. He reached out a hand to my face.

"There are tears in your eyes."

"Only because I cannot believe how clever you are, how precisely you have captured me."

All these years on, the memory is still painful.

"Marianne?"

My eyes swivel to Shona.

"He was obviously a very interesting man," she says.

I do not know what expression Shona catches on my face but whatever it is, it prompts something unexpected in her reaction. I see wariness in her eyes. Fear, almost. It goads me further.

"Would you like to know HOW interesting?"

She does not answer.

"But it is a secret. Can you keep a secret?" I lean forward slightly towards her.

"Raymond was accused of murder."

She does not know how to react. I can see that. She has gone very still. She does not know if I am making it up, or am mistaken, or worse, if it's true.

"Oh surely not, Marianne!"

"Yes!"

"Murder? Who?"

Out in the hall, the lights begin to flash again.

Buzz. Buzz. Buzz.

Shona turns, almost with relief at the sound.

"We'll talk again, Marianne. Will we?"

Buzz. Buzz. Buzz. The noise is so insistent.

Annie wakes suddenly.

"I want to go home," she wails. Her voice drops to a whimper. "I want my mum."

Buzz. Buzz. Buzz.

It is the doorbell. It will be Charpentier again. Charpentier and his sidekick.

"If it is a Frenchman," I call to Shona, "do not tell him I am here."

CHAPTER EIGHT

Zac

Zac couldn't reach her. Abbie was curled up on the sofa with a magazine that he knew she wasn't reading, refusing to meet his eye. He wasn't sure whether her retreat from him was straight-forward revulsion or a form of punishment. Women's punishment was so silent. Perhaps he wasn't wholly feminine after all, he thought, staring at the television screen. The possibility held a glimmer of promise.

"Do you want some coffee?" he asked.

"No thanks." Abbie did not look up.

In the kitchen he flicked the switch on the kettle and sat down at the table. He was used to a feeling of alienation. But alienation was a quiet feeling inside, a permanent fixture that sat imperviously, like a rock on the beach with the tide moving in and out around it. This was different. The gnawing anxiety, the constant tension, the feeling of impending doom. His stomach churned constantly these days, his insides twisting into spasms like a clenching fist. He didn't want Abbie to reject him. He didn't want to be back on the outside.

But do you love her - he asked himself. To avoid answering the question, he got up and took a mug from the cupboard, busying himself with spoons and jars.

He did not hear her come into the kitchen. She was simply there when he turned round. She walked towards him, saying nothing, and laid her head on his shoulder. He realised she was crying silently and the guilt rose inside him like a tidal wave. He put his arms round her and the faint smell of vanilla rose from soft, freshly washed hair. Her femininity should make him feel protective, even aroused, but he recognised instead the faint pang of jealousy. He wondered what it felt like to smell that way, what it felt like to have a man hold you in his arms. To be the held instead of the holder.

Wasn't this what he wanted? For her not to reject him? Abbie looked up at him.

"Zac," she said, fearfully, "what's going to happen?"

He gently replaced her head back against his chest.

"It will be all right," he said, and he felt the sobs begin to shudder silently through her. Wasn't that what men were supposed to say?

"It will be all right, Abbie," he repeated desperately, though somewhere deep inside, he suspected it wouldn't.

———

Zac retched, then coughed with the violence of it. His stomach bubbled and burned. Doctors were always vague about the cause. Irritable bowel syndrome they always said, reaching for an umbrella term and their prescription pads. Zac reached out his arms, clutching the cold porcelain of the sink and tried to straighten. Mornings were bad. He ran the cold tap and splashed a little water onto his face, watching his reflection in the mirror as the water ran in rivulets down his chalky skin. He looked awful.

Abbie was still sleeping when he left for work, curled like a child into his pillow, arm stretched across the empty space where he had lain. Their fears had sparked off each other last night, a comforting hug, a chaste hug developing into something more frantic and desperate in a bid to block out what the past was and what the future may hold. Abbie's fear that her femininity had failed to satisfy him and she would be left alone, that she was useless as a woman; Zac's fear that his masculinity had failed to satisfy her and he faced a lifetime of loneliness, that he was useless as a man.

He could never work out the sex. It wasn't that he couldn't be aroused as a man, just that emotionally, it wasn't truly satisfying. The body was wrong, the sexual role was wrong. The mechanics all worked, but he felt trapped inside them. He leant his head against the grimy window of the bus as it trundled out of town towards the care home. Abbie had asked if he was gay but it wasn't as simple as that. He WAS attracted to men as well as women; that much was true. But he didn't want to have sex with them as a man himself. That would be just as incomplete as having sex with Abbie. He wanted to have sex with them as a woman.

It was too confusing. All these labels that people would apply. Was he gay because he liked men? Or bisexual because he could be attracted to both? Or should he really be a heterosexual woman? And if so, did that mean he was having a lesbian affair with Abbie? He couldn't find the right label. It was as if he didn't actually fit anywhere.

A sudden image of his father came into his head and Zac's cheeks flushed with a sense of shame. Imagine if his father could read his mind right now! If he had proof of how revolting his son really was, instead of just suspecting it. His father always seemed embarrassed when he was with Zac and met colleagues from the station unexpectedly. His police mates usually clocked Zac with a stare that was quizzical and lasted slightly too long for politeness. "Your boy?" one of them had said, once, a mixture of disbelief and amusement spilling out of his voice.

Zac sensed that his father disapproved of everything about him, including his career choice. Not that it was entirely choice in a rural area like theirs. There was a small fish factory, a few pubs, some shops, a small office for the local council, and a care home. He wasn't going to spend his life stinking of raw haddock, that was for sure. Shops were fine, easier than a care home in many ways, and occasionally he wondered if he'd made the wrong choice when he was wiping shit from some old man's backside, but there was a broken bit inside Zac that made him want to heal others.

Broken but tender.

Besides, he had never intended staying here this long. He knew he could have gone to university if he'd made an effort. Another year at school and he would have made the grades if he'd forced himself to break sweat. But somehow, half-way through his school career, he just lost heart. It was his intention when he left to break free, leave the country and move to the anonymity of the nearby city where he might blend in more. Then Abbie had come along. Abbie had no intention of going anywhere.

She was a small town girl, always would be, Zac thought. At times, her complete lack of ambition had exasperated him – frightened him, even. It made him feel there was no escape. Was she, he asked, content to work as an untrained assistant in a small nursery forever? The unasked question inside him was whether that meant he had to stay here, forever, too. Abbie's eyes had hooded with a mixture of hurt and resentment.

"What's wrong with that?" she had demanded.

Zac had been stricken with remorse when he saw how belittled she felt, and wrapped his arms round her.

"Nothing," he had whispered against her hair. "There's nothing wrong with that."

There was a fear in Abbie, he realised. Not a specific fear, like a fear of spiders or rats or the crack of thunder overhead. Unless it was of life itself, maybe. She was close to her mother and her two sisters and that made her feel safe. She didn't need to see the bigger, wider world and maybe, just maybe, Zac considered, that was a kind of strength. To know who you were and what you were and what made you happy… Zac, after all, couldn't answer a single one of those questions.

The bus jolted suddenly and Zac's head banged painfully off the window. He sat up. It was so warm this morning, and he still felt nauseous. He needed another shower already. He peered through the grime into a playpark where a small boy was kicking a ball with his dad. Zac watched the man's delight as the little boy's foot connected with the ball, the man's hands shooting into the air in triumph. He smiled in spite of himself. Had his father ever had such an innocent moment of pleasure with him? His father had played football semi-professionally as a young man and now coached the local under-15s with a seriousness that made his young players fear their trainer as well as revere his credentials. Zac had never been one of them.

He still felt like a child in front of his father: the hopeless, hapless eleven-year-old who claimed he wanted football boots for his birthday. The boots had been flash, black and green with small hints of white. He smelled the leather as he opened the tissue paper in the box and his father grinned at him conspiratorially. It was the best bit of acting Zac had ever done. He grinned back at his father with a kind of desperation. He had asked for them but now he had them, he didn't know quite how to react. Should he try them on in the house? He took one of the boots out and slipped a foot in. The studded sole felt strange beneath his foot and he was conscious of everyone watching him.

"Thanks," he said simply, as if his excitement had made him tongue tied, and his parents smiled hopefully at each other and then at him.

"Here," said his dad, as Zac struggled with the never-ending lace, "not like that daftie! I'll show you..."

It was one of the few times he could remember affection in his father's tone.

"Maybe you'll play for my team one of these days," he said.

Zac remembered how his heart had sunk.

The bus turned into a quiet avenue lined with trees where Zac had to get off. It was a five minute walk to work, past a row of fine, Victorian sandstone houses with handsome bay windows and embellished glass doors. They were the kind of houses few people could afford any more and some had been converted into student flats. Zac looked across to the playing fields in the distance. The schools were out for summer and there were already some kids kicking a ball around. In his mind as a child, he'd thought the football boots would be the answer to the unresolved question in his mind. Just the act of asking for them, of being a proper boy, would change things.

But nothing had changed. How could it? Team picking at PE remained what it always was.

"Jim!"

"We'll have Martin, then."

"Joe!"

"Tim!"

Until there was only one left. Zac, standing in his shiny boots, trying to look unconcerned while staving off sharp tears of humiliation.

"Okay... Zac then," the captain who'd drawn the short straw would say reluctantly, and the pack would be off, running across the pitch before Zac could even join them. Then the excruciating ordeal of pushing and shoving and sliding in mud, and being always in the wrong place at the wrong time, and hearing the muttered anger of team mates. "Fuck's sake, Zac!" "Why do we always get him? "Get out of the fucking way, poofter!"

Zac's phone vibrated in his pocket as he turned in at the open wrought-iron gates of the home. Blossoms from the rhododendron bushes fell over the top of the gate, and there was a low drone from the bees swarming into the heart of the flowers. The noise always felt a little menacing, a distant threat that could become an immediate one at any second. He took out his phone. **Sorry. Never heard you leave. Empty here without you. Love you, zac. Ax**

Love you, Zac. The words did something to him. It was the acceptance he craved and yet he knew that it wasn't the real him that Abbie loved. How could it be? She didn't know who he really was. It was like reading a message that had actually been written to somebody else and trying to claim it as your own. His stomach twisted and he stopped abruptly on the path, winded by the physical pain.

Abbie was relieved that there had been rapprochement and Zac knew that she would now pretend the whole episode hadn't happened. There had been revelation, but no resolution and she would gradually come to terms with it by pretending that there hadn't even been a revelation. She would make subtle changes to what had happened to enable her not only to live with it, but to go back to the way things were. The morning sun hit his face as he moved forward and Zac squinted in discomfort. Why, he asked himself, was he feeling so despondent? Because he was back in exactly the same place as he had been before - except now he had lost his privacy.

Abbie was so needy; it vaporised out of her and it made him feel protective because he understood need. It almost matched his own, but as a man, he had become used to hiding his insecurity. It was just a shame, he thought, as he walked through the front doors, that his needs and Abbie's needs were so entirely contradictory.

Shona's office door was open as he passed.

"Zac!"

He popped his head round and smiled. He liked Shona. She was a kind woman. He couldn't understand Marianne's antipathy to her but then Marianne was a woman of definite impulses and opinions.

"I want to talk to you about Marianne."

"What about her?"

"Has she ever talked to you about her husband?"

"Raymond? A little."

"Is there a story there?"

For some reason, Zac felt nervous. A story? His stomach tightened and he looked blankly back at Shona. He felt the same whenever Marianne mentioned Raymond. She always spoke about him as if he should have such significance to Zac, yet he was a dead man he'd never known. There was something almost spooky about it.

Shona motioned at him to close the door and Zac came properly into the room, pushing the door behind him and leaning back against it.

"What do you mean? All I know is that he's dead."

"Has she ever mentioned murder?"

Zac's dark, almond-shaped eyes widened.

"What?"

"Never mind, "said Shona, waving a hand dismissively, as if she had been foolish to mention it. "I… she was probably havering. Forget it. I think she's deteriorating a bit."

"Raymond was murdered?"

"No… he… I think Marianne got a bit confused, but she said it so deliberately."

"Said what?"

"That Raymond had been accused of murder." She looked at Zac uneasily, as if looking for reassurance.

"Oh my God!"

"She's a strange woman," she added. "Don't you think?"

"I suppose so."

"She says things that somehow make you shiver, yet you don't quite know why."

"She's very astute," said Zac.

Certainly there was a feeling of some mystery radiating from her, Zac thought, as if there was much you did not, and could not, know about her. But he had always had something of a bond with Marianne.

"Those glittering black eyes," Shona said with a slight laugh, and Zac sensed that the laugh covered a feeling of revulsion. "She almost frightens me."

—◆—

"You look sad today," Marianne said.

Zac took her hands in his and tried to warm them.

"It is so hot today and yet your hands are freezing," he said, rubbing her fingers gently in his.

"Are you sad?" Marianne persisted.

"Oh, no more than usual," Zac spoke lightly.

"Yes, that's true. You are often sad."

"No Marianne, that's not what I meant!"

"Yes. Yes it is. It is exactly what you meant."

Her fingers felt like twigs, hard and knobbly beneath Zac's soft fingers.

"Sometimes," she added, "we hide behind the truth rather than lies."

Marianne's gaze was uncompromising.

"We pretend the truth is a lie," she continued, but Zac did not speak.

"How is your young lady?" she asked, after a moment.

"Fine."

"Oh dear."

Zac found himself almost irritated. Why could Marianne not simply follow the submissive pattern of the other old ladies? When their strength failed them, their courage went. But Marianne's assertiveness seemed undimmed by physical frailty. It was hard - physically and emotionally - working here, but Marianne made it challenging mentally too.

Marianne reached out a finger to Zac's chin and gently forced it round towards her.

"Why are you sad, Zac? What troubles you?"

"I don't know."

"I understand," she said, not lifting her eyes from his.

"Do you?"

She dropped her hand.

"Let me tell you something. There was a night, a night with Raymond. The first night I knew." She stopped, adding almost to herself, "No, not the first night I knew. I *always* knew. The first night I admitted I knew."

70

Zac held his breath.

"We were going to a fancy dress party. Everyone else did things half-heartedly. Hastily borrowed items. In my case, an unconvincing moustache, a pair of wire-rimmed glasses and an old tuxedo from a charity shop."

Zac scanned her face as she spoke, his eyes darting nervously.

"Groucho Marx," she said.

The smile dissolved on her lips when he did not reply. "Of course," she murmured, "you are too young."

"I know who he is."

"Raymond," she said, as if Zac had not opened his mouth, "unlike the rest of us, went to endless trouble. He hired a wig. A costume. He spent an hour locked away getting ready, applying makeup, and when he emerged it made me gasp. He was stunning."

"Who?"

"Marilyn. Marilyn Monroe."

Zac's stomach tumbled.

"Everyone's ideal woman," Marianne continued, "yet he pulled it off. There was a man at the party who spoke to me. He barely looked at me because he could not take his eyes off Raymond, but he thought that underneath my slicked-back hair and grotesquely unconvincing moustache, that I really was a man. 'Your wife,' he said, 'is a very beautiful woman.'"

"Were you jealous?" Zac asked curiously, before he could help himself.

Marianne laughed lightly. "Jealous? Murderously so! How could I hope to keep such a beautiful creature? Especially when I was so plain."

"Marianne, why are you telling me this?"

"Because we were talking about being comfortable in your own skin."

"No we weren't.

"Well," said Marianne, fixing Zac with a look that made it difficult for him to avert his eyes. "Then we should have been."

CHAPTER NINE

Marianne

It was a year, perhaps eighteen months, after Charpentier's visit that Raymond relaxed enough to find another outlet. It is human nature. You vow never to do something again, but over time the rock of your resolve is washed away by a tide of longing that simply wears you down like the sea. That is how it was with Raymond. He was not strong enough to resist who he really was. I'm not sure any of us are.

I disliked Sebastian from the start with his tanned skin – fake, I may say – and his crocodile smile. I doubt his name even was Sebastian; I am fairly certain that was some affectation that he had adopted to make himself sound more interesting. He had a brittle, bitchy quality that did not seem to disturb Raymond, but which he turned on me mercilessly. In every way he was a shade off colour, from his pink shirt to the slightly-too-large diamond stud in his ear. No class. I had no idea what Raymond saw in him; he was far too camp to be his usual type. I suspected that he chose someone as far away from Patrice as he could so that he seemed less of a threat to me.

And the ego! He swanned around the place with the physical confidence of a prize fighter, despite the slight bulge around his middle and the thinning hair. Oh, he was good-looking enough in his way, I suppose, but deeply unattractive. Perhaps someone more generous than I am would put it down to an entrenched defence mechanism, brought about by his 'otherness', but his slightly grandiose approach to everything, his air of superiority, made me grit my teeth.

"What do you do, Sebastian?" I asked, when Raymond first anxiously introduced us.

"Oh, I'm sort of in showbiz," he said with an excitable little squeal that characterised his speech and which I would come to loathe. "I work in radio."

"Really," I said. "Where?"

"I don't work full time at the moment," he added. "But things are going well."

Raymond smiled encouragingly at him.

"I see. Where do you…?"

"I believe you're a lawyer," Sebastian interrupted. He said the word with a slight sneer. "Oh my God, Marianne," he said clutching his hand to his chest, "How do you work in an office all day? It would drive me CRA…azy!" Up the voice soared and then down again. "I'm too creative, I think."

I was not to be diverted.

"So you work where…?" I said.

"In radio."

"Yes, but where?" It was the lawyer in me.

Sebastian eyed me resentfully.

"At the moment, I work in hospital radio," he said archly.

He meant he was an occasional volunteer. The most creative thing about Sebastian was his imagination.

Sebastian and I were rivals from the start and we both knew it. But the events in France tempered any volatility in this triangle, at least for Raymond and me. We had been through too much to make the same mistakes again. Besides, I knew instinctively that Sebastian was no Patrice. No grand passion. He was a diversion, a dalliance, a silly entanglement.

Working in a school made Raymond cautious about where he socialised. That's why he had gravitated to the south of France in the first place. I think that sometimes he couldn't help it and dipped into places that he shouldn't - seedy clubs and an infamous strip joint in town that included transsexual strippers - but I deliberately didn't ask and he deliberately didn't tell. On the whole, having Sebastian around was enough to moderate his behaviour for a while and I accepted him on that basis.

If only he could have moderated Sebastian's behaviour. I hated coming home from work and finding he had taken up residence on my settee. Sometimes he would have his head resting on Raymond's shoulder and would look up at me with eyes heavy with both contentment and spite.

"You don't mind if Sebastian stays for dinner, do you?" Raymond would ask, a little anxiously.

"Not at all."

Strangely, I think Raymond thought he was doing me a favour. Including me, letting me see what he was up to rather than disappearing in secrecy as he had once done. We both knew where that had got us. But for his part, Sebastian never missed an opportunity to make me feel like an intruder in my own home: the gooseberry. Nor to try to shake my confidence by making me feel like the ugliest woman on earth.

"Oh my God, Marianne, come and sit down," he would say, his high, effete voice rising and falling in that over-dramatic way he had. "You look awful! So grey and tired. Are you feeling all right?"

"How considerate you are, Sebastian, but I feel fine, thank you."

"Really? That job is too much for you, Marianne. It's ageing you prematurely."

His blue eyes swam maliciously in a muddy sea of tan.

"Well, we certainly couldn't say that about yours, Sebastian."

Raymond got uncomfortable, I know. Sometimes, I would bite my lip, frightened that the animosity between me and Sebastian would force Raymond to choose. Even with a creature like Sebastian, I was never confident enough of Raymond's choices to push him towards a permanent decision.

In some ways, perhaps I only had myself to blame for the sudden appearance of Sebastian in our lives. There was a short spell – it didn't work out – when we moved from our quiet village, which was a relatively short drive from the city, to a seaside town an hour away. The move had been at my insistence. I thought if I kept Raymond away from the temptations of city life, it would help, but of course, it didn't. He was like a dieter who had realised his secret stash of chocolate biscuits had been removed from the cupboard and panicked. The result was Sebastian.

We moved back from the seaside to the village in time – I have come here like a homing pigeon all my life - but it was an unhappy period. I hated the spells in summer when the sea haar would creep round us like rancid breath, barely lifting for days on end. The air was warm, the sun beneath the cloud fighting and failing to get through, and I'd sometimes get tired of waiting for the sunshine and go for walks on the hill above the beach, where the delicate pink- and vanilla-centered wild roses would loom suddenly through the mist. I'd arrive home, sticky and uncomfortable, my hair limp on top and frizzy at the ends with the moisture. Those days epitomised an ugly period of miserable discomfort.

"Dear GOD, Marianne! What have you been doing?" asked Sebastian once on my return.

He followed me into the kitchen.

"I have a friend who is a hairdresser. I could see if he could fit you in some time," he said, with too much tender concern to be genuine.

I turned.

"Well I don't suppose there's enough of yours to keep him busy," I retorted, deliberately looking him up and down disdainfully. It was the look, I think, rather than the words, which infuriated him.

Sebastian drew closer to me.

"Face it Marianne," he hissed, so that our raised voices would not be heard in the other room. "You are a mess! My God, Raymond makes a more convincing woman than you do!"

I bent to take some washing out of the machine so that he would not see how much his words hurt. I could feel his eyes burning in my back.

"Why don't you leave him, Marianne?" Sebastian taunted. "He doesn't love you. You are just a burden. You have nothing to offer him."

Nothing to offer him. The phrase circled my mind, returning over and over to me during the course of the next few days. I did not answer Sebastian and I am sure he thought he had defeated me. Inside, I began to make my plans.

Shona is less keen to talk since our little chat about Raymond. She smiles a lot in my direction, but moves on as quickly as possible.

There is something about her that provokes cruelty in me. I enjoy the power; I have so little in other ways.

"Would you like to know more about Raymond?" I asked her today as she doled out medication. She flinched slightly and I watched her try to stifle the movement as it rippled through her.

"Tell me whatever you like, Marianne," she said uneasily. "Tell me more about his painting…"

"No, no," I whispered. "About the secret. The murder."

"Oh Marianne! Are you certain about that?"

"Certain."

"Who did he murder?"

"I didn't say he murdered. I said he was accused of murder."

"And did he?"

I merely smiled.

"Who… who was he accused of murdering?"

"A Frenchman. A man called Patrice."

Shona looked at me uncertainly.

"His throat was cut and he bled through the floor to the ceiling below. Bled like a pig."

"Oh my God…"

Shona looked round.

"Zac!" she called.

"It was the ceiling of a bar."

"Now Marianne, let's talk about something nicer, shall we?"

Zac came over then and I smiled at him. He looked at Shona enquiringly.

"Maybe you could help Marianne with the rest of her medication, Zac," Shona said. She lowered her voice and turned away slightly but I heard what she said perfectly well. "I think she just plays me up. She's better with you."

I smiled inwardly.

"Sure," said Zac, though I could tell he was a bit puzzled.

"Right then Marianne," he said, as Shona walked away. "You've had the pink ones, haven't you?"

I nodded.

Zac started to unscrew another bottle on the medicine trolley.

"What have you been up to?" he said, glancing at me.

"Nothing."

"Shona seemed…"

"She's a little squeamish. I was telling her about blood seeping through a ceiling."

Zac paused as he emptied out the tablets.

"Why were you talking about blood on a ceiling?"

"I can't remember."

"I see."

"Oh yes I can …I've just remembered what it was."

"Really?" Zac looked at me a little dryly. "What?"

He handed me a glass of water.

"It was a book," I said, "The plot of a detective book I am reading. I offered to lend it to Shona."

"Marianne," Zac said, "you have a very fertile imagination."

I merely smiled.

Chapter Ten

Zac

It was the sudden mental image of his mother's face that made Zac hesitate momentarily as he emptied the tablets out of the bottle into his hand. Soft brown eyes hiding in a worn face, dark streaks and shadows lending an air of permanent tiredness. Conchetta's skin seemed to be stretched thinner over the bone these days, as if her face was losing all its stuffing, and though her hair was still thick and mostly dark, wiry grey hairs straggled through the blackness, like weeds through a rose garden. The physical changes, her vulnerabilities, made Zac feel more tender towards her than ever. He loved her. A few tablets fell back into the bottle from his hand.

But she would be better off without him, he thought. The thoughts in his head were exhausting, whirling like drifting snow-flakes from every direction so that he could no longer see clearly. Such overwhelming guilt, so much unhappiness that he caused just because of who he was. Conchetta was a conflict avoider and with his father around, there was plenty of conflict to avoid.

Zac always felt her pain reaching out to him when his father was at his most scathing. Of course she would be devastated at first by Zac's death. He never doubted that she loved him. But the conflict would be gone, the sense of division, the feeling that she was torn between her husband and her son. Surely that must be a good thing?

He looked at the tablets. He was not afraid to die as much as he was afraid of *how* he would die. If he could be certain that it would simply be oblivion, then he would not hesitate. To be away from his own thoughts, to be released from inside his own head, to sleep peacefully. But if he made a half-hearted attempt and was discovered... well, he could not face the consequences. And if he botched it and caused enough damage to permanently disable himself, but not enough to die, then it would be yet another burden on Conchetta. A flame of anger flared inside him. He would probably botch it. He was useless. What had he ever done properly in his life?

Nothing, his father would have said. His father, who watched him silently and turned from him with barely a word, while Conchetta fluttered round trying to appease them all and pretend there was some normality in this fractured family. When he was little, Conchetta would hold Zac's hand under the table at dinnertime, or smile at him with her soft eyes, or stroke his knee soothingly when his father's silent disapproval was at its most withering. Little gestures, bird-like and furtive, that told him she loved him, even if she could not openly take his side. Zac felt a surge of guilt. How exhausting Conchetta's life had been. He wondered what hope she had felt when she first held him as a baby, what disappointment had followed.

He had ruined Conchetta's life with his freakish instincts. And then there was Abbie, who thought she loved him, but loved someone who didn't exist. Zac looked down at himself, at his own body, as if looking at a stranger's. It felt disconnected from the rest of him, as if he, Zac, finished somewhere round his neck. The rest of it was…well, he didn't know what it was. Flesh. Bone. Muscle. That was all. He would be doing Abbie a favour. The way things were, they were destined for years of tension that could only end one way. If he died now, she could move on, love someone else who was capable of loving her the way she deserved.

He picked up a tablet, then hesitated. The God factor. He didn't believe in God until he contemplated dying and then it became not so much a belief as a fear. He was sinful. An abomination. If it all just… *ended*… the pain and the anxiety and the self-loathing, then that would be one thing. A long, silent sleep. Judgement was another thing entirely.

Zac looked up from the table, the tablet still in his hand, his attention caught by movement. He glanced out of the window. How strange the cloud formation was, like a giant dragon's head belching fire. Slowly it drifted, changing shape so quickly, yet he was barely conscious of movement. The dragon became a more benign horse, and then the shape spread slowly outwards, the flanks of the horse spreading until the whole thing was… what? An angel. An angel with wings, that loomed towards him. He felt suddenly moved by the enormity of everything round him, the way it all fitted together, had some kind of unity. Except for him.

He closed his eyes. Was it possible to go on, simply to change shape like the clouds in the sky, adapt into something else? He couldn't see how. It was unbearable even to think about the struggle involved in change. It was not seamless like the clouds. A wave of tiredness swept over him. How good it would be to sleep properly. His nights were restless and the mornings eaten up by pain and nausea and he felt washed out with the retching. Empty. It would be simpler if he just erased the problem. Better. It would truly be better for everyone. He moved his hand to his mouth and tried to concentrate simply on the swallowing action, not the effect of that action. Don't think, he thought. Just do. Just do. Just do, do, do.

———

Shona half hoped that Marianne would be asleep when she went into the lounge with the tea trolley but the old woman was sitting alertly at the window, dark eyes gleaming as she looked out into the garden. She was so absorbed, Shona thought, frowning. She was not so much lost in thought as consumed by it. There was a difference. Marianne might get confused, but at moments like this, Shona thought the old woman was every bit as sharp as she was. Maybe that was why Marianne frightened her.

"Where is Zac?" Marianne said, without turning her head. Her gnarled hands twisted absently at the ends of a pale pink scarf that hung loosely round her neck.

"He's off sick, Marianne."

"You said that yesterday. And the day before. And the day before that."

Was she right? Shona wondered. Had Zac been off for three days now? Tuesday… Wednesday, yes… three days.

"Would you like some tea?" Shona asked.

Marianne turned to her at last.

"What's wrong with him?"

"I… he… he's just not feeling himself."

Marianne studied Shona's face. She had not missed the lack of specific illness in Shona's answer.

"When will he be back?"

"I'm not sure."

Marianne's intent gaze dropped and she turned back to the window dismissively.

"He might be off for a bit longer, but I'm sure he'll be back when he's properly well."

Marianne did not answer, already absorbed again in her own private thoughts.

Shona began to busy herself with a cup and the teapot. She would pour one for Marianne and simply leave it by her side. She did not want to mention Zac again. The staff had been told not to discuss his situation with residents. It was too upsetting for them. Poor Zac. He was such a gentle boy. Unusual. A movement outside the door caught her eye.

"Angie!" she called.

The figure in the hall, stopped, turned reluctantly. A sullen faced girl of about nineteen appeared in the doorway. Her long dark hair was scraped back into a limp ponytail, glistening with sweat and grease at the temples.

"I'm just off for a quick fag," she said sourly, waving a cigarette and defying Shona to interrupt.

"Mary in the blue room needs seeing to first."

Angie's eyes bore venomously into Shona as she slipped the cigarette back into the pocket of her pale blue overall. She turned away towards the lift and Shona heard her mutter something.

"Old fucker."

Shona was not given to temper but she felt a surge of anger, even though she was not sure if it was her or Mary in the Blue Room that Angie meant. This was another reason she missed Zac. Most people were unsuited to this work, only took it because they had nothing else. Zac was different.

"Angie!"

Angie turned back, and looked at her coolly.

"Yeah?"

"What did you say?"

"I didn't say anything."

"Yes, you did."

"I never heard anything."

Shona turned in surprise. It was Marianne who had spoken. Shona lifted the cup of tea from the trolley and put it by Marianne's side, banging it slightly as she put it down so that a trickle of tea spilled over the edge of the cup. When she turned back to deal with Angie, she saw a flash of pale blue uniform and the lift doors closing.

Her lips tightened and she pushed the trolley away, hearing Marianne's voice trailing belligerently at her back.

"I never asked for this tea."

———

As his brain returned to consciousness, Zac could hear muffled voices swimming towards him from somewhere in the distance. The effect was not unlike being under water, he thought, but he had not the energy to open his eyes to investigate. A sniffle, a rustle of tissue, a sudden burst of sobbing as though a dam of tears had suddenly burst.

"Oh for God's sake, Conchetta," he heard his father say wearily. "Is that going to help?"

"He is my BOY!"

Even in the state he was in, Zac could recognise the mixture of resentment and hurt, the edge of desperate hysteria, that Conchetta so often displayed around his father. Poor thing, Zac thought vaguely, from wherever this place was that he was trapped. Why did his father treat her this way? Why did he care

85

so little what she felt? Or seem to. Zac felt too exhausted and nauseous and overwhelmed to continue the thought.

He was alive.

The realisation made Zac keep his eyes tight closed, unwilling to face the scene at his bedside. A mixture of relief and despair surged through him and he didn't know how to separate the two, or how to gauge which was the stronger emotion. He only knew that he had the same problems as before to confront but now they were worse. He had failed. He always failed.

"He is not a boy," said his father. "He is a grown…" He stopped.

"Say it!" said Conchetta with such venom that Zac found himself half opening one eye, in the tentative way you might cautiously part the slats of a blind. Conchetta had jumped to her feet, her normal pallor warmed with two hectic flushes of anger in her cheeks. "SAY IT!" she screamed. "You cannot even say the word! Man. He is a MAN!"

"Sit down," said his father flatly.

Zac closed his eye again. All that emotion in Conchetta and his father could not deal with it, let alone benefit from the power of it. How much she could have loved him!

"He is a man," repeated Conchetta defiantly, unwilling to give in.

"What is it that's wrong with him?" persisted his father. "Is he gay – or worse?"

Zac's heart skipped a beat. He was feeling very sick now, wanted to retch, but told himself to keep perfectly still.

"Why must there be something wrong with him? Why must you always see it in that way?"

"He is unlike any man I have ever known."

"So? SO?" demanded Conchetta. "He is a little different but

am I supposed to love him less for that? He is my boy and he will always be my boy – whatever you say."

"Yes," muttered his father. "That's the problem. It was always Zac, Zac, Zac…"

"Are you jealous of your own son?"

Zac had never heard his mother speak this way, so angry and so… confrontational.

"Don't be ridiculous Conchetta!"

"Ridiculous? I'll tell you what is ridiculous. It is ridiculous to think that someone can change who and what they are by sheer willpower alone. You believe that you can think yourself 'normal?' Make a choice? Now that IS ridiculous!"

"You can never be reasonable when it comes to this."

"So what are you saying? That it is my fault?"

"You mollycoddled him…"

Zac hold his breath in the ensuing silence.

"You are beyond stupid."

Conchetta spat the words out coldly. Zac could not believe his ears. What had got into her?

"Am I? Am I really?"

"You seriously think a mother can change what her child is inside because she loves him too much?"

"Conchetta, he behaved like a girl! He ran to you, clung to you, hid behind you. You never forced him to face what he is - a man."

"It is you who cannot face what he is. YOU."

Zac heard the impatient scrape of a chair. His parents' angry voices began to swim and recede. He had to be sick, couldn't hold it much longer. His stomach burned.

It was true Conchetta had been his refuge as a child. He remembered so clearly running to her when things were wrong, as they often so were, and the sensation of sitting in her lap with his head on her chest while her fingers caressed his hair so softly. "My poor boy," she would murmur, "my poor little chap." 'Chap' was such an English word and it sounded strange in her French accent. Her adoption of the foreign expression touched him, somehow.

Tears began to smart behind Zac's closed eyelids. Had it not been for her acceptance… The pain in his stomach was so intense now he was going to throw up for sure. Then his mother's voice came into focus again, cutting suddenly through his discomfort. It had a tone he did not recognise. Goading. Cruel, almost.

"And you…what about you? Perhaps it's your fault, hmm? Perhaps this 'femininity' you are so afraid of is because of your genes?"

Zac heard Conchetta's heels tapping on the floor and then her voice hissed. "If being exposed to masculinity is so important in all of this, perhaps then you were not man enough. Hmm?"

"There was nothing…"

"Nothing you could do? No, of course not! It was all my fault and you could not combat my malign influence over our son. So you did nothing but hover like a dark presence over all of us, making your disapproval so obvious the boy did not know what he could possibly do to make you accept him."

"Accept? You want me to accept that my son is… is…"

"Yes! Yes I want you to accept! Whatever comes after 'is', I want you to accept. Is gay… is different… is feminine… is Zac. Whatever it is, I want you to accept because he is your son. Your child. And you know why else? Look! Look in that bed… No, you can't, can you? You are not brave enough to face the truth. That… THAT… is where not accepting gets you. He nearly died.

Zac felt so bad about himself that he nearly died. Is that what you want?"

"Perhaps it would have been better…"

His father's voice sounded strange. Zac felt his heart constrict, as though someone squeezed it in his hands. His father squeezing the life out of him.

There was silence, then Conchetta muttered an obscenity in French. A door banged shut. Zac lay rigid. Had his father gone? He heard a sniff, then the sound of stifled sobs again. The sound pained him. Even now, he could not bear to hear his mother cry without comforting her in the way she had always comforted him. A hand gently touched his head. He forced his eyes open in time to see a figure turning from the bed. But it was not Conchetta. He realised, with a wave of confusion, that it was his father.

What should he make of that, he wondered. It was too difficult to work out. Zac closed his eyes, drifting, drifting far away. The door clicked softly.

CHAPTER ELEVEN

Zac

Outside the door, Zac steeled himself. He didn't want any awkward questions. Marianne looked up, her face clouded by irritation as the door opened but she broke into an instinctive smile at the sight of the tall, dark-haired figure who entered.

"Zac!" she exclaimed.

"Hello Marianne. How are you?"

Marianne's smile faded as she looked closely at his face. It was grey, as though every drop of blood had been sucked from it.

"Better than you, by the looks of things."

"I'm fine."

"You're even thinner than before."

"I'm fine."

"Why were you off for such a long time?"

"I've come to take you out for a walk. Shona said you had asked to go out into the garden?"

"Why were you off?"

"I wasn't well."

"What was wrong with you?"

"Shall we put your cardigan on or would you like your jacket?"

"What was wrong with you?"

"I wasn't well, Marianne!"

Zac felt a rush of emotion. Perhaps that was a good sign. For the last week, it had seemed as if everything inside him was dead, but Marianne… he felt invaded by her scrutiny. It was as if she could reach him in the dead place inside, perhaps because she knew that dead place existed. Zac suddenly wanted to sit down.

"You still talk like a lawyer!" he scolded, trying to sound light-hearted.

"You are not off for more than three weeks with something trifling," said Marianne, motioning that she wanted her blue cardigan that had been discarded on the end of the sofa.

Zac reached for the cardigan and began to help Marianne into it, pushing her right hand through the sleeve first.

"Well, I'm fine now," said Zac.

Marianne reached out her hand and unexpectedly grasped Zac's.

"You do not need to pretend with me, Zac," she said quietly, with more tenderness than Zac expected or was used to.

He felt his eyes sting. Perhaps the doctors were right. It was too soon to come back to work. But he could not stay in the house any longer. He had returned to his parents' house after his release from hospital so that Conchetta could look after him while Abbie was at work. He had found it a difficult period. They had never discussed his reason for trying to end his life but that was what he would have expected. It was only Elicia who ever spelled things out in his family but even she had been quiet. They had all been too afraid to talk, his father's eyes following him silently, his mother's thin, hopeful smile and quivering fear lacerating him with guilt. Elicia laughed even more than usual.

Conchetta had found him, arriving at his door entirely spontaneously with some post that had arrived at the house for him. She knew it was Zac's day off but had thought he was out when he did not answer the doorbell. She was disappointed, but let herself in with the key Zac had given her, hoping he would return before she left. Sometimes, she did a little light cleaning and cooking for Zac and Abbie and as she opened the door, it occurred to her that she could surprise them by leaving a meal for this evening. Perhaps a tagine, she thought as she opened the door, something that would cook slowly. Instead, she walked into unexpected horror.

The last thing Zac recalled before slipping into unconsciousness was Conchetta's scream, the high-pitched hysterical scream that told him he had got it all so wrong. Even as he drifted into no-man's land he understood the primitive nature of her anguish. He had heard a cow once, bellowing long into the night when its dead calf had been removed. Conchetta's scream had reminded him of that. In the weeks since the overdose, the memory of that scream had been the only thing to pierce Zac's indifference. Until Marianne.

"You do not need to pretend with me," Marianne repeated, dropping his hand.

Zac said nothing, placing her left arm awkwardly into the other sleeve of the cardigan. Pretence was his whole life. He was used to it.

"You are skin and bone, Zac."

"I have always been thin."

"Not like this."

"I know I look awful."

"What? You do not look awful! That is not what I am saying. I am saying you must look after your body."

"I hate my body." The words were out before Zac could think about them. He flushed.

"Hm," said Marianne, non-commitally, her gaze unflinching.

"Don't look at me like that!"

"How long have I known you, Zac?"

"Oh I don't know… two years maybe. Three?"

"Whatever it is, long enough."

"Long enough for what?"

"To observe. To know something of your struggles."

Zac said nothing.

"When I first met you, I felt as if knew you already. I thought perhaps it was because you reminded me physically of Raymond. The same black hair and flashing dark eyes. But then I realised that it was more than that."

"What was it?

"There was something familiar about your spirit."

Zac's fingers stilled in his wrestle with a cardigan sleeve. He looked at her almost fearfully.

"I don't know what you mean."

"I think that what I recognised in you was a quality that Raymond had."

"Oh? What was that?"

"A sense of otherness. He knew what it was to be an outsider and I think you do too, Zac."

"I don't know what you mean."

"Okay Zac." Marianne's voice was soothing, like she was stroking a fretful child, which made Zac feel more uptight than ever.

He pulled the cardigan over her shoulders.

"Shall we go? Perhaps to the bench by the rhododendrons? You like that bit of the garden, Marianne."

Marianne sighed. "Very well, Zac. Let's go."

Marianne looked almost feverish, Zac thought when he entered the residents' lounge, pink-cheeked and bright eyed.

"At last!" she exclaimed.

"What's wrong Marianne?"

"I have been waiting for you to arrive."

"Well, it is nice to be needed!"

"What kept you?"

"This is my normal starting time. What on earth is wrong with you? You want to go out, is that it?"

"No. Well yes. But not yet. I have something to show you first. Take me up to my room."

Zac looked at her uncertainly. She seemed so agitated it concerned him.

"I have had an idea," she continued. It has been playing around my head while you were off and today I feel more sure of it. I want to show you something in my room. Quickly. Come on Zac!"

Zac wheeled her chair out of the lounge and up the corridor.

"Close the door," Marianne commanded as he wheeled her into the room.

Zac hesitated. He did not like to close doors when dealing with residents on his own.

"Close it!"

He stuck out a foot and lightly pressed the door behind him as he wheeled the chair through.

"Over to the dressing table."

Zac sat on the edge of the bed while Marianne reached for a jewellery box and placed it on her knee, before using her hands to push against the dressing table and manoeuvre herself round to face Zac.

"Why do you hate your body, Zac?"

"What?"

"You said you hated your body yesterday."

"Did I?"

"You know you did!"

"Oh, everyone hates something about themselves, Marianne. It is no big deal."

"We share something in common, Zac. We are both trapped inside our bodies. Me by illness and old age, you by…." She paused. "Please tell me why you were off for so long."

"I…"

"Please."

"I took…" Zac came to an abrupt halt. He could not say it. "I just got unwell. A bit stressed." He smiled half-heartedly. "Looking after you Marianne – that's wot done it!"

"You took… what?"

Marianne waited but Zac did not reply.

"Perhaps," she continued, "you tried to find a way out."

"Perhaps."

"Raymond too," she said.

Zac's head jolted up to look at her.

"Raymond?"

"I'd like to tell you about Raymond."

"Tell me what?"

"He was a transsexual."

Zac felt his throat constrict. He did not want to hear that word.

"That was Raymond's 'otherness'. I am not certain what yours is Zac. But I know it's there. At first, I assumed you were gay. Then I realised that did not quite fit. There was something deeper, just as there was with Raymond. It is a hard thing to define, but when you have lived with it, you recognise it. I think you are struggling as he struggled."

"No... I... why are you saying such a thing?"

"Denial is dangerous."

"I am not in denial," Zac said desperately.

"Well, I am wrong then." Marianne fingered the box on her knee thoughtfully. "Raymond and I made so many mistakes."

"Why did...?"

"Why did he marry me? I think you can tell me that better than I can tell you, Zac. Why are you with Abbie?"

"I..."

"Because a little bit of you loves her. And a big bit of you wants her because she is your chance of normality. Isn't that the case?"

Zac looked so stricken by the question that Marianne reached out a hand to his cheek.

"You are the son we could have had, Zac. Raymond and I. You remind me so much of him."

"When did he...?"

"He has been gone a long time."

Zac was silent for a moment.

"I wasn't going to ask the question you thought I was."

"What question?"

"You thought I was going to ask why he married you, but I wasn't."

"So what were you going to ask?"

"Why you loved him."

"Love does not cover what I felt, Zac."

Zac looked at her curiously. Such passion she spoke with. Unabated, unchanged, flickering inside the rubble of her ruined body as it must always have done.

"You loved him even though..."

"Even though, in spite of, because of. All of them. I could live with what Raymond was. It was he who could not live with what he was."

Zac wondered for a moment if all this meant that, unlike him, Raymond had been successful in his suicide attempt, but he did not like to ask. There was something about confronting the question that made him uncomfortable, scared even. He looked at the bright rays of dancing dust and light that streamed in the window and felt suddenly cold.

"I tried to encourage him to live part of his life as a woman but to include me," Marianne continued. "For a while it was enough. But he needed more. He wanted to transition."

Zac shivered.

"Transition?"

"To become a woman. Take hormones. Have surgery."

Zac's stomach was beginning to tighten into the familiar twisted knot. Perhaps that was how Raymond died. He felt nauseous and needed to move from his seated position. He wished he could lie back, stretch out on Marianne's bed.

There was a short knock and the door pushed open. Shona popped her head round.

"Ah Zac…" she said. "I wondered if you were here. I'll just leave this door open."

"Close it!" screamed Marianne, enraged.

But Shona disappeared, leaving it open.

"She is kind, Marianne," protested Zac. "You are so awful to her."

"She is a ninny."

Zac sighed.

"We need to go. But you were going to show me something?"

"This," said Marianne. Her thin gnarled fingers twisted at the lock of the jewellery box on her knee. A burst of tinkling music from 'Doctor Zhivago' played as the lid opened. Zac watched as she lifted something out, something on a pale, delicate lilac ribbon. Then he saw that it was a silver key.

"What is it?" he asked

"We had a flat, Raymond and I. In the south of France. It is still there."

"Really?" said Zac, surprised. "Who looks after it?"

"An old friend."

"A wonderful place to have a flat. Marianne. What a shame you can't use it."

"Yes."

Marianne fingered the key greedily.

"Shall we go out to the garden now?" asked Zac.

"I want you to go," said Marianne.

"Oh…" said Zac, standing up.

Marianne held the key up.

"No, no… to the south of France. You need a holiday. You have not been well."

She held the key up, dangling it at the end of the lilac ribbon.

"I can't do that. Marianne. I…" Zac faltered. "That's very kind of you but… I can't possibly. I've been off work already and …but thank you. Thank you for the offer."

"It's a key to more than a flat, Zac. This place… it will show you things, help you discover things."

"What things?"

"Yourself. Whoever you are."

"I can't."

"Why not?"

Zac was silenced.

"I don't know anyone in the south of France," he said eventually.

"You know me," said Marianne. She looked up at him, her eyes luminous with animation. "This is not all selfless, Zac. I have a plan. I want you to go, but I want to go too. No, no don't look at me like that! I have thought hard about this. I have unfinished business there. Take me with you. Go to the south of France and take me with you."

Chapter Twelve

Marianne

Nothing to offer him. Sebastian's words consumed me. I poured all my frustration and hatred into him while appearing to tolerate him in my home for Raymond's sake. It was our wedding anniversary in September and I smiled enigmatically - and what I hoped was sexily -as I pointed out over dinner one night that Raymond and I would have special plans for that night. Plans that naturally did not include Sebastian.

I took a day off work and visited the hairdresser and beauty parlour for some treatments. It was not that I was stupid enough to believe that a haircut, or a facial skin treatment, or a full body massage would in themselves make me beautiful. But they made me FEEL beautiful and confidence is power.

My short, dark hair fell back perfectly into place when I moved, gleaming like a rich horse chestnut. I lined my eyes with kohl and slicked my lips with soft pink gloss. My stockings slipped smoothly over my moisturised skin in a soft caress and I slid my feet into high heels. Even the mirror did not dampen my enthusiasm tonight as it might usually do. The reflection was closer to the blossoming of my youth than I had ever achieved in recent years.

Ten minutes before Raymond was due I ran him a bath laced with oils.

"Upstairs," I called as I heard the door bang.

Raymond wandered into the kitchen first. I heard his bag drop on the wooden floor, the sound of his feet on the stairs and I felt breathless with the anticipation of having him closer to me.

"Hi," he said popping his head round the bedroom door.

He looked at me in surprise.

"You look nice," he said. It was an academic assessment.

"For you," I said with a smile, indicating the bath. "I have booked a table for this evening."

"Where?"

"It's a surprise."

He seemed almost disconcerted - but I think in a pleased way - by my attentions, and I helped him slip out of his clothes and into the bath. I deliberately made my attention sensual rather than sexual. Perhaps it was a repetition of my beauty parlour experience but this time for Raymond. In any case, I knew that anticipation was a key weapon in sexual desire, a build-up of tension. The most important sexual organ is the brain.

Raymond emerged from the bath with his dark hair sleeked back, water dripping from the ends. The soft white towel was wrapped around his waist and he padded into the bedroom and over to the wardrobe but I got there first. We had two banks of wardrobes in our room, one for him and one for me.

"No, no," I said, smiling teasingly at him as he went to open his side. My hand lay on his.

"This side."

I opened my wardrobe and Raymond looked at me.

"Anything," I said.

"But we…"

"Anything."

"I thought we were going out?"

"We are. I have booked a table an hour's drive away."

There was an air of incredulity about Raymond's expression that made me enjoy the moment in a real rather than a forced way.

"You are really prepared to…"

"Yes."

Raymond made a strange little sound, a combination of a gasp and a laugh.

"Truly? You mean it?"

I could sense his excitement at my attitude. Neither of us would ever mention France or Bar Patrice out loud to the other, but I knew he must be thinking that the churlish acceptance of his habits - the sulky tolerance of them - was being replaced by something else. He pulled out a silk dress with a black and grey rose print on it and held it up to me questioningly.

"Perfect."

I selected some underwear and he slipped it on. I took out a long blonde wig and sat him down in front of the mirror and did his makeup. As I applied some blusher with a broad brush, I caught sight of his reflection in the mirror and stopped suddenly. It was hard for me to see him this way. I felt almost as if I was opening the door of his cage myself and telling him to fly away. But he looked so happy, so alive, that I smiled at his reflection and he lifted his lips to kiss me in an instinctive way that he had not done for a long time. I laid my lips lightly on his and he pulled me closer. He was grateful, I knew that, but I pulled away. I would exploit his gratitude later. Build the tension a little more.

"Later," I said. "We have to go."

Raymond looked at himself in the glass.

"We are really going?"

"Yes."

He was trembling when he stood up. This was so different from the times he sneaked out to Bar Patrice's, dressed up. This was his home. He worked here. He could not afford to get caught. And yet the danger of it was exhilarating and I knew that inside the danger was an element of sexual provocation that excited him.

Most men risk looking ridiculous dressed as a woman, unless they take hormones to feminise their appearance. The clothes, the make-up, the mannerisms, they are all simply a veneer, an added top layer. But they became part of Raymond, or he became part of them - I'm not sure which. Like Jasmine, he was a good-looking man in a feminine kind of way but as a woman, he was beautiful. Perhaps it was not to his advantage that he made people stare because on closer examination there were small clues to his true gender: he had beautiful skin but up close, perhaps it was slightly coarser than a woman's. But on the whole, if there was anything masculine about Raymond I would say it was boyish rather than mannish. He was tall, willowy, fine-featured. If anything, he had more presence as a woman, more authority. More drama.

We were surprisingly quiet on the journey. I drove and Raymond looked out of the side window as the countryside flashed by, the first tinges of autumn colours staining the tips of the trees. The yellow and burnt orange reminded me of the landscape in the south of France. I don't know if it was the same for Raymond – I don't suppose it was – but I kept finding reminders on that journey of the night Patrice died. The colours, the highly charged tension, the sense of anticipation. The only thing missing was the jealousy, though I suppose somewhere in the mix, my feelings about Sebastian provided an element of that.

As we drew up outside the restaurant, I turned to Raymond and smiled, then noticed he had sweat on his brow.

"I can't, Marianne," he said, his voice full of panic. "Someone will know…"

I did not answer him. Calmly, I took a powder puff from my bag and dabbed at his brow, then opened the car door. I stood outside waiting, feeling less calm than I looked, and eventually his door opened.

"Good evening ladies."

Ladies. The doorman swung the door open and I saw Raymond draw himself up and take confidence from the single word.

He looked at me sideways as we walked down the corridor and I saw the glimmer of elation in his eyes. For the rest of the evening, he immersed himself in his new identity. We ordered the best of everything. Creamy scallops with a mint and pea puree; fillet of beef and dauphinoise potatoes; dark chocolate truffles dusted with caramelised strands of red chilli pepper. It felt like foreplay, sensual indulgence that made us both flirt quite outrageously. I leaned across the table.

"Your name is Rosalyn," I said.

"What do I do?"

"What would you like to do?"

He laughed.

"I would like to be… an actress."

"Ah…you would like to be loved, Rosalyn."

"Yes."

"I love you."

"I know." Raymond's eyes softened. And I love you too, Marianne."

It was the gratitude talking. And the champagne. But he did love me in his own way. Neither of us would be sitting here if there were not love between us. A strange kind of love, some might say. I didn't care. I didn't expect anyone else to understand.

"What do you think people take us for?" I asked. "Friends? Colleagues?"

"Sisters?" said Raymond.

"You are too attractive to be my sister."

"Don't be silly."

The restaurant was warm, softly lit and intimate and I had deliberately booked a corner table. It felt like a cocoon which held us safely while we peered out at the rest of the world. Then I spotted a man who kept looking over at Raymond.

"There is a man in the corner," I said under my breath, "and he certainly thinks you are attractive. I think he is trying to catch your attention."

Raymond smiled and after a few seconds, casually glanced sideways. The thought that he was being watched by a man both pleased and excited him.

I leaned across the table and said seductively,

"But for tonight you're mine. That man cannot see I have wrapped my legs round yours under the table like a chain. He can't have you."

Raymond giggled. He was alive, enjoying the challenge of our flirtation, of being allowed to be a woman. Secrets are sexy, I thought. Something shared and intimate and bonding.

But a moment later, Raymond glanced sideways and I noticed his expression change subtly.

He turned his chair slightly towards the window so that he could be viewed less easily. It was dark outside now and the chandelier lights of the restaurant danced in the inky blackness of the glass. Raymond kept his head angled towards the darkness, even when the waiter brought the coffee and truffles.

"What is the matter?" I asked, unnerved by the sudden change in temperature.

"That man you mentioned," he said.

"What about him?"

"Don't look round. Marianne, don't! He suspects."

"No he doesn't!"

"He knows. I'm telling you he knows."

I kept my eyes fixed on Raymond, as if deep in conversation and oblivious to everything else.

"Raymond, calm down. He is watching you because he fancies you."

"Calm down! My God Marianne, he knows. I should never… never… it was too risky. What was I thinking of? There's going to be a scene."

It surprised me how scared Raymond was. He was never scared in France. I suppose the risk of exposure made our expedition all the more exciting, but now at the moment of imminent exposure, Raymond was a mess. In just a few minutes he had gone from coquettish to terrified and an unladylike sweat was back, glistening on his brow like raindrops.

"Marianne, I teach children. What…"

In the corner, the man pushed his chair back and scrunched up his napkin, stuffing it into his coffee cup. Raymond's nerves were catching and I swallowed hard as he walked towards us. Raymond didn't move a muscle.

"Goodnight," said the man as he passed the table. But I saw him look back curiously in Raymond's direction.

"Night," I said.

Raymond said nothing, terrified his voice would reveal everything. He bent down to his feet, pretending to rummage in his handbag. I think that was the terrifying thing… that if, at any point, he had to open his mouth, everything was over.

"He's gone."

"Let's go," said Raymond. "I need to get out of here."

"No, wait. Wait a few minutes."

I did not know if the man turned his head back because he liked the look of Raymond or because he guessed the truth. We sat in silence until I saw the lights of a car outside head towards the window and then turn away.

"Waiter! Could I have the bill please?"

Raymond leant his head back on the car passenger seat and breathed deeply. Neither of us said anything as I turned the car out into the open road. Darkness sped by, a blur of lights as we hit villages, a skim of summer rain on the window. After ten miles or so, I felt Raymond relax. Then I heard a noise and I turned in surprise. I thought he was crying at first but as we passed a streetlight, I saw that he was snorting with nervous laughter.

"Oh my God, Marianne!"

I grinned.

"Did you see him…? Jesus, the look! He definitely knew."

"No he didn't."

"He bloody did!"

By the time we reached home, we were shaking with laughter and nerves. We sat in the drive outside the house for a moment.

"But we did it," said Raymond, his voice tinged with exultation.

"Yes, we did. Together."

Raymond stopped laughing.

"Thank you, Marianne. It was the best present I ever received. The acceptance…."

He said no more but he reached a hand out and touched my cheek, and I caught his hand and held it.

"Let's go in," I said.

We were both giddy with champagne and hysteria and relief, and it provoked something reckless in both of us. We kissed the moment we got through the door. I thought briefly of Sebastian's words…nothing to offer…and felt a surge of triumph. I just hoped that whatever was released between us, would take root and grow.

———

"This is very good of you Sebastian," I called. I lay back contentedly on the wicker sofa in the conservatory and watched him through the open door. He had an apron over his peacock blue shirt and his cuffs were rolled up. Steam rose from a saucepan on the front ring and a lid rattled on the back over a pan of boiling water that hissed and spat.

"Not at all," he said smoothly. "Nothing fancy. "

"Do you want a hand?" asked Raymond, opening a sleepy eye.

"No you're fine. It's just some pasta."

"Good," murmured Raymond, and his eyelids closed again.

"It shouldn't be overcooked," said Sebastian primly, busying himself emptying black peppercorns into a grinder. "Even Italian restaurants overcook it. Sometimes it's shocking the slop they serve up as Italian food."

"You should tell them, Sebastian. I'm sure they'd appreciate the feedback."

"Don't be arch, Marianne. It doesn't suit you."

I curled myself up on the sofa, the wicker creaking beneath me as if sighing at the weight.

"What was your connection with Italy again, Sebastian?" I asked him. "Oh yes – you holidayed there in 1962."

"Marianne," said Raymond reproachfully, opening one eye again.

"Or is it just that you visited Rizza's ice-cream parlour in town once?"

Sebastian banged the pepper grinder down on the table.

"It's ready," he said.

"Smells good," said Raymond.

"Onions, garlic, peppers, tomatoes, cream and pepperoni with some parmesan shavings on top."

"Ooh, parmesan shavings. No mere cheddar for Sebastian," I said. I uncurled myself from the sofa and stood up, stretching like a cat.

"Yum," said Raymond, patting Sebastian on the back as he drained the pasta into the sink... "I'm starving."

"Me too," I said.

Sebastian half turned.

"You have such a good appetite for a woman, Marianne," he said. He lifted the pot from the sink. "I did notice that little tummy of yours is getting bigger."

I grinned inwardly. I had been waiting for this moment.

"I know," I said, "just like yours Sebastian. But I'm pregnant. What's your excuse?"

The pot clattered to the floor and two heads turned towards me. Raymond looked like he might faint. Sebastian looked like he might murder me. Pale worms of spaghetti straggled across the floor.

"Well," I said, "that was a show stopper." I linked my arm though Raymond's.

"Are you pleased?"

Sebastian left shortly after. It was me who had to clean up most of the pasta from the floor. It was worth every last minute of effort. It was perfect, really. A celebratory meal cooked for us and I didn't even have to suffer Sebastian's presence while eating it. I poured two glasses of wine and handed one to Raymond who was stunned and silent.

"To our new arrival," I said.

CHAPTER THIRTEEN

Zac

Conchetta looked at her son with a frown.

"But Zac," she said gently, her eyes dark pools of concern, "you are not well enough yet to go off by yourself. You need to get stronger."

"I won't be by myself. I have to take one of the residents on holiday."

"That sounds most strange and irregular."

Across the table, his father stayed silent but his eyes flicked over his son, then back to his own plate.

Zac tried to chew a lump of meat that was turning into an obstacle in his mouth. It was impossible to swallow. He looked up miserably. He was back in his own place with Abbie and he wished he had never agreed to come home for dinner. Elicia caught his eye and winked.

"Who is this resident?" persisted Conchetta.

"She is called Marianne. She is wealthy and has a flat in the south of France. She has asked me to be her chaperone and do some nursing duties but there will also be a carer in France who will help look after her."

"And what are the managers of the home saying?"

"They have insisted she sign a disclaimer, absolving them of any responsibility. And I have to take it as my own holiday, nothing to do with them."

"But you have just been off."

"That was ill-health. It does not count as holiday entitlement."

"Sounds ridiculous to me," said his father, pushing his chair back. There was a clatter as he opened the dishwasher and put his plate in.

Conchetta glanced up nervously.

"Well," she said, "irregular I suppose, but perhaps… perhaps it will be pleasant enough to have some sunshine." Conchetta thought it a bad idea, but as soon as her husband said it was, she felt obliged to retreat from her own opposition... Smooth things over for Zac.

"I think Zac's lucky," said Elicia brightly. "I would love to go to the south of France." She scraped the last mouthful from her plate and put her knife and fork down with a clatter.

Her father muttered something nobody could hear and went out, closing the door behind him.

Conchetta and Elicia looked at one another.

"You will be careful, Zac?" Conchetta said. "You won't do anything foolish when you are on your own?"

Zac flushed scarlet and shook his head.

"Of course not."

"You won't ever… I couldn't…"

"Mum…" said Elicia.

"I know," said Zac.

"You have to eat," said Conchetta, watching as he scraped the remains on his plate into the bin.

112

"He'll eat croissants, won't you Zac?" said Elicia. "And French bread."

"And pâtisserie," said Conchetta more brightly. "Beautiful cakes."

Zac tried to smile.

"Yes," he said.

He couldn't wait to be gone.

Marianne was different, Zac thought, watching her. There was still a feverishness about her, a sense of anticipation.

"What are you doing?" he asked.

"Writing a letter," she said. She looked up from the table. "Writing a letter," she repeated, "to someone I have not seen for forty years."

"Goodness me! Who is that?"

Zac looked at the sheet of azure writing paper and saw Marianne's thin scrawl spidering shakily across the page. Her motor skills were deteriorating badly.

Before she could answer, a figure from across the room started to walk unsteadily towards them, leaning heavily on a Zimmer and looking around her as she moved. Annie's hair was wilder even than usual, a startled halo of white around her head.

"Do you know where my mother's house is?" she asked Zac plaintively.

"Go away Annie," snapped Marianne.

"I want to go home," said Annie. "Please."

Zac put his arm round her. "Come and sit down Annie. Shall I get you a nice cup of tea?"

"You are wasting your time," muttered Marianne, returning to her letter.

"What do you think, Annie?" said Zac. "A cup of tea?"

Annie brightened suddenly.

"Oh that would be lovely, dear," she said.

Zac helped her over to the chair but Annie suddenly stopped.

"Where are you putting me?" she demanded fretfully. "You're keeping me from my mum. She'll be angry with you."

"I told you that you were wasting your time," said Marianne, without lifting her head from her scribbling.

"No, no," said Zac soothingly. "Your mother will be here soon, Annie. We will sit and wait for her here and I will get you some tea until she comes."

"That's a good idea," said Annie, all compliance again. "I hope she comes soon."

"What are you telling her that for?" demanded Marianne.

Angie popped her head round the door.

"Zac. Mary-in-the-Blue-Room. Your turn."

Mary was never just 'Mary', always 'Mary-in-the-Blue-Room', her identity now defined by her location. Zac nodded but flinched inwardly. He hated having to feed Mary-in-the-Blue-Room.

The Blue Room was the last room at the end of a corridor on the second floor. Mary never left it. For the three years Zac had worked here, he had never seen her downstairs and Shona said Mary had been there for five years before that without being out of the room. Not even at Christmas. Mary-in-the-Blue-Room had almost mythical status and new staff were always scared to go in there by the time they got appointed to look after Mary. Eight years, Zac thought, as he walked down the corridor. Eight years in one room.

He opened the door hesitantly. Mary was propped up by pillows, a misshapen bundle of bones and shrivelled skin. How could you look like that and still be alive? Zac wondered. She was doll sized which made the parched wrinkles of her skin seem even more incongruous. The only part of her that moved freely was her eyes. Zac had never seen anyone who looked as old as Mary. Yet there were young people dying of cancer who looked like there was nothing wrong with them until the final weeks. Shona said Mary was 88, but she looked even older to Zac. Her eyes found him as he opened the door, following his movement.

"Time for lunch, Mary," Zac said loudly.

He busied himself with the pillows trying to prop her up more securely, but she simply slid back after each attempt.

"I wonder what there is today," he said brightly. "Are you hungry?"

Mary said nothing but her eyes followed him still. They had a vacant quality, Zac thought, were almost translucent in their emptiness. It was as if the colour had been washed out of them and meaning had seeped away too. He wondered if she was constantly trying to make sense of where she was because that's the way it looked, as if she was constantly trapped with strangers in an unknown place. How frightening that place must be.

Zac lifted the lid on the plate and his stomach heaved. The food was liquidised into different coloured heaps. There was a fortified cream dessert, too, but he left the lid on until the last minute because he knew from experience that the smell of it was disgusting. He placed a bib over Mary's chest to protect the sheet and placed a teaspoon of liquidised carrot to her mouth. Her lips parted automatically.

His nose wrinkled involuntarily as he spooned it into her mouth and he saw her shudder as she swallowed, before her face contorted. It was lukewarm, Zac thought despairingly. He slid the spoon back into the mush.

"Is that nice, Mary?" he said.

Her eyes bore into him. Zac pressed the spoon to her mouth again, hoping her lips would part but they stayed closed. A trickle of carrot coloured saliva dribbled from the corner of her mouth.

"It's been a beautiful day today," said Zac, wiping her face gently. "Can you see from your bed, Mary? How lovely and sunny it is?"

He tried a spoonful from a different coloured heap. Mary's lips automatically parted slightly before she realised and turned her face from the spoon.

Perhaps the dessert, he thought, pulling open the lid. At least it was fortified with vitamins and calories. He gazed down at the pink goo. Fruits of the Forest, it was supposed to be. Mary accepted a few spoonfuls, seemingly oblivious to the nauseating smell of it.

"Come on Mary," he coaxed. "Try another spoonful. It's good for you."

Mary's eyes swivelled up to his face.

"All right, Mary?" he said, smoothing back her hair from her forehead.

Mary opened her mouth to speak, but only a hoarse whisper emerged.

"What was that?"

"I want to scream," whispered Mary.

Zac felt his heart tumble.

"I know, Mary," he said gently. "I know." He took her hand on the cover and held it between his own, rubbing her fingers. Mary watched their entwined hands intently for a minute, and then her eyes swivelled back up to his face with an intensity that made him instinctively shrink back. She looked up at him expectantly, as if waiting for something.

"Go on," Mary croaked, her eyes never leaving him. "You do it."

"Do what?"

"Scream for me," she said insistently, as if bewildered by the delay of his response. Her eyes bore into him. "Scream for me."

Zac stroked her head, pushing the wispy hair back from her face.

"I'll put the television on, will I?" he said.

Mary looked at him, uncomprehending, betrayed.

Voices might help, he thought. Signs of life. He looked round the room. Was this it? Was this what life was, where it ended, what it amounted to? A wave of despair washed over him. Maybe it would have been better if he had succeeded in ending it all. Better than sloughing through the shit of it all, only to end up like this.

He looked at the little pile of human rubble in the middle of the bed. He wasn't the only one trapped inside a body, as Marianne had put it. Whoever Mary was, whoever she had been, was trapped inside this wreckage. Perhaps we are all trapped, Zac thought.

He picked up the remote control on the bedside table.

"Let's see what's on, Mary," he said. He flicked through the channels, stopping at an old black and white film on channel 4. Mary did not even turn to the voices.

"I'll leave this on for you," he said. "I'll take the dishes away and you can tell me what it's about when I come back."

Mary made no acknowledgement of the fact that Zac had spoken and he stood up, removing the tray from beside the bed.

As he passed the lounge, he saw Marianne still writing.

"Not finished Marianne?" he asked.

"Yes, yes I am. Do you think you will be able to post it for me?"

"Of course."

He picked up the envelope.

"South of France?" he said.

"Yes," said Marianne. "I want to let an old friend of mine know when I will be arriving. She has the key to the flat and will air it for us."

Her eyes were bright.

"Her name is Jasmine. Jasmine Labelle. 1118 Rue Matin, Saint Estelle."

It was strange, Zac thought, that Abbie seemed so untroubled by his visit to France. She obviously thought that looking after an old woman would occupy all his time and prevent him doing anything stupid. Ironic that she thought Marianne was 'safe'. She thought that he wouldn't lose himself in France with such a responsibility - of course she had no idea that Marianne had promised he would find himself there.

Abbie had clung to him since the suicide attempt, part terrified by the level of his despair and part mortified at what she considered to be a public declaration of her inadequacy. She hadn't let him out of her sight since.

"It wasn't about us," Zac had protested when he finally got home from hospital.

"What was it about then?"

"Me."

She had looked at him fearfully but had not dared to voice her true feelings.

It would not last, Zac thought, this tiptoeing round him, but perhaps it would buy him some time.

He was preparing to roast a chicken, rubbing oil into the skin and grinding coarse sea salt over the top when Abbie came into the kitchen. There was something soothing about the physical nature of the task, the way the oil clung to his fingers. He smiled at Abbie as he ran his hands under the tap.

"Okay?" he said. He took a lemon from the bowl, halving it with a sharp knife and licking the juice that trickled over his fingers and onto the wooden board. He looked up at Abbie as he stuffed the lemon into the cavity and sprinkled rosemary on the top. She was transmitting something, a kind of optimism he hadn't seen for a while.

"I've been thinking," she said, "do you want me to take some holiday and come with you to help with the old lady? Will it be too much for you on your own?"

Zac's heart stopped. He could think of nothing worse. Going to France had become a necessary escape, a breathing space, and it could not be snatched from him like this at the last minute. He tried to suppress his horror.

"Thank you," he said, going over to Abbie and wrapping his arms round her so that his face was hidden, "but there is no need to do that. Much better for you to take some holiday when we can do something together without anyone else there."

"I don't want you to take on too much."

"I won't."

"If you are sure…"

"Completely."

He kissed the top of her head and moved back to the chicken.

"Zac…. I've been reading something today."

"Yes?"

"About transvestites."

Zac opened the oven door and placed the chicken in carefully, glad to have his back to her. If that was all it was, things would be so much easier. As he closed the oven door, he felt Abbie beside him gently rubbing his back.

119

"It's okay Zac – really. I'm not… this article… it said most men who were transvestites were heterosexual."

"That's true," said Zac, before he could stop himself. It *was* true but…

"Many of them are in macho occupations, like the police and the army and the dressing up is just a way of releasing tension."

"I'm hardly in a macho occupation," said Zac, before he could help himself.

"No, but…"

Abbie put her arms round him, burying herself in his chest. The idea that he was gay was Abbie's biggest fear. How simple it would be if he were, Zac thought.

"Some people play sport to unwind and some play with train sets and some…well, some dress up. I can live with that Zac. I can."

He felt a sudden surge of affection for her, for the effort she was making. Given her first reaction to seeing him dressed as a woman, the instinctive disgust.

"We can be good together, Zac. Grow old together, have children… I just want to see you happy. When I thought I had lost you…"

Have children. He could say nothing and he ran his fingers over her hair to compensate. Maybe there was selfishness in her response, and fear, and a need for security but there was love too and whose motives were ever entirely pure? Were his?

The picture she painted was, in its own limited way, appealing. But for how long? He wanted to let Abbie believe that this was just about dressing up, that he was a transvestite. But it wasn't true. He wondered if she even knew the word transsexual. How could he explain? The truth was he didn't want to be a man assuming a part for an hour, a day, even a week. He didn't want to pretend. He wanted his body to match what his brain had always known that he was: a woman.

Chapter Fourteen

Marianne

Sebastian had lost his power. I knew it and so did he.

"Dirty trick, Marianne," he said when we were alone.

"Having a child with my husband is a dirty trick?" I said. "You just need to face facts, Sebastian. I have so much more to offer him than you have."

If Sebastian recognised his own words being thrown back at him, he betrayed no sign of it. He was not the most self-aware person at the best of times and most people have no idea of the bombs they release in what they say. He may have forgotten; I had not.

Sebastian's hold over Raymond annoyed me. He was no Patrice and I knew it, so in that sense, he did not threaten me emotionally but I could not understand the appeal. In a way, I recognised the level of stability he offered Raymond which was why I didn't make more of a fuss. He was a convenient outlet for a part of his life that needed to be fulfilled. Turning everything upside down with a child was a risk. I thought I knew that, that I was taking a calculated risk, but it was only when I told Raymond I was pregnant that I realised quite how much of a risk I had taken. I began to doubt how in control I actually was.

At first, Raymond's reactions were all over the place. Shock, euphoria, fear, depression… it was I who had to be the stabilising influence on his emotions.

"Our life," he said one night when we were lying in bed. "How can we bring a child into this life?"

"We are no less capable of looking after a child than anyone else."

"Sebastian…" he said, and sighed.

"Sebastian may have to be around a little less," I said carefully. "But I think we will survive."

"Shall we ask him to be godfather?"

I felt enraged.

"No we shall not!" I said tightly.

Raymond turned onto his side to face me.

"Marianne I can't suddenly turn into someone else. I can't be Mr Average reading 'Baa, Baa, Black Sheep' at bedtime every night. You know that. We agreed…"

Our agreement was longstanding and it was this: he would stay with me if I let him be who he was.

"I'm not asking you to be someone else," I protested.

Raymond rolled onto his back again and looked broodingly at the ceiling.

"How can I be a father, Marianne?" he asked eventually, his voice small and despairing. "Me… a father? What if it's a boy? What can I teach a boy about being a man?"

"Stop thinking about being a father and think of being a parent," I said.

"Can we be two parents instead of a father and a mother?"

"Of course we can!"

Raymond turned and looked at me curiously.

"You really want a child Marianne? Really, really?"

"Not *a* child. Your child."

"Why?"

Before I could answer, I felt the baby kick for the first time.

"Quick, Raymond," I said, so urgently that I gave him a fright

"What is it," he asked, sitting bolt upright

"Give me your hand."

I placed it on my stomach and watched his face.

He looked startled, then a smile spread slowly across his face and he gave a little hiccup of laughter.

"Oh my God!"

"Look!" I said, looking down at my stomach and laughing. The small bulge of my stomach was moving, the baby writhing inside.

"Oh my God," repeated Raymond in wonder. "It's like a little animal is trapped in there!"

"It IS a little animal," I said. "OUR little animal."

Raymond stayed stock still, in a state of wonder, feeling the movement underneath his hand.

"I wish," he said, "that I could experience what that feels like." He looked at me with a mixture of wonder and pain. "I would love to be a mother."

Life is about power, gaining it and losing it. The only power I have now is the power of memory, retreating inside it to a time when I was whole, deliberately shutting out Shona, and Annie's relentless screams for her mother, and the incessant buzzing, and the furtive whispers about the horrors of

Mary-in-the-Blue-Room. I don't want to consider that one day, and before too long, it might be Marianne-in-the-Blue-Room.

But this trip with Zac has changed things. For the first time in years, I am content to live in the present as well as the past. I have a sense of longing and anticipation. I feel alive in a dead body. The past is meeting the future. When the smell of cooking lunch unfurls from the kitchen, wafting its silent way up the stairs and into the lounge, I no longer simply gag at the vile stench of cooked cabbage or baked fish. I am conscious, too, of the nice smells, the warm vanilla filled scent of biscuits baking for afternoon tea, and my mind turns greedily to the thought of France, and the afternoons we will spend there in the flat above the pâtisserie.

Everyone disapproves, especially Shona with her limp, colourless, concern. I know she has tried to talk Zac out of it. If she managed, I swear I would kill her. I spent so many years refusing to think about that flat in Saint Estelle but in my final years it consumes me and I long to go back. There is nothing left to fear there except finality. It will almost certainly be my last trip on earth, though Zac got flustered and uncomfortable when I said so.

"Don't talk like that Marianne," he said.

But he does not understand. I am not upset by the prospect because I thought the last had already been. This is such a wonderful bonus and the sense of anticipation outweighs any possible sadness.

"Marianne?"

Zac's voice is full of concern when I glance up at him.

He bends down beside my chair.

"I have been trying to talk to you for a few minutes," he says. "You seemed very far away. Are you feeling all right?" His cool hand steals across my brow.

"Yes," I say, looking round. For a moment, a fraction, I feel confused and cannot quite remember what day it is, or what I am to do.

"Is it time to go?" I ask.

"No, Marianne," he says gently, "it is another week before we go."

"Well I know that!" I snap, because I feel foolish. "I meant time to go into the garden."

I didn't mean that at all.

"Oh I see," said Zac uncertainly. "Sorry. Well, yes, I suppose we could take a quick stroll."

These moments of confusion frighten me. They seem to be happening more frequently. I do not dare to look too far ahead. Most women lose their looks as they age but I lost mine a long time ago. To lose the brain that compensated for them is too cruel. It proves to me that there is no order in the universe, that there is only anarchy. I do not believe in God.

The rhododendron flowers are falling from the bushes, a pink velvet carpet on the path.

"It will be hot in Saint Estelle," I caution Zac. "You must pack lightly."

"Yes."

His voice is full of unease.

"You are worried about being on your own and responsible for an old woman."

"No, no." He smiles but I can see it is half hearted.

"How is your French?"

"It's pretty good because of my mother but my father always insisted she spoke in English to us, so it's not as perfect as it might be. My comprehension is better than my spoken French."

"Mine was good... a long time ago."

"We will manage, won't we?" he says.

"There will be help in France. It is being taken care of, I promise. There will be someone staying in the house to help." I hesitate. It is hard for me to show emotion but I want to thank Zac. "I… I am grateful to you," I say. "This chance… it means everything."

It is not like me to be meek and I can see that Zac is surprised. He smiles at me, so very sweetly, as if I have made all his effort worthwhile.

"It will be good to get away for a little while. You are doing me a favour too."

"I have no-one else. No family…"

"I know, Marianne." He lifts my hand for a moment and squeezes it.

"Did you…?" he starts his sentence but then hesitates as if he has thought better of it.

"Did I…?" I prompt.

"Did you ever want children?"

"I was pregnant once."

"Were you?" Zac's voice is full of surprise. He clearly does not think I was the maternal type.

A breeze ripples through the bushes, whispering.

"I was told that the baby probably had Down's syndrome."

Even all these years later, it feels strange to say it so matter of factly. Like it was nothing when actually, it was everything.

"I am sorry."

"It was a long time ago."

It was and it wasn't. The past is never far away. I can feel Raymond's devastation still. Having allowed himself to let go, to have the dream of being a parent that he always believed was beyond his grasp, the news was too cruel. He felt he was being punished. I think he felt our baby's abnormality was some kind of payback for who he was; it was nature's way of rejecting him, of telling him he didn't deserve to be a dad.

As for me, everything crumbled then. My sense of security with Raymond, my power over Sebastian, my dream of what my marriage might become. The tests were not conclusive. There was a chance that the baby would be born healthy but neither Raymond nor I really believed that to be possible. Somehow, it seemed destined that we were not to be allowed to walk the normal path in life.

What I had to decide was whether I was prepared to look after a handicapped child – and whether I was equipped to. I felt differently about the baby's movements inside me. They were no longer a joy but a reminder of a predicament. I felt invaded, like the space inside me was being taken up by something alien.

"Don't tell anyone," I warned Raymond, "particularly not Sebastian." But when I came in one night I knew that Raymond had talked, just by the calculated look of concern that Sebastian shot in my direction. He could not hide his triumph.

"Marianne…" Zac is talking quietly and I look up into his kind, dark eyes. "Don't cry Marianne," he says, wiping my cheek softly with his finger.

"I am not crying," I tell him. "When you get old, even the slightest breeze makes your eyes rheumy. It is most inconvenient."

The girl in the café fingered her pearl earrings, and then moved her hands to stroke the trailing scarf around her neck, in a way that fascinated me as I sat at the next table. It was so sensuous the way she took pleasure in the feel of the smooth pearls beneath her fingers, in the brightness of the silver strands of her pink scarf as the café light hit them. It was the fact that she had Down's syndrome that made me notice her first, I suppose, but within minutes she absorbed me for her own sake. She looked like a child and yet I realised after a few minutes that it was hard to place her age. She could have been fourteen or twenty four, or even thirty four. It was impossible for me to say.

She sat on her own, preening herself like a grown-up lady while her mother and brother sat at a table next to her. I was so mesmerised by the girl that I did not at first realise I vaguely knew her mother, who had consulted me after her divorce, looking for advice about drawing up documents concerning provision for her children should she die. It was simply a legal exercise to me at the time, but here were the children she had been providing for. When I caught the woman's eye, she nodded at me briefly, with a half-smile of recognition.

The girl's brother was disabled too, his body enormously fat - presumably because of whatever syndrome he suffered from - and his face permanently contorted into a grimace that looked almost like pain. He scared me, that boy. I felt the baby inside me kick against me as I looked at him, as if in protest. If I had a child like that, I would be constantly terrified, uncertain how to help him, how to keep him alive. But the girl was a different matter, her exaggerated femininity both instinctive and enchanting. She, too, was heavy – as Down's children often are – yet there was a delicacy, a daintiness about her movements, and her dark eyes darted lightly, like beams of light.

I could not take my eyes off her as her fingers twirled and stroked, and primped and prettified. She clearly revelled in colour and texture and she liked the effect of adornment. When she smiled, it was in a way that managed to be simultaneously coquettish yet sexless. It was obvious that she felt like a woman, despite having a limited understanding of what being a woman was. Was gender all about instinct? For the girl, it was about pearls and scarves and pretty pink lipstick, and for a moment I wanted to cry that it was not really so.

If only the accoutrements of gender could solve Raymond's problem.

Her mother indulged her little display of independence, the sitting-alone-but-together, simply flashing an occasional smile in her direction. She was a large woman with a round, pleasant face and an air of calm. Her clothes were immaculate, if a little old-fashioned, an expensive tweed winter coat with a fur collar draped over her chair, and a scarf that I recognised as designer wound round her neck. Her children, too, were in the finest of clothes. Money was clearly no object. Much good it had done her.

"You have your hands full," I said, when I caught her eye.

"That is why I had to make arrangements… in case anything happened," she said, then looked at me tentatively. "You remember me?"

"Yes, of course."

She smiled.

Her daughter ignored our conversation completely, lifting a delicate china cup from her saucer with great care, pinkie finger rising into the air.

"Is it very difficult for you?" I blurted out.

The woman looked startled at the directness of my question.

"I'm sorry," I said instantly. "I… that must have sounded strange." I indicated the vacant seat beside her. "Do you mind? There is something I would like to ask you."

She looked a little taken aback but she was such an accommodating woman that she pulled the seat out for me.

"Of course," she said.

"Forgive me – I have forgotten your name."

"Harriet."

I held out a hand.

"Of course. Marianne."

"Yes," she said, shaking hands.

Her son tugged at her jacket, grimacing, and she ran a hand soothingly over his hair. I watched, lost in my own thoughts.

"You had a question for me?" she said after a minute or two.

I am pregnant," I said. "My baby has been diagnosed with Down's Syndrome."

A look of compassion – she finally understood why I was talking to her – crossed her face.

"I see."

I noticed she did not say she was sorry like most people. There was no uncomfortable pause, no suppressed, embarrassed horror, no sense of searching for words.

"I have to decide…" I left the rest unsaid.

"You are frightened."

"Were you?"

"Yes."

"Did you consider…?" I looked across at her daughter who smiled back at me

"I didn't have the choice. I only knew when Millie was born and she came out blue and still and the nurses tried to revive her. She had heart problems too. And then the doctor came and told me that she had Down's."

"But you loved her?"

As the question leaves my lips, I realise that is the one I needed to ask most. That is my fear. I have only loved – really loved – Raymond in my life.

"No," said Harriet.

I was startled by her response but at this point Millie left her seat and came to her mother, wrapping her arms round her and whispering in her ear. Harriet stroked her short, elfin hair in an instinctive gesture. All this time, her son simply sat grimacing and wriggling in his chair and every so often Harriet reached out to touch him reassuringly in some way: stroking his knee, or his cheek, or fixing his hair which was so short it did not need fixing.

"How…?" I said, inhibited by Millie's presence.

"Look at the little dog, Millie," said Harriet. "Look…outside the window." Millie rushed over excitedly and looked out as a small, lively black dog leapt up at the window. She bent down, placing her hands where his paws were.

"I screamed," said Harriet quietly, "and cried, and told them to take her away. I did not want to see her."

Her answer created turmoil in me.

"I said I hated her. I wanted her dead."

Harriet looked at me and smiled.

"You are shocked. Or perhaps reassured?"

I was not reassured, as it happens. This woman, who exuded such love, had rejected her child and I do not know where that left someone like me. What chance did I have?

"When did you change?"

"When I saw her wheeled away for surgery and I knew I wanted her to return. When I saw her poor little blue face scrunched up in pain. When I watched her gasp for breath and every breath she took constricted the air in my own chest. I wanted to blow life into her. I knew I would kill to save her."

I had never met anyone who talked as starkly as this woman.

"And then, when she grew, she showed me how to love her by the way she loved me."

132

Millie rushed back excitedly, all business, telling her mother about the dog at the window and we could not say more. I did not know how much Millie understood but perhaps enough for us to remain silent round her. I watched the interaction of this little family silently, drinking in the gestures and the glances and wondering if there was a new man who completed it.

"Your husband left…" I said tentatively.

"Long gone," said Harriet matter-of-factly.

"Yes, I remember."

She smiled. "But his money isn't. I kept the best of him."

"Nobody new?"

"With my two?" She did not sound resentful and merely shook her head.

Millie's show of independence was over now, suddenly and completely, and she hung on her mother's arm, nuzzling her head into Harriet's shoulder and looking up at her face, waiting for Harriet to look at her and respond. I had never seen such adoration in another human being's eyes as I saw in Millie's. I am not a woman who cries often. Perhaps it was simply hormones from my pregnancy but I had a lump in my throat watching her.

Her capacity for affection seemed limitless. But your life, I thought to myself, your life will never be the same. And the boy… the boy… what if… I glanced again at the way Millie held Harriet's arm, and the grip seemed metaphorical as well as physical. Was it, I wondered, claustrophobic to have her there always?

"Do you ever get… tired?" I said to Harriet. "Tired of being needed so much?"

Harriet's fingers stilled suddenly on top of Millie's head where she was smoothing her hair down. Then she smiled at me.

"Do you ever get tired of love?" she replied.

CHAPTER FIFTEEN

Zac

Zac rested his head back on the seat as the aeroplane engine throbbed. Spots of rain splattered onto the small round cabin windows and the world outside seemed grey and somehow far away. It had been an enormous effort to get Marianne here, so much of an effort that frankly, he had wondered why on earth he had agreed. At the other end, it would all start again, the medical assistance, the wheelchair, the interminable waiting and snail's pace progress. He wasn't sure he could cope.

Beside him, Marianne's eyes were closed but he knew that she was awake, waiting. With a lurch, the plane suddenly surged forward, trundling down the runway, faster and faster, the overhead locker doors rattling with the vibration. There was that familiar feeling of contained power, the surge of expectation, the delayed moment of climax until the wheels finally lifted and the plane tilted upwards. The inevitable release of energy when the gathering momentum simply exploded into lift-off.

Zac turned his head sideways on his headrest, just at the same moment Marianne turned hers towards him.

"Things will happen now," she said.

He felt a knot of apprehension in his stomach and turned back towards the window as the plane headed into grey cloud. All he could do was brace himself and wait for the inevitable.

———

Sweat dripped down Zac's back as he tried to negotiate the narrow, unfamiliar streets of Saint Estelle, impatient horns blaring at his back. The light was bright and harsh in his eyes as he hit the square where a sprawling farmers' market was in full swing. He inched forward round an array of stalls and gaily striped awnings, fruit piled high and cheese covered by nets to escape the flies, an untidy assortment of scattered empty boxes and crates littering the way and forcing him to edge out past them. A horn blared as an oncoming driver shouted angrily at him through his open window. Zac looked round desperately, trying to find an exit.

Marianne sat silently beside him, drinking it all in greedily. Another horn blared.

"Round the back," she said. "Take the next road to the right."

Zac wondered if she could possibly remember any meaningful directions after all this time but he was not in a position to argue.

"Down there," Marianne continued, "past that pizzeria then go left into the cul de sac. "Bar Patrice," she murmured, turning her head to look more closely. Her voice seemed full of wonder to Zac, reverent almost. She tried to turn to him. "Bar Patrice," she repeated.

The road was quiet and Zac paused, relieved to be able to

look around unimpeded. He had no idea where he could legitimately leave the car but it didn't look like legitimacy was much of an issue. Cars were parked higgledy-piggledy on pavements, crammed into corners and left at odd angles in spaces that were too small to properly contain them.

"There should be some parking spaces further on," said Marianne, and he pulled forward before spotting a tight space and coming to a halt. He would take her up, they agreed, and then come back down for their bags.

It was almost impossible to push Marianne's chair over the small cobbled stretch of the alley and Zac heaved and sweated as the wheels caught in the ruts. But even in the absorption of the task, he noticed Marianne's fascination with Bar Patrice, the way she turned her head towards it and peered in closely as they went past. As far as he could see, it was just a rather dingy traditional bar with an assortment of older Frenchmen sipping black coffee and aperitifs. He was not sure why it was of such intense interest to Marianne and he soon turned his attention back to the difficulties of manoeuvring the chair.

He was relieved to reach the pavement and feel the wheels run smoothly again.

"There it is," Marianne said eagerly.

"Where?"

"You see the pâtisserie?"

Zac looked down the road and saw a stylish, black painted façade with a striking black and pink striped awning.

"The entrance is just to the side of the door," said Marianne.

Zac could feel her agitation now, a sense of anticipation, that same feeling they had sitting on the runway when the engines throbbed with potential power. There were two high spots of colour in her cheeks and for a moment he felt a sense of panic, wondering how he would cope if Marianne became ill on this trip. God forbid, but what if her heart gave out? What if she had a heart attack with all the excitement and died? Had he been foolish in agreeing to come here?

He pushed her forward, past the pâtisserie and chocolatier. The left hand window was decorated with summer roses, pinned in garlands across the top of the glass. Pink and red petals were scattered on a table that was piled with white and dark chocolate truffles, topped with red roses at the pinnacle. In the right-hand window was a selection of pâtisserie, miniature pastries and tarts filled with vanilla custard and chocolate cream and almonds, topped with drizzled raspberry coulis and fondant icing.

In an attempt to calm Marianne down, Zac slowed slightly at the window.

"How beautiful," he said. "Would you like me to buy you something, Marianne?"

Marianne shook her head.

"Later," she said, unable to say more. She pointed a finger at the entrance. "There."

Zac hauled the chair over the lip of the entrance and wheeled her towards the lift. It was old fashioned and cumbersome, with a metal grid chain door that had to be pulled across before the outer door was closed. Zac pushed for floor one and waited as the lift moved fraction by fraction, ascending slowly.

"You must have been in this lift many times, Marianne," he said, to break the silence.

She shook her head.

"I always ran up the stairs."

The simplicity of her answer made Zac sad. So much made him sad these days, he thought with a frown. At last the lift lurched to a halt and he opened first one door then the other and wheeled Marianne out onto the landing.

He saw her gasp slightly, trying to take a deep breath and he put a hand on her shoulder. She pointed to a door opposite but said nothing. The door was red, freshly painted, not the look of an abandoned apartment at all. With one hand still on Marianne's shoulder, Zac pushed forward and knocked.

CHAPTER SIXTEEN

Marianne

I feel almost as if I cannot breathe as Zac wheels me past Bar Patrice. I know that if I look up, I will see the window where I watched Patrice with the blonde woman the night he died. I do not yet dare to look up and see the empty space.

The bar looks ordinary enough, perhaps even more rundown that before, but then it always did look normal during the day. The old men sitting in the front section look much as they ever did, though obviously they are not the same old goats who used to prop up the bar. New old goats. Last time I was here, I walked in that door under my own steam. I find it hard to understand what has happened to me since then. Time passing is inevitable and yet it is one of the most confusing things about life. I was that – and now I am this. The simplest of concepts and the most complex.

The pâtisserie, on the other hand, is different. The pink and lilac candy bar appearance has been changed to something smarter and more sophisticated. Zac is very attentive, kind the way he offers to buy me some treat. I know that a trip into that pâtisserie will be very special but now is not the moment. I cannot wait to get upstairs and see who will be waiting. My heart is hammering and the sense of anticipation is taking away my ability to speak.

I wonder what Jasmine will look like now. Will time have been as hard on her as it has been on me? I feel almost ashamed that someone from my past will see me like this, withered in an old chair, reliant on someone else for almost everything. Why do I want to see her when I used to run from her? I suppose because I want to recapture something: a time, a place, an emotion. I want to hold it in my hand and look at it again. See what it really was. The urge to go back is always so powerful.

In the lift with Zac, all I can think of is Raymond and I standing, side by side, in the empty apartment the first time we came to view it. It is strange because I am now sitting but Zac is standing, looking like Raymond, and it is almost as if time has swallowed me up but not him. Raymond and I used the lift only that once in all our years there, because we were on the first floor and even back then the lift was slow and it was quicker to walk.

The lift seems to take an eternity. It inches slowly upwards and the turmoil of memories of my past life spins inside my head.

———

There are always, in life, events that change everything. I thought my pregnancy was going to be that event, but strangely it was what happened afterwards that was the catalyst for change.

After his initial fears about the possibility of Down's syndrome, Raymond became buoyant, optimistic in a way that I had not seen since the night Patrice died. It was as if he had been given a little bit of himself back. I felt so relieved. I thought that I had made the right decision, that having a child was finally going to allow us to move on. I was not naïve enough to think that the events of Saint Estelle would be wiped out completely; you can never rub out shadows. But I thought that I had found a way to create a new life, and that the old one would recede further and further until we rarely thought of it.

The day had started without any sign of how momentous it would be, which is the way momentous days start out, more often than not. I was due for a scan and Raymond was coming with me. He was in good form, joking in the waiting room about how conventional we looked. Mr Average Schoolteacher and his wife. Inwardly I thought there was nothing about Raymond that could ever deceive anyone into thinking that he was average but I simply smiled.

"Imagine if they knew!" he whispered as we waited.

"Knew what?"

"About the night… you know… our anniversary… when he was conceived." He started to laugh. "Oh God… that man…"

"It's not a he."

"Isn't it?"

"No. We're having a girl."

I picked up a magazine and started to leaf through it.

"You sound very sure," he said.

"I am." I placed a hand on my stomach absently, waiting to feel a kick but there was nothing.

"Why so sure?"

I just shrugged. Ever since the day in the café when I had watched Millie, I had convinced myself that this was a girl I was carrying. My Millie. I felt it. I had tried to tell Raymond about that day but somehow I couldn't convey to him what it had meant and I gave up.

141

"Marianne..." I looked up to see a nurse smiling at me and followed her into the room.

"How are you today?" she said, helping me up on the bed in the small room where the scanning equipment was. "You've brought your husband with you this time."

She glanced at him and smiled.

"This is Raymond," I said and she held out her hand to him.

"Pleased to meet you Raymond. I'm Val."

I lay back and she pushed up my top to expose my rounded belly, squirting some jelly on. The cold made me gasp.

"Sorry," she said, and she flicked out the lights so that she could examine the screen. She turned to Raymond as she worked.

"So what do you do, Raymond?"

"I'm an art teacher."

"Oh I loved my art teacher at school," she said. "He was so quirky and different."

"Really?" said Raymond, sounding almost neutral but I, who knew him well, detected suppressed amusement in his tone.

She chattered on, but after a moment I noticed that she was concentrating, not engaging so freely any more, and answering only briefly when I asked a question.

"I won't be a minute," she said and she left the room, returning with a man that I recognised as the consultant I had seen only once before. He looked at the screen and then examined me and I began to wonder about the quality of the stillness that had developed in the room. I could tell that Raymond was oblivious to any sense of danger and I could not understand how his senses did not alert him to what was happening.

"Is everything all right?" I said.

"You can sit up now Marianne," said the consultant. "I'll let you get yourself together and then we can have a chat next door."

He went out and Val helped me up again. I pulled the top down and slipped my feet into my discarded shoes. Val had resumed her chat and for a moment I was slightly confused. Perhaps everything was all right after all. But I knew as I walked out the door that it wasn't, not because Val said anything but because of the way she smiled at me. It was full of pity, that smile, and my heart missed a beat.

We sat in front of him, this stranger in his white coat and he spread some notes in front of him.

"I'm afraid it's gone," he said.

The effect on Raymond was remarkable. We weren't touching, yet I could feel his body stiffen without even looking at him.

"Gone?"

It was as if someone had breathed on him and he had turned to marble at my side, cold and unflinching.

"What's gone?" His voice was tight.

I suppose the consultant – I can't even remember his name – was a clever man but you would never have known it.

"There's no movement," he said.

He didn't speak unkindly. Just carelessly, without any apparent insight into how we might be feeling. Perhaps he thought we would be relieved because we had already known the baby had Down's.

Raymond looked at me.

"The baby is dead?" he said, ignoring the doctor.

His expression terrified me and I grabbed his hand. His fingers were like ice.

"I think it's best if we induce, but there's no immediate rush. Go home and take a day or two to get used to everything and then we'll bring you back in. I'll get Val to go through everything with you when you're ready." He wrote something in the notes and then looked up at us.

"It's for the best," he continued. "The pregnancy wasn't viable and this is nature's way of taking care of it. She tends to get these things right, Mother Nature."

He couldn't have said anything worse. Raymond shot out of his chair like a man possessed. The consultant looked up, startled, his pen poised over the page. Raymond leant his hands on his desk and leant towards him.

"Fuck Mother Nature," he said quietly, through gritted teeth.

He went out, closing the door ever so carefully behind him.

———

Raymond cried in his sleep. He did not want me to see him break during the day because I still had the birth to go through, but at night, when his subconscious dictated his behaviour, he sobbed until the pillow was damp. I stroked him without waking him, trying to soothe him. There had been a lot of loneliness for both of us in our marriage, but I don't think either of us had ever felt lonelier, each protecting the other from the violence of our feelings.

I did not need to be induced in the end. A few days after we discovered the baby was dead, my labour started and Raymond, white faced and grim, ushered me to the car in the middle of the night. We drove in silence through the dark but every so often his hand gripped mine.

The pain was unlike anything I had ever experienced, a metal corkscrew turning inside me, ripping me open in a way that I knew was more than physical and would never heal. The staff wanted to give me every possible drug to blunt it, because the baby couldn't be harmed now and there was no need for me to suffer, but somehow, pain was all I had left of this child. Every excruciating contraction forged the only relationship I would ever have with her, and I refused to give it up. I screamed, not just with the physical pain, but with the agony of loss, and the nurse finally ignored my protestations and injected me with a sedative to calm me. When the baby slithered out of me, blue and mottled with purple patches that looked like bruises, the room was silent, and my world would never be the same again.

The midwife bundled her up and without even looking, passed her behind like a rugby ball to a waiting nurse who rushed her from the room. I was left, empty and exhausted, blood trickling down my thighs, wondering if I could not have held her for just a few seconds even. But things were different then. There was no photograph, no print of the baby's little hand or foot as there would be now, no keepsake box of mementos. There was simply silence, the rustle of the nurse's stiff uniform and the sound of the door closing on my dreams.

There was a moment, a sudden rush of emotion, when I tried to raise myself from the bed, follow, track the baby down, and Raymond held me back desperately, murmuring my name soothingly against my hair.

"Marianne... Marianne... Marianne..." The sound of the words combined with the hum of the air conditioning became a song in my head, a requiem for my dead baby. Marianne, Marianne, Marianne.

"I want to see her," I said, surprised by how strong my voice was. "I want to see the baby.

"Best not," said the nurse, in such a way that it made me feel ashamed for asking. As if my request was morbid or indulgent.

"The baby." I heard Raymond croak. "What was it?"

"It was a little boy," the nurse said, and I wondered why she was saying that about my baby Millie. I knew, whatever they tried to tell us.

"A little boy." Raymond repeated, nodding, and I stopped struggling suddenly, lying back against the plumped up pillows. I rolled over, turning my back to everyone in the room, staring intently at a spot on the wall until my eyes felt strange, burning deeply, and the spot began to shimmer.

"We'll take care of the burial," the nurse said to Raymond, talking in a low voice as if that meant I would not hear. I wanted a funeral, a proper funeral, but I didn't have the energy to fight and I believe they buried my baby in a plot of land in the hospital grounds that contained a number of stillborn babies. There was nothing to name her, nothing to mark the fact that our baby had ever existed.

I wanted to go home but they convinced me I must stay for a night so that they could keep a check on me. I only agreed because Raymond remained at my bedside in an armchair, all night. The light in the room was switched out and I kept my back to him, pretending to sleep, watching the light filter in from the corridors and listening, dry eyed and bereft, to the sound of babies crying lustily in the maternity ward next door.

—⁂—

The lift jolts. Moves again. Jolts.

I have thought so much about my lost baby this last week. The memories of that time flood back as I travel up in the lift with Zac to see Jasmine – and whoever else might be with her. Please, I think fervently, let it not just be Jasmine there. Let my message have got through and been understood.

When the lift doors finally open, the freshly painted, glossy red door that meets us seems bright and cheerful, at odds with my memories of when I was last here. When Zac knocks, my heart thumps. Everything else is still.

CHAPTER SEVENTEEN

Zac

Zac rests his hand on Marianne's shoulder as he hears the sound of movement behind the door. The double lock turns. Click, click.

As the door swings open, Zac sees a striking, elderly woman, slim and tall with dyed black hair swept up into a bun. She is elegant but very thin, her fine features angular in the taut pallor of her face. Her eyes are very fine still, despite her age, large and well-shaped and expressive. For a second, she looks as though she might lose her composure when she sees the figure in the wheelchair.

"Marianne," she whispers, leaning forward to grasp Marianne's hand from the chair, and pressing her fingers momentarily to her lips.

Marianne murmurs something in French that Zac cannot catch and looks up expectantly. The hectic flush in her cheeks is still intense.

"Oui. Elle y est," says the woman soothingly, pointing to a closed door.

Marianne breathes out heavily.

Zac hesitates, uncertain what to do. He can see how agitated Marianne is. He feels like an onlooker in a private drama, an outsider, until the woman glances in his direction and smiles faintly.

"You must be Zac," she says, extending her hand in a way that strikes Zac as faintly theatrical. Her accent is heavy but the tones so deliberately musical and well-modulated that Zac wonders if she teaches speech.

"My name is Jasmine."

"Pleased to meet you."

"Come," says Jasmine.

She opens the door and holds it for Zac to push Marianne through. There is another older woman, well dressed and handsome with soft, ash blonde hair, standing at the fireplace, watching the door. Zac estimates that she is at least in her seventies. She is tall, so tall, he thinks. As tall as he is – perhaps taller. Zac hesitates, aware of something arcing silently between this stranger and Marianne. He does not know whether to push the chair forward further. The stranger's hand has flown to her mouth at the sight of Marianne, her lips trembling. Zac sees her eyes fill momentarily.

"Time has not been kind to me," murmurs Marianne.

Her pride, her spirit is struggling; Zac can feel it. His sense of it is so powerful that he almost physically flinches.

The stranger moves forward, lowering herself to her knees in front of the chair, and

Marianne lifts both her hands and places one on each of the stranger's cheeks, a gesture so intensely intimate, somehow, that Zac looks away. He catches Jasmine's eye but cannot read what he see there. Some combination of emotions that Zac does not quite understand, but he thinks he recognises both empathy and jealousy in the mix.

"You are still my Marianne," says the stranger. She leans her head forward and rests it on Marianne's and they talk this way for a moment, excluding everyone else in the room.

"You look wonderful," whispers Marianne against the stranger's hair. "I knew you would."

"It is so good to see you again."

"I think of you every day."

"Don't say that."

"Why not? It is the truth."

"It makes me feel like I abandoned you."

"You did."

"We agreed."

"I know."

Marianne moves her head away from the stranger's and takes her hand, then catches sight of Zac looking curiously at them.

"I would like to introduce you to someone," she says. "Zac, you have not met this lady before but you have certainly heard of her. "This is Rae."

Zac can feel Marianne's eyes boring into him.

"You have heard me speak of her."

"I don't think…" says Zac hesitantly, uncertain what to say.

"Yes, yes," says Marianne, cutting in. "It is just that you have heard me talk of her as Raymond."

Zac's gasp is lost in Marianne's continuing introduction.

"She was once my husband. Rae, this is Zac. He looks after me. He is the boy we should have had together."

———

Marianne was slumped in a corner of the settee, exhausted. Her body had no resistance and the cushion had slid forward under her, forcing her into an awkward heap.

"You don't look very comfortable," said Zac. "Here, let me push those cushions up." Marianne offered no opinion on the matter as Zac hauled her upwards, propping the cushions behind her back to stabilise her.

The flat was empty now. Jasmine and Rae had left them to settle in, promising to return later.

"Emotional effort is always more exhausting than physical effort," said Zac soothingly. If anyone knew that, he did.

Marianne nodded.

Zac hesitated.

"Why did you tell me Raymond was dead, Marianne?"

"I didn't."

"Didn't you?"

"I said that he was gone. Gone a long time ago. And he was. Anyway, he might as well have been dead."

"When did he go?"

Marianne closed her eyes.

"Are we having lunch?"

Zac took so long to answer that Marianne opened one eye and squinted at him. Zac almost laughed.

"Yes, we're having lunch. Will you tell me about Raymond after we've eaten?"

"Yes, after lunch."

"What would you like?"

Marianne perked up. "Crusty bread from the boulangerie below, pâté from the delicatessen, rocket salad with fresh tomatoes drizzled in oil." She had imagined it so often.

Zac looked surprised.

"You eat like a bird at home."

"Can we go now? Down below to buy the things?"

The similarities between childhood and old age struck Zac

as they stood in the pâtisserie: the fixations and obsessions, the self-centred absorption, the lack of inhibition and the dependency… Marianne, holding a stick of French bread from the boulangerie side of the shop, gazed into the pâtisserie cabinet with a sense of unbridled wonder that touched Zac. It was not the wonder of seeing something new, but the wonder of seeing something that she had thought she would never see again.

What would you like, Marianne?"

Marianne did not answer immediately but her lips moved. "Chocolat," she murmured, "Crème anglaise, noix de coco, amandier…"

She looked up at the assistant, a young, dark-eyed girl who could not relate in any way to the heap in the wheelchair and avoided Marianne's eye.

"Avez-vous du ruban lila?"

The girl shrugged sullenly. "Oui."

She opened the drawer from which rolls of curling ribbon trailed and took out a new one. Lilac.

"Celui-là,"Marianne said, pointing a finger into the glass beside a chocolate tarte, thin and dark and elegant, topped with raspberry and a dusting of icing sugar.

"Deux," nodded Zac, holding up two fingers. The girl's dark eyes flashed up at him admiringly and she opened a box. Marianne watched as she pulled and cut a length of lilac ribbon, curling it quickly and deftly with the scissors. Marianne held up her hands to Zac to ensure she got the box, and placed it proprietorially on her knee.

Back in the flat, she would not let lunch begin until she had fulfilled every detail of the fantasy she had so often dreamt of.

"Lay it out on the little table," she told Zac, when he brought through the rocket and tomato salad. "Here, beside my chair."

"Like this?"

"Yes. And the window… open the window so that the breeze lifts the curtain and I can feel it on my face."

Zac sat opposite, a plate and fork in his hand and ate, watching her.

The room was warm, even with the window open.

Marianne was so lost in thought that she did not notice that her fingers rested in the food, covered in pate and tomato seeds, warm and sticky.

"You have hardly eaten a thing," Zac said, when he had finished his own meal. "Here, let me wipe your hands."

Marianne looked down at the plate.

"It tasted better in my dreams."

———

Marianne wound the lilac ribbon round and round her thin fingers as they talked.

"Cut just a sliver off the chocolate tart for me," she had told Zac, but even that lay almost untouched beside her, alongside the remnants of a discarded cup of coffee. The strong espresso had been the only thing to cut through her jaded appetite and the metallic residue left by her medication.

"They seemed so pleased to see you," said Zac.

"Yes," agreed Marianne, with what seemed to Zac to be surprising neutrality. He didn't understand this triangle.

"Why did Raymond leave you, Marianne?"

"Luke died. Our baby. We called him Luke though he was never christened. Or buried properly come to that."

"I'm sorry."

"You want to know because you want to know how to leave Abbie."

"No, no! I…"

"Don't you know the song, 'Fifty Ways to Leave Your Lover'?" Marianne began to sing quietly.

"The problem is all inside your head she said to me,

The answer is easy if you take it logically,

I'd like to help you in your struggle to be free,

There must be fifty ways to leave your lover."

"It's not that easy," said Zac. "Besides, I don't know that I want to leave my lover."

"Just jump on the bus, Gus, make a new plan, Stan."

"Stop it, Marianne!"

Marianne tried to move the wheel of her chair.

"Please wheel me into my bedroom now. I want to sleep for a little. They will be back this evening." She looked at Zac.

"Do not look so offended Zac. You know I am right. Come here. Please. No, sit down here for a minute, next to me."

Zac sat on the edge of the seat.

"Zac, tonight we will go to Bar Patrice. Things will be clearer. I promise."

"You want to go to a bar?" he demanded, unable to keep the incredulity from his voice. "Are you sure?"

"I cannot come here without going to Bar Patrice. And neither can you. It will explain things to you. And you… you will not be the same again."

Zac felt frightened suddenly. Alone. He wished Abbie had come after all.

"No don't be frightened."

Zac looked at her almost resentfully.

"Let Rae help you. And Jasmine."

"Are they…" Zac asked curiously and then stopped. Perhaps he was being indelicate.

153

"Are they what?"

"Partners?"

"Not really. They just live in the same place."

Zac was uncertain how to interpret that.

"He did not leave me for Jasmine if that is what you think," she continued. "But I can see that something has happened between them at some stage. Whatever it was, it is over now."

"I see."

Marianne smiled. "Do you?"

Not really, thought Zac.

"Isn't that just life?" said Marianne thoughtfully. "Jasmine wanted me but got Raymond. I wanted Raymond and got no-one. And Raymond… Raymond wanted someone who died a long time ago and has been looking ever since."

Died long ago. Did she mean Luke? Zac wondered.

"He might as well have had me for all he found in his search. Isn't that ironic?"

Marianne began half-heartedly pawing at the wheel of her chair and Zac stood up to help, pulling the chair round and pushing her towards the door.

"But who gets what they want in life when it comes to love?" murmured Marianne as they walked through the doorway, her eyes half closing already.

Chapter Eighteen

Marianne

The bedroom is calm, still painted white and furnished simply as it always was. There is a small vase of roses on the heavy, dark wood chest of drawers, pink and vanilla, the pink buds singed at the tips with crimson and bending slightly into the glossy lake of their reflection in the polished wood below. Jasmine has left them there, I am sure, not Raymond. They are so beautiful and so artfully positioned.

The effort of moving through from the sitting room and transferring onto the bed has awakened me but I am glad when Zac closes the door and leaves me alone. He has left the window open for me and the traffic whirls below, the sound of a world I cannot join. Despite closing my eyes, sleep will not come with all this emotion resurrected inside. Seeing Raymond again… the pain of witnessing his shock at my condition. How ugly that look made me feel! How old and ugly and discarded. It was like the time I was confronted by his portrait of me, all over again. The looking glass of someone else's cruel observation.

The years drift backwards again so easily. Raymond was attentive after Luke died. Attentive but remote. I knew that this artificial state could not last forever and tried to prepare myself for life changing again in some way. But even I had not guessed what was coming next.

"I need to talk to you."

I was putting a cup in the sink and I turned to see Raymond standing in the doorway of the kitchen. He had just come in from school - late - and he was dressed in black jeans and a black shirt and he held his jacket in one hand and his keys in the other. I knew looking at him that he had talked himself into this conversation on the way home and felt he could not delay one more minute or his courage would desert him.

I did not rush. I dried my hands carefully, knowing that something momentous was about to happen, and sat down at the table, motioning him to do the same. Raymond sat — or his legs gave way - his keys clattering onto the table. He stared down at the wood for a moment while I waited for him to speak.

"I want surgery," he said. "I want to become a woman properly. No more pretending."

"Raymond…"

"No, don't Marianne," he said. "Don't tell me this is not what I really want because I do."

"You are still grieving."

"Yes, I am still grieving but that is not why I want to do this. Well yes it is… but not for the reasons you think. I am not confused by grief. It has clarified everything. Life is too short. I cannot… I simply cannot…"

His voice was cracking already and I grabbed his hand.

"I am sorry Marianne," he whispered.

"Raymond," I pleaded, desperate for him to stop talking, "we have got through this before. Go and lie down for a little."

"No, I need to talk Marianne! You can't change my mind on this."

"But Raymond, nothing has changed."

"Yes, yes it has," he said, and I realised that perhaps he was right.

"I need to be who I am before it is too late."

"Who you are!" I said scornfully, dropping his hand. I flinched inwardly at the hurt I saw on Raymond's face but couldn't stop myself. "I KNOW who you are, Raymond. I have loved you for who you are."

"I know."

Raymond was miserable. Guilty and miserable.

"You cannot have surgery without having hormones, without living as a woman for a year," I told him. "How can you possibly do that and keep working?"

"I don't know," he said shaking his head. "I don't know but I know that I have to. Even if it means losing my job. Losing everything."

"Me?"

"Even you."

We clung to each other and I knew we were frightened, both of us, of what was to come. There was more serious intent in Raymond's voice than I had ever heard.

"I can't bear to hurt you," he said. "But I can't bear to live this way anymore. I simply cannot waste any more of my life. Please tell me you understand. Please Marianne."

I knew how desperate he was but I could not give him the reassurance he needed.

I put my head into my hands on the table and refused to look at him.

"And how do I fit into this plan?" I said, finally looking up.

"I don't know."

"You want to leave me."

It was a statement, not a question. For a moment he refused to look at me.

"I don't know."

"We agreed," I said.

"He is still between us."

He means Patrice but I refuse to mention him by name. A surge of anger rises in me. Damn Patrice!

"You will be an outcast," I spat. "Do you understand that? A deviant!"

"I am not a deviant!" he retorted angrily.

"You think men will want you? Do you? Well?"

"Some."

"Some! Do you know anything about men, Raymond? Real men? For God's sake, you have been living in a male body for long enough, surely you know something of their ways!"

I was shocked at my own cruelty, but could not stop.

"You think they want a woman who was once a man? A kid-on woman, a sort-of woman, a woman who was once the same as them? What kind of man wants *that*?"

I was killing Raymond inside, but I could not stop.

"You will fit nowhere. Do you understand that? Heterosexual men will not want you. Homosexual men will not want you. Women will not want you. You will not belong to anyone, Raymond. What sort of life is that?"

"A more honest life than this."

"Raymond…"

"If straight men don't want me," Raymond said with a sudden defiance, his eyes brilliant with unshed tears, "and gay men don't want me... well, there are those who are attracted to transsexual people like me."

I banged my hands on the table in anger.

"Like Sebastian? Like SEBASTIAN!" I screamed. "You would be content to live your life with a creature like him? The men who want 'a girl with a little bit extra'."

Raymond's hands literally flew to cover his ears.

"Don't Marianne!"

"Yes! Yes I have to. You are going to turn our lives upside down because you have some misguided fantasy about who will be in your bed?"

"This is not about sex!"

"No? What is it about then?"

"Identity. My identity. And I do not feel myself to be a man. I never have. You know that. You *know* that Marianne."

His voice dropped. "Nobody knows me better than you, Marianne."

"Nobody loves you like I do, Raymond."

"Not any more, no."

If he had not said those words, perhaps I would have thought there was a way to survive together. But when he said them, I knew that what happened the night Patrice died had never gone away, that it was as much that as anything that drove Raymond. Nobody but us knew the truth of what happened - and that had both kept us together and driven a wedge between us.

I could not hide my devastation.

"Marianne..."

"Don't touch me!"

I wondered if he knew. I wonder if he realised then that I would love him no matter what, that my love transcended gender. I would have stayed with him, even if he had become a woman, though it would not have been my choice. But events were taken out of my hands. And whatever he said, gender was more important to Raymond than it was to me because he was determined to change his.

Raymond let his hands drop from me and shrugged helplessly.

"I cannot speak about this anymore," he said, turning from me wearily. "Perhaps when you are calmer we can try again."

"He never loved you like I did," I said bitterly. "He wasn't even faithful. He wasn't faithful to anyone. If you were different, if he loved you, why did he treat you like that?"

I watched him walk from me and I crumbled.

"Raymond!"

He stopped dead, waiting for another attack.

"What?" He turned round when no answer came.

I could barely speak. I have never been a person who could easily beg.

"What?" he repeated.

My voice when it came was cracked and small and made me ashamed.

"Don't leave me."

Professor Ralph Mitchell was unlike any doctor I had ever consulted. I would have said he was about sixty at the time I first met him, a quietly spoken, unassuming man quite without the usual levels of arrogance of medical men at the top of their profession. He would not have spent a lifetime in a Cinderella branch of medicine if he had not had special levels of empathy, though I suppose there is always a certain glamour and prestige in being a pioneer. He was London's top man in gender reassignment.

I was always struck by the gentleness of his voice, which was often barely above a whisper. Sometimes it was a strain to hear him. I wondered if he had developed it as an antidote to the high emotion his working life was surrounded by: the inevitable outpourings of angst; the deluges of tears. But when you really listened he also had a slight speech impediment, a soft lisp that gave an occasional whistling quality to his speech. Sometimes, it is these tiny little imperfections that make you understand other people's problems, though God knows there is a difference between embarrassing diction and having a brain that's a different sex from your body.

Now that there is more open discussion of the transsexual condition, people talk about being 'trapped' in the wrong body. That never seemed quite right to me. It was more a mismatch. It was a bit like wearing the green jacket of one suit and the red skirt of another. Each was fine its own way – they just didn't go together. That's the way it felt with Raymond: that he was an amalgamation of the brain of one person and the random body of another.

I remember some self-appointed guardian of public morals on television once, talking about the 'immorality' of providing transsexual surgery on the NHS. Doctors, he said, were creating 'Frankenstein monsters' with their work, abominations of nature. Personally, I wasn't sure why it should have been any more immoral than sorting out a twisted intestine, or a hare lip. It is nature that tends to create monsters in my opinion - not surgeons.

I accompanied Raymond to all his appointments with Professor Mitchell. He had just begun his course of female hormones and was about to commence what was called his Real Life Experience: living as a woman for a year before surgery. It was a pre-requisite that was insisted upon before any operation could take place.

I knew all about the physical process of surgery: the removal of the testes; the construction of a vagina using skin from the penis and scrotum. You must realise, Professor Mitchell said, - 'realissse' as it came out with his whistling's' - that the removal of the erectile tissue and the testes is irreversssible. He spoke with a profound sense of calm that tended to eliminate panic, but my heart sank at the word 'irreversible'. Raymond had beamed.

"How many regret surgery?" I asked and Raymond glared at me.

"A tiny percentage," Professor Mitchell answered patiently.

But then there came a time, not long before Raymond's surgery was scheduled, when I wanted to see the Professor alone. I rang his secretary to ask if he would see me, and heard a muffled exchange at the other end of the line. A brief meeting was agreed for a week later.

"Please sit down, Marianne," said Professor Mitchell courteously, waiting until I was seated before taking his own place behind his desk. Given his job, it always amused me how conservative he looked, this little, grey-haired man with his light-coloured, machine washable trousers that rose at the ankles to reveal beige, diamond-patterned socks. He was not a man you could imagine discussing sex with when you first met him. Yet he never looked fazed by any conversation that took place in his consulting room. He would simply nod encouragingly no matter what was said, listening intently, waiting calmly for you to continue, so that you felt by the end of the appointment that you were the most normal person in the world, that your particular problem was nothing he had not heard before. Sometimes, I felt the most terrible urge to tell him about Patrice Moreau, just to see if finally he was shocked. I did not, of course. Survival depended on nobody knowing about Patrice.

"How can I help?" he asked.

"I wanted to talk to you about what will happen after Raymond's surgery."

"Of course," he said, nodding. "Though you must understand, Marianne, that there are limits to what I can discuss about Raymond without his permission."

"I know."

It was not the physical process that I needed to know about now. I did not want further information about the ways to reduce infection, the outside possibility of rectal damage, or the supreme importance of daily vaginal dilation with a stent to keep the newly formed opening from closing over. What I really wanted to know about was what would happen to our relationship.

"Will he still love me?" I finally managed to blurt out.

"Does he love you now?"

I was taken aback by the question, wrongly interpreting it as a challenge, Professor Mitchell's way of casting doubt on what I thought Raymond felt for me.

"Yes. Yes he loves me," I said, a little stiffly.

Professor Mitchell nodded.

He looked at me almost expectantly, like he was waiting for me to grasp some truth.

"What is Raymond's favourite colour, Marianne?"

I shrugged. "Black... purple... perhaps...."

"Black and purple will still be his favourite colours after surgery."

Professor Mitchell's head tilted and he looked at me keenly.

"You understand what I am saying, Marianne? His eyes held that combination of professional detachment and personal compassion that made him so effective at what he did.

"I will not be operating on Raymond's brain, switching on one emotion and turning off another. You ssss…ee?"

The word whistled into the silence between us.

"I will be operating on his body."

I looked at him hopefully and I suspect he understood what was in my mind because I sensed his slight unease then, a rush to clarify.

"But that is not to say that certain things will not change," he continued.

"What things?"

"You know, Marianne, that sexual identity and gender are different?"

I nodded.

"Post-surgery, Raymond's gender will have changed. He will be female. But what his sexual orientation will be… that is not certain."

"It will be different to now?"

"What would you say Raymond's sexual orientation is now? Does he prefer men or women?"

I knew it was not a question he knew the answer to. It was not a trap but a genuine query. There was no point in lying though it pained me to answer truthfully.

"I think he is bisexual."

Professor Mitchell looked at me without judgment and yet something about his stare made me qualify that.

"Though his preference," I stuttered, "would almost certainly be for men."

"So how would you describe your sex life?"

"Sporadic."

It was an overestimate that my pride insisted on. 'Rare' would have been more accurate.

Professor Mitchell did not react in any way. His tie was closed right to the neck and his beige jumper sat neatly in a little fold over his stomach. He looked so conservative that I found it hard to imagine him spending his life operating on genitalia, discussing sex, and then going home to peel off his diamond-patterned socks for a grey-haired wife in a Marks and Spencer dress. But other people's sex lives are always a surprise.

"After surgery," said Professor Mitchell, "patients sometimes find that their sexual orientation has changed."

"In what way?"

"Some who have previously been attracted to women, continue to be attracted to women and live their lives as lesbians. But some find themselves more attracted to men after their transition. Another group again find themselves almost asexual."

In a way, that was my best hope. No potential rival to pull Raymond away from me.

"How many?" I said. "How many are in each of these groups?"

Professor Mitchell picked up a sheaf of papers from his desk and put on a pair of glasses to read.

"This a recent study," he said. "In a study of 3000 transwomen."

"Is that a lot?"

"It is a reasonable study." He looked over the top of the glasses at me and then resumed. "In a study of 3000 transwomen, 23% described themselves after surgery as heterosexual, 31% as bisexual and 29% as lesbian. 7% described themselves as asexual."

"How many…" I said hesitantly, "how many will stay with the partner they were with before transition?" It was by far the more important question.

"It is hard to be specific with all these figures, Marianne. They vary." He took his glasses off and placed them, legs spread, on the desk.

"Roughly."

"Eleven per cent."

Just over one in ten. The odds were not good.

"I understand that this is as traumatic a time for you as for Raymond," Professor Mitchell continued. "Let us get down to basics. What is it that you are worried about, Marianne? What are your biggest fears…sssss?"

His voice was soothing, and I did not need much coaxing, but it was hard to put into words. I thought for a moment. Raymond and I were drawn together by so many things; inadequacy, hurt, rejection, insecurity, as well as love. And secrets. We were protection for each other's secrets. Particularly Moreau. But if Raymond gained new confidence in who he was, then what need was there for me?

"What do you fear, Marianne?" Professor Mitchell repeated gently.

"That Raymond will be reborn and I will die."

"Yes, I see."

"Do you?"

"You fear abandonment. It is a very common human fear."

I smiled weakly. There… I was normal.

"Where do you think your abandonment fears stem from, Marianne?"

I froze in my seat.

"Your childhood was quite normal?"

"Relatively."

I lied.

The memory flooded through me. A worn blue babygro wrapped in crushed, yellowing tissue, presented tentatively to me when I was 14 by what I came to understand was actually my adopted mother. I always wondered why it was blue, not pink.

Strangely, it was that little detail that made me feel most rejected. Not the fact that I was enough of an inconvenience to be left, wrapped in a towel, on the doorstep of the council social work department. It was that I mattered so little that anything had been good enough to dress me in. Or perhaps that there had been another baby before me who had had clothes bought for them, who was being kept, while I was discarded. Isn't it a foolishly trivial emotion to bother about colour in the face of something far more significant? Even I can see that. It's especially ironic when you consider the significance that gender was later to assume in my life. But emotions are not logical.

Professor Mitchell did not push.

"You can tell me anything you want, Marianne."

I shook my head.

"It doesn't matter now."

I had fought to stamp that memory out all my life. I wasn't about to dredge it up willingly. It was not who I was. I had done well for myself. I owned designer suits. Real pearls. I didn't wear rubbish; I wore expensive to show I was worth something. And Raymond. I had Raymond. I had done well.

"There are two things to remember, Marianne."

"Yes?"

"Firstly, abandonment is not inevitable. And secondly it is ssss…survivable. Almost everything is ssss…survivable. The fear is almost always worse than the reality. Remember that, Marianne. Please. Remember that."

Raymond's face was swollen like a boxer's, his top lip thick and raised almost to his nose on one side. One eye was half-shut and blood trickled slowly from his nose, splashing every so often in thick, red splodges that were instantly lost in the autumnal coloured swirls of the silk dress he wore. The top of his nose was encrusted with the dark red of congealed blood that had been smeared, then dried, and the bruise on his left cheekbone was a livid purple under the pearlised glimmer of bronzer. I had never seen Raymond ugly but this was the closest I ever got: his whole face was blown out monstrously. Yet somehow, the ease with which his face had been changed only served to underline his delicacy. I screamed instantly when I opened the door, a cocktail of pain and anger rising in me because I could not bear to see him hurt. I hated whoever had laid a finger on him.

"No, no, no!" I punched the wall, beside myself with rage. "Bastards!"

The sense of pain that anyone could harm Raymond felt primal. He stood impassively on the step, trails of blood leaving caterpillar tracks of red slime on his face. The shock had left him speechless and I could see that he had lost more than mere blood.

I put out a hand to touch him, but he shrank back before I made contact, and my hand hovered uncertainly, wanting to stroke and reassure him, but knowing I could not touch the bloated cushion of his face without causing him great pain.

"Come inside," I said and he moved past me obediently and sat down on the bottom step of the stairway in the hall. I knelt down in front of him, resting on my heels, and took his hands gently in mine.

"What happened?"

"A group of teenagers. I… some of them from the school, I think, I…" he stopped.

"Tell me."

"I was in a bar with…with Sebastian. I saw one of them stare. I could tell he was trying to place me and then he realised who I was."

Raymond was no longer working at the school by this time. He had left in a ghastly whirl of publicity that had immediately involved a tabloid newspaper and a clutch of photographers who, for four days, had taken up almost permanent residence outside our home. They were a degenerate-looking little gaggle of unkempt wasters – a mixture of the unshaven and the badly shaven - who spent an inordinate amount of time handing round a hip flask. They would have been better served finding themselves a decent job. Occasionally they were joined by a reporter, a brittle-looking blonde woman with bags under her eyes like a bloodhound, who came to our door several times, rattling the letterbox in a way that frankly I considered an incitement to violence. Then a note fell onto the carpet assuring us she wanted to do a "sympathetic" piece and offering money for our story. Raymond was tempted just to get rid of them all, but I told him not to be ridiculous: he might just as well cosy up to a rattlesnake.

The piece that eventually appeared juxtaposed a photograph of Raymond's school with a picture of him trying to sneak out of the back of the house – and therefore looking furtive – accompanied by the uninspired headline, "Please Miss!"

"These people have no imagination," I had said to Raymond, who sat slumped in a chair, watching me with dead eyes. He had a similar look tonight, as if another little piece of himself had gone.

"How many?" I asked.

Raymond shrugged.

"Six, seven. Not all of them hit me. Some were just…there."

"Cowards. Against two of you?"

Raymond leant back slightly against the stair and looked up at the ceiling.

"Sebastian," I said. "What about Sebastian?"

"What about him?"

"Where is he?"

"I don't know."

He flashed me a look that seemed full of something shockingly akin to dislike.

"Go on, Marianne."

"Go on what?"

"Say, I told you so."

I was silent.

Raymond glanced briefly at me as he stood up painfully.

"Sebastian ran."

He turned and leant against the banister, wincing, then hauled himself slowly upstairs.

"Shall I…?"

But before I could finish, he shook his head.

"I am fine. Thank you."

Between the two of us, I had always felt like I was the strong one, the half of the partnership that was in charge. There was something about Raymond that always gave in a

little too easily. The part that was prone to say, oh well… It often worried me that people might think he did not have much backbone. But in that period of being a 'trial woman' he developed a strength I did not recognise and could only admire. He would not back down.

"You have developed balls only to get them cut off," I said.

He was not amused.

He got up as normal the day after the attack, though it was a Sunday and we did not need to be anywhere other than home.

I tried not to watch him too obviously as he gingerly put some light makeup on over the bruises. His left eyes was bloodshot and his face was swollen, his top lip blown out to twice its normal size on the right hand side. It gave him a peculiar, lopsided look. He selected a soft, bottle green jersey dress from the closet, a colour that normally gave a beautiful greeny tinge to his grey eyes.

I touched his back gently as he stood in front of the mirror.

"Nice," I said.

He said nothing but smiled faintly at our joint reflection in the glass, and brought my hand round to cover it with his on his left shoulder. I thought that smile was resolute.

I was wrong.

It was the around the fifth month of his real life trial that I found him on the floor, bleeding with cuts on his wrists. I think the year-long wait for surgery simply felt interminable at that stage and he grew weary. In many ways, I would say that he was happier than he had ever been in those five months, more at peace, and yet the practicalities were so difficult: his inability to make a living and his subsequent financial reliance on me; the certain knowledge that nothing other than his gender identity would be solved by his forthcoming operation.

He was frightened and weak when I found him but he begged me to simply bind up his wrists and tell nobody. To seek medical help would delay the surgery even longer while psychiatrists investigated his mental health. With some misgivings, I did as he wished. I tried to understand, to suppress my anger with him. Why was I never enough?

I remember that when I found him, he was lying on the dark blue carpet in the bedroom, rather than on top of the white bedding. It really hit home, that morbid little bit of etiquette.

He might have been willing to put me through the trauma of finding his corpse, but at least he did not wish me to endure the inconvenience of having to get the blood stains out of the sheets.

"Shhh. Shhh. Shhh, Marianne."

Zac's voice is soothing me, his fingers stroking mine.

Where am I? Dark furniture and white bedding, pink edged roses. I can still feel the gloopy stickiness of blood on my fingers.

"It's all right, Marianne. Shh."

"Is there blood? Is there blood on the bedding?"

"No, no, everything is fine."

"On the ceiling then? Is the blood staining the ceiling? Look up!"

"No Marianne. There is no blood, I promise. You must have been dreaming but it is all right now. I am here. Everything is fine."

Zac smiles at me, his face beginning to come into focus.

"My goodness Marianne, what lurid dreams you must have been having," he says softly, stroking my hair. "How loudly you were shouting!"

"Was I?"

"Never mind. Shall I take you through again to the sitting room and we will wait for Rae and Jasmine to come? They will be here soon."

Wait for Raymond. Yes. Let's wait for Raymond. I have, after all, spent a lifetime waiting for Raymond.

CHAPTER NINETEEN

Zac

It was a relief to Zac that he was not asked outright. Rae simply took him to the wardrobe and asked him what he would like to wear. There was an assumption made that he had neither to explain nor falsely dispute. No doubt Marianne had spoken to him, Zac thought. His fingers trembled as he took out a plain, black beaded dress. Rae put his hand briefly over Zac's to still the tremble, to say, without speaking, that he understood.

"Good," he said, removing his hand.

Zac breathed deeply. These women… Jasmine, Rae… they were unlike anyone he had ever met. For the first time in his life, he felt he wasn't entirely alone. The feeling elated him, gave him strength.

Jasmine handed him a wig, lustrous dark curls that tumbled on his shoulders.

"You look like April Ashley," she said. "Don't you think, Rae? Remember those old photographs?"

Zac looked up questioningly.

"One of the first like us," explained Jasmine. "She became a Vogue model."

(I prefer the original version of the question – it has a sense of wonder.) How was that possible, thought Zac. Possible to be so convincing as a woman that you became the epitome of feminine glamour: a Vogue model? He caught his breath. There was something about this place, these people that made him feel the universe had suddenly expanded. Was it just being away from home? Would it last?

In the home, being with old people was like being with children. Their world was small and narrow and it was your job to keep them safe. And yet being with these elderly people was different. The world got bigger every minute he was with them.

He did not know how to interpret Marianne's look when she saw him. It was she who knew him best, who had made all this possible after all, yet she looked shocked.

"Raymond," she whispered.

"Yes?" said Rae, who was standing beside her chair.

Marianne looked up as if surprised.

"May I…" she began. "May I have some water before we go?"

"Of course."

Zac stood awkwardly.

"Come here," said Marianne. "Let me fix your brooch."

He knelt down beside her and she unpinned the clasp of a diamante spider, re-pinning it on the shoulder of the black dress as if it was crawling over his shoulder.

"See," she murmured. "It is better there."

"You have a good eye, Marianne," said Zac, looking in the mirror.

"Yes, so I have been told," said Marianne impassively. "But nobody ever told me I had a good heart. You think about these things when you get old."

Rae returned, handing her a glass of water.

"Is it wise?" she asked him, holding the glass but not drinking.

"What?"

"You and Jasmine must have been in Patrice's many times over the years."

Yes."

"But is it wise for you and me to go together?"

Raymond was silent for a moment. "Do we have a choice?" he asked.

Marianne shook her head and handed the glass to Zac, untouched.

The light in the back room of Bar Patrice was dim and blue, neon blue, like the light of a casino strip. It shimmered from giant video screens on the walls as the pulsating beat of music, bass turned up high, boomed dully around the room. There was a woman on the screen, a woman in a long cream lace dress with a fish tail, lips stained vermilion red, her arms snaking into the air as she sang.

Marianne stared at the screen, mesmerised, as Zac pushed her chair through the door.

"Why is she up there? Where is she standing?" she demanded.

Even in the semi-dark, Zac caught a glance between Rae and Jasmine. He bent down to talk softly in her ear so that the others did not hear.

"That is a screen, Marianne. It is a music video playing."

"Yes. Yes, of course," said Marianne, flustered. She glanced round looking for Rae. "It is so different." She held out her hand to him.

"Come in, come in!" said a man in a velvet dress, lurching drunkenly past them. "Close the door behind you. Keep the riff-raff out!"

"Or perhaps not," murmured Marianne, looking at the stranger sharply.

"Maurice," the man said grabbing Zac's hand. "Maurice. And you are?"

"Zac."

Zac watched the man disappear. He might be wearing a dress but he had made no real attempt to look like a proper woman. Dark shadow stubbled his chin and despite the livid pink lipstick slashed unevenly across his mouth, and the smudged mascara in the pouches under his eyes, there was something very masculine about him: the broad features and solid breadth of his shoulders; the way he moved and carried himself.

What a strange place this was, thought Zac, looking round at the bizarre trio of Marianne, Rae and Jasmine. It made him feel both excited and uneasy, but behind that there was a sense of being deeply alive. He was aware of every pulse of blood through his veins. He made his way across the room. There was a small bar at one end, a barman leaning across the counter watching the new arrivals. He held Zac's gaze a second or two longer than necessary. He was tall, muscular. Very masculine and self-contained. Attractive. Zac looked back levelly, then felt unnerved when the barman looked away first. Perhaps he had misunderstood the look, Zac thought, feeling foolish. Perhaps the man thought he looked ridiculous. Even for this place. He looked around, drinking it all in.

He asked for drinks without looking directly at him again, feigning interest in the bottles behind the bar.

"Just visiting?" said the barman as he poured vodka into a glass.

Zac flushed, then nodded. His ear was becoming accustomed to the language again but he still hesitated to speak. He glanced up,

176

letting his eyes dart over the man and away. The barman was older than him, perhaps pushing forty, Zac thought, lifting the glasses from the counter and going back to the table. The barman said nothing but nodded briefly to him, an acknowledgment that felt more than just a gesture.

Zac turned round and almost walked straight into Maurice in the velvet dress.

"Sorry," Zac said instantly.

"Pray, hope – and don't worry," said Maurice intently.

Zac looked blankly at him.

"Pray?" said an arch voice behind Zac. Jasmine had come over to help him carry the glasses.

"Jasmine!" said Maurice, reaching to grasp her hand. "Pray, hope – and don't worry," he repeated.

"Ah, Maurice, it is always so lovely to see you," said Jasmine in tones so beautifully modulated that the self-conscious affectation of it left Zac feeling uncomfortable. Maurice seemed oblivious to the insincerity, walking unsteadily behind them and falling into a chair beside Rae. He gathered himself and leant across the table, looking meaningfully round the company, as though about to impart something of great significance. Rae looked at him expectantly.

"Pray, hope - and don't worry," said Maurice again, with all the sincerity a bottle of Bourbon inspires.

A bubble of laughter escaped from Zac before he could stop it.

Maurice grinned at him with drunken amiability.

"Pray to whom?" asked Marianne.

"To God!" said Maurice

"Oh dear," said Jasmine. "You still believe in God, Maurice?"

"Certainly."

"Well, perhaps He exists," says Jasmine. "But I doubt it. And I am not sure He is very interested in the likes of us."

"He made us," said Maurice.

"Well!" murmured Rae. "I think something went a little wrong somewhere."

Jasmine snorted.

"How can you be religious?" said Rae with curiosity rather than disapproval. "The God brigade hate people like you and me!"

"There is no judgement in heaven," declared Maurice.

"Did he say no judgement under heaven?" Marianne asked, turning to Rae.

"IN heaven," said Rae.

"We are all imperfect beings in different ways," said Maurice.

Nobody else seemed to be listening but personally, Zac found that poignant. Perhaps this strange, drunken man had something there. Was imperfection of the body - as he had always felt his own mismatch of brain and body to be - a more significant imperfection than an imperfection of character? Greed, say. Or selfishness. Or hatred. Surely not. He felt a surge of optimism. Looking up, he saw that the barman was watching him intently, but he glanced away quickly when Zac caught his eye.

None of it will matter in the next life," said Maurice. "Don't you see? There is no gender in heaven either."

"How dull," said Jasmine cuttingly. She glanced at Marianne.

"Do you think there is a life after this one, Marianne?"

"I hope not," muttered Marianne.

Zac looked on silently. It seemed a peculiar thing for Marianne to say at her age but he did not like to interrupt to ask what she meant.

Maurice leant across and rested his arm on Marianne's chair.

"You must pray, hope…" he began, while Marianne stared a little vacantly at him.

"And don't worry, yes, we get it," interrupted Jasmine, rolling her eyes.

She turned to Rae.

"It's like some awful verbal tic," she said, as if Maurice wasn't there. "Or Tourette's."

Maurice looked at her almost soberly.

"Who said that?" Rae asked Maurice.

"Said what?"

"Pray, hope… that stuff."

"A holy man," said Maurice vaguely.

"Who?"

"I can't remember. Padre Pio maybe."

Zac was still thinking about imperfections. His own had always felt so all-encompassing because his identity was at stake. He had always thought this… this thing, problem, imperfection, whatever it was he had, was an indication of his own moral failure. But perhaps it was simply a biological failure. And that was out of his hands.

"Zac!" said Jasmine.

"Sorry?"

He looked up to find them all looking at him.

"Do you believe in God?"

"I don't know."

"Ah." said Maurice, nodding sagely. He drained his glass. "But God believes in you."

"Deep," said Jasmine sarcastically. "That's why he is so good to us, obviously. Takes away our struggle."

"Jesus permits the spiritual combat as a purification, not as a punishment. The trial is not unto death but unto salvation," said Maurice. "That's Padre Pio as well," he added, then frowned. "If the first bit is."

Spiritual combat, thought Zac. That is certainly the way it feels. A movement at the corner of his eye made him look over. What was wrong with Marianne, he wondered. She was trembling.

"I want to go home," said Marianne suddenly.

"What's wrong?" asked Jasmine.

Marianne looked at Zac. "Take me home."

"Of course," said Zac.

"But we've only just got here," muttered Jasmine.

Rae took her hand silently.

Marianne looked at him.

"You cannot see the joins," she said, suddenly impassioned. "Can you?"

Rae stroked her hand, letting her eyes caress Marianne's face.

"What joins, my darling? What joins can you not see?"

"The joins of time." For a moment, Zac thought she might cry but she did not. "One minute we were here, young, in that time, that moment. And now we are here in this one. And I cannot see the join, the transition, the path between the two. Not really."

"We have not been here together since…" said Rae.

"No," said Marianne quickly. "Not since then."

She glanced at Jasmine and then at Rae with a question in her eyes for Rae. Have you told her - the look asked. Rae shook his head and Zac could see some of the tension leave Marianne.

"You wouldn't," said Marianne.

What did she not want Rae to tell Jasmine? Zac wondered.

Rae put his fingers on Marianne's lips in reply.

"I loved you then," said Marianne softly.

"And now?"

Boom, boom, boom. The volume of the music shot up suddenly and Marianne glanced up again at the woman in the cream lace dress on the screen.

"Don't ask me," she sang, "what you know is true."

"She belongs in here," says Marianne. "Doesn't she Rae? With her fishtail and her scarlet lips and her seedy glamour. Don't ask me what you know is true. That is your answer."

Rae smiled.

"And you can never, never, never tear us apart," sang the woman.

"I cannot see the joins," repeated Marianne, resting her head on his.

"Perhaps there are none," whispered Rae.

"Are we expected to play gooseberry all night?" demanded Jasmine acerbically.

Rae kissed Marianne's fingertips and laid her hand back carefully on the arm of her chair.

"Take me home, Zac," said Marianne.

As they left the room, Zac was aware of the barman, lifting a hand, looking directly at him. His stomach tightened. He had a sense of something yet to come.

Zac almost did not recognise Maurice in a tired business suit, his tie loose around his neck and his brow beaded with sweat. He looked badly hung over. He was sitting on a stool at the front bar in Patrice's with a cold espresso and a cigarette that he barely touched, but which curled smoke up through nicotine-stained fingers. He coughed and took a sip of coffee.

Marianne was having lunch with Rae and Jasmine, and Zac had only come in here on impulse, glad of an hour or two to himself.

It was the only place he knew, he told himself. But there was another draw. The dark eyes of the barman flashed into his mind. Almost black they were, Zac thought. Watchful and deep.

"Maurice?" he said tentatively.

Maurice looked up in surprise.

"Bonjour," he said blankly, before recognition suddenly flooded his face.

"My God! Yes!" His voice dropped and he looked round, but the bar was almost empty. "Beaded dress... Zac, was it?" He indicated the seat opposite him.

"I am surprised you remember my name!"

"Quite a night." Maurice smiled weakly. "Suffering," he said, wiping his clammy brow.

Maurice turned to the bar.

"Alain!"

The barman emerged from the back of the bar. Zac felt surge a flutter of nerves.

"Two coffees. This is Zac. Zac, this is Alain who owns the bar. My best friend, aren't you Alain?"

Zac wasn't sure if Maurice was being sarcastic about the amount he spent at the bar, or if Alain really was his best friend.

The barman smiled, nodded at Zac, his eyes appraising.

"We met last night," said Alain.

So he remembered.

"You always notice the good-looking ones, Alain!" said Maurice.

Alain merely smiled.

A man of few words, Zac thought, watching his retreating figure.

Maurice rubbed his eyes with tiredness, then blinked at Zac.

"I didn't recognise you when you first came in today," he said.

"Me neither. You, I mean."

Maurice looked less physically substantial as an ordinary man, Zac thought. It was strange the way the woman's dress and the heels, the facial stubble and the lipstick, had somehow combined to emphasise the masculine side of him rather than the feminine. It had made him look larger than life, as if his masculinity was bursting out of a thin feminine shell. But today he looked like any other insipid, overweight, middle-aged man in a slightly crumpled shirt.

"You look… different, too," said Zac hesitantly.

Maurice lifted his cup and glanced up at him with bloodshot eyes. His hand trembled slightly.

"The dress wouldn't go down well at work," he grinned.

"What do you do?" asked Zac, unable to take his eyes of the cup as it shook in Maurice's hand.

"It doesn't matter."

"Sorry."

"No, I didn't mean it like that. I work as a sales rep as it happens. But it doesn't matter, if you know what I mean."

Zac nodded.

"You?"

"I am a carer in a home for the elderly."

"My God! Good for you."

"Do you have a partner?" asked Zac, then flushed. The question sounded more intimate than he had meant it to.

"She left me."

'She', thought Zac with a flicker of interest.

"She couldn't stand my funny little ways anymore."

Zac thought of Abbie and felt his spirits plunge immediately.

"I see," he said.

"Oh not the frocks," said Maurice, waving his hand dismissively. "I just left the top off the toothpaste once too often. That kind of thing."

Zac stared at him, then laughed suddenly, instinctively.

Maurice smiled and held out his hand.

"Shake! We will be friends, Zac. How long are you here?"

"Two weeks."

Maurice's hand felt clammy.

"A good length of time for a friendship. Complete but not stale."

He smiled. There was something sad about his smile, Zac thought. It held too much resignation.

"Those people," continued Maurice curiously, "the ones you were with last night. Are they your family?"

"No. Long story. I am a carer for Marianne. She and Raymond came here many years ago and I have brought her..." He stopped short. "For her last visit," he was going to say. He supposed it was, but he left it unsaid.

"She has connections here?"

"Emotional connections, yes. A flat, a past...but she has not been here for many, many years."

"She..." began Maurice, then hesitated, saying a phrase in French that Zac did not understand. "She is looking for part of herself that she left here?" he said.

"I suppose you could put it like that."

"And you," said Maurice, "you are looking for part of yourself, too?"

"Maybe."

Maurice looked over his shoulder.

"Alain!" he shouted. "Have you forgotten the coffees?" Alain did not appear.

"You like men or women?"

Zac swallowed.

"I..."

"I understand," said Maurice encouragingly.

I understand. So simple but the phrase unlocked something in Zac. He had never talked about himself in his life and heard that response. Not even with Conchetta. Nor with Marianne, come to that. But he suspected he could tell this new best friend, this stranger, anything. Because in two weeks, Maurice would be his past. He would never see him again and that idea of a temporary soul mate was very liberating.

"I… I want to be a woman."

"That is not what I asked."

Maurice lit another cigarette.

"Don't make the mistake of confusing your gender identity with your sexuality, Zac."

"But if I am really a woman…"

Maurice shrugged.

"Perhaps you are a lesbian. No, don't laugh. I didn't mean it as a joke." He took an almost furtive puff of the cigarette from behind a cupped hand. It was strange how masculine some of his mannerisms were, thought Zac.

"I have a partner," Zac said suddenly. "Her name is Abbie. And I love her but I'm not sure if I'm IN love with her." He felt a rush of adrenaline hearing the words aloud, literally a ringing in his ears. He'd said them. Maurice did not even appear to realise their significance. He simply nodded, accepting what he said without question.

"And you?" Zac asked curiously. "Who do you like?"

"Women," said Maurice instantly. "But.." Maurice raised his hands helplessly and blew out a quick burst of smoke. "They find it hard."

Zac understood the frustration and the helplessness of the gesture.

"They find it hard that you want to be a woman?"

"I don't want to be a woman. I want to dress like a woman – occasionally. I am transvestite, not transgender."

"I see."

Zac looked more closely at Maurice's face. How old was he? Fifty perhaps. Fifty-five. His hair was receding and grey at the temples, and there were bags under his eyes that gave him a lugubrious quality without the makeup. The rush of fire in Zac's belly, the excitement of acceptance, abated. He looked at Maurice and felt suddenly overwhelmed. Fifty-five and he hadn't done it yet; he hadn't found peace. It was obvious.

"Alain!" shouted Maurice again in the silence.

"So you live alone?" said Zac.

"With God... and myself," said Maurice, in a tone that suggested to Zac that he had said it many times before. "Do I need anyone else? " He turned and shouted over his shoulder. "Alain! Where the hell is our coffee?"

"I need more than God and me," said Zac.

"Or you think you do," said Maurice. He stubbed out the partially smoked cigarette. "It is amazing how little you can survive on. Your family... are they supportive?"

"My mother is. She is...very special. And my sister, though of course she's less invested in my happiness than my mother. But it's hard for them to understand. How could it not be? Not even I understand. And my father..."

Maurice sighed. "Yes, fathers are a problem. As far as they are concerned, if you question your sexuality, you question theirs too."

"He doesn't like being in my company," said Zac.

"Do you like being in his?" asked Maurice.

No, answered Zac in his own head, but he remained silent.

"You are allowed to dislike him as much as he dislikes you."

Maurice's words suddenly flicked a switch. This was not just about what his father felt; what Zac felt was important too. It surprised him that such a simple exchange could hand him back some control.

Alain arrived from the kitchen with two cups.

"Sorry, the machine broke down."

"No matter," said Maurice. "We have been getting to know one another. Zac was telling me about his difficult father."

Zac felt uneasy. It was one thing to say these things aloud, another to hear them repeated. "You two have something in common then," said Alain.

"Is your father still alive?" Zac asked Maurice.

"No. He died, maybe ten years ago. I was not part of his life, until the end, that is."

"What happened?"

"He asked to see me when before I had not been welcome." Maurice picked up his discarded cigarette and relit it unthinkingly. "Insurmountable problems suddenly become surmountable when death knocks on your door. It is a shame that we have to wait until then."

A bead of sweat was rolling down his forehead. Maurice fished in his pocket and took out a checked cotton handkerchief and wiped his brow.

"I think I am going to die," he said to Alain. ""Remind me never to touch your filthy alcohol again!"

Alain glanced at Zac and raised his eyes with a sarcastic smile.

Zac smiled back at Alain. It was strange, he thought, how he and Alain had addressed very few words to each other yet there was silent communication flowing between them. He knew that he was being appraised, and that he was doing the same in return:

quietly watching and interpreting the nuances of Alain's expressions and reactions.

"What about *your* father?" Zac asked Alain. "Are you close?"

Alain glanced at Maurice.

"Alain grew up without his father," Maurice said to Zac. "He died when Alain was a baby."

"I am sorry," said Zac awkwardly.

Alain shook his head.

"I never… knew him," he explained. "Long time ago."

"What happened?"

"Mon père…" he said before turning away. His voice dropped and all Zac could hear was a mumble.

Zac looked at Maurice for explanation.

"What did he say?" he asked with a frown.

Maurice drew the handkerchief over his eyes and face.

"He said his father was murdered."

CHAPTER TWENTY

Marianne

Memories fill this flat; the elusive scent of the past. When you first spray perfume, the vibrant, pungent cloud fills your nostrils and assaults your senses, sometimes not altogether pleasantly. But after a while, when the wearer has long stopped smelling it, it settles into something more mellow and mature, a vague residue that every so often catches you unaware, drifting softly into your consciousness when you turn this way or that. A puff, a whiff, a moment when the scent is real, then gone again. My memories feel like that; mature now and settled into something richer but slightly evasive. But oh, every so often I can smell them clearly, the lingering intensity of what they once were.

Strangely, there was no euphoria when Raymond had his surgery. Not at first anyway. There was too much pain for that. The morning he was due to go into hospital, I found him sitting at the French window in a shaft of sunlight, watching the world quietly. He had turned when I came into the room and smiled, holding out his hand to me without a word. I joined him and we looked out at a sky still streaked ominously with the deep red of dawn.

"I watched the light come up," he said, "watched it rise to create a new day."

I squeezed his hand.

"The two-spirit people of the native American Indians had a special role in sun dances," he said.

"Two-spirit people?"

"People like me. Those with a male and a female identity."

I suppose he was telling me that transgender people were in every culture; that he was not some abomination of the decadent West.

It was not as if Raymond left that morning as a man and returned as a woman. Really, it was already all over by then. The surgery was simply the final icing on the cake. After a year of hormone therapy and extensive electrolysis, he already looked more female than male. I had grown almost accustomed to his outwardly female persona, though I cannot lie: even now I find it difficult to think of him as Rae - as anything, in fact, other than my Raymond. But we had settled into an almost sisterly existence, and I did not dare to say that I missed the masculine dimension, even though I did.

"Any second thoughts?" I asked and he simply shook his head.

"Are you scared?"

"A little."

We held one another for a moment, my cheek on his, and his skin was soft and feminine. I longed for the stubble that had once rubbed like an emery board against my cheek.

"Time to go," I murmured, but he kept his hold when I tried to move.

"Thank you, Marianne," he murmured.

"For what?"

"For always accepting me. For being here."

"Who else was going to be here?"

"Only you," he said.

I had hours and hours to replay that conversation as I sat in a bare hospital waiting room with a selection of well-thumbed magazines. The place was warm enough but the walls were painted in a pale, cold blue that made me feel chilled and anxious as the seconds, minutes, hours ticked interminably by. Who else was going to be there? Only me. We seemed to alternate, Raymond and I, between moments of intense intimacy and solidarity, when he appreciated me as the rock he clung to in every storm, and moments of anger when he wanted his freedom and saw me as part of his problem: the obstacle blocking his way.

I was allowed to sit by his bed when he came back from theatre, just watching him breathe. In and out, and in and out, until I was terrified that an 'in' would not be followed by an 'out', or an 'out' would not be followed by an 'in'. Sometimes, there seemed to be a pause when his breathing hung, suspended, and I lurched forward only for him to take a sudden gasp. He's fine, a nurse had said lightly, with what seemed to me to be careless indulgence, when I asked. In the end, I had to stop watching him. I took hold of his hand which lay on a starched white sheet and a peach coloured blanket that was the shade and roughened texture of fabric Elastoplast.

When his eyes opened, I leant over him immediately – leant over HER I suppose I have to say from this point on – and smiled.

"How do you feel?" I asked softly, stroking her hair off her forehead.

Her lips barely moved and I could see they were dry and uncomfortable.

I leant closer.

"What?"

"Bloody awful," she murmured.

"Don't try to talk any more. Close your eyes. Rest."

She was hooked up to a morphine drip for 24 hours but it was then removed - to avoid dependency, the nurses said.

"I'll risk it," Rae pleaded, but they replaced it with only Paracetamol and Ibuprofen which would have struggled to see off one of Rae's headaches on a bad day. It was increased to a stronger cocktail when she was unlucky enough to get an infection and her temperature was raised. She lay, miserable and still, and I watched her silently as she tried to move her flushed cheeks to a cool part of pillow. I suppose it was the anticlimactic nature of the transition that distressed her most. The genital area was swollen horribly and the whole thing was seeping blood and pus. She was miserable, and eventually the tears began to cascade. It was not as she had imagined; the butterfly emerging effortlessly from the chrysalis to be the creature nature always intended. The blossoming of Rae's new identity didn't quite happen in the calm, triumphant way she had dreamed of.

"You feel bad?"

She nodded miserably and I took a risk.

"Oh pull yourself together," I said. "You're a woman now - you can't whimper at the least little thing like men do!"

She giggled through her tears and turned her face into the pillow when the laugh turned into a painful cough that put pressure on her stitches.

"Sorry." I lifted her hand and held it in mine and we sat in a bubble of silence.

"This will pass Rae," I said eventually, soothingly. "In just a short time, it will seem like nothing at all."

"Promise?"

"I promise."

A nurse came in, carrying something in her hand.

"Rae," she said, "we need to do your first dilation."

<hr />

Losing Raymond was like a bereavement. I mourned for him and the awful thing was that I had no-one to share that pain with. I certainly couldn't tell Rae. But I recognised that essentially, Raymond was still with me and I had to be grateful for that. I imagine it was a little like losing someone to one of those awful dementia illnesses, where the person appears to still be there physically but in reality is quite gone. The person who is left is still them – and yet is an imposter too.

When I battled with those feelings, I tried to work out the nature of love. What it meant. What it depended on. I only ended up with a headache. I knew that I loved Rae partly for Raymond's sake, rather than her own. But I would have taken any part of Raymond that I was allowed to keep. If he'd been paralysed in an accident I would have loved him still. If he'd become ill with a debilitating disease, I would have loved him still. The spirit would have been the same inside the changed body. Was it so different to have the same spirit inside a body with a different gender? Rae was enough for me. She had to be. How did Shakespeare put it? "Love is not love which seeks to alter when it alteration finds. Oh no, it is an ever fixed mark, that looks on tempests and is never shaken."

<hr />

She was grateful, so grateful. For a time. But it is a fickle emotion, gratitude. It co-exists with dependency, and when dependency flees, it drags gratitude with it. Like a reprieve from illness, or narrow escape from an accident, when you swear you will live your life differently, be marked forever with the stain of thankfulness on your forehead for the gaining of a life that might so easily have been lost. Until the process of living drains your good intention, and eventually you forget it was ever there. So it was with Rae.

In the weeks of painful vulnerability, when Rae needed me, we were as close as we had ever been since before Patrice Moreau died. It seemed impossible that we would ever part. She leant on me, both physically and metaphorically, and I gladly accepted her weight and supported her as best I could.

But gradually, she blossomed, both physically and emotionally. I kept hearing that conversation with Professor Mitchell in my head. *"What is your deepest fear, Marianne?" "That he will be reborn and I will die."* Rae's new body was everything she had wanted and she could not pass a mirror without looking in it and smiling.

"Oh Marianne, I look like *me*," she said, turning this way and that in front of the glass. "At night, when I dreamt, I was almost always a woman. And I looked like *this*."

"You never told me that," I said, "about your dreams."

"Didn't I?"

She was happy, brimming with the confidence that fulfilment brings, and her need for me waned. It was not as conscious, as deliberate, as simply discarding me. It was casual thoughtlessness, rather than deliberate cruelty. No matter; the effect was the same. She was not aware of how much she was changing, whereas I saw every tiny detail: the first morning she failed to consult me anxiously on what she was wearing; the day I found her giggling coquettishly with a delivery man on the doorstep.

I walked past her into the kitchen and waited until I heard a cheery 'goodbye' and the sound of the front door closing.

"Is that your impersonation of a woman?" I said, when she walked, humming to herself, into the room. I couldn't help myself.

"What?"

"Oooohhh," I simpered, mimicking her giggle. "Oooohhhh!" Rae flushed with hurt.

"You're just jealous," she said, walking back out past me.

I was.

It didn't happen overnight; these things rarely do. And it didn't matter how many deals we'd done over the years, or how many promises we'd made, or what was right and what was wrong. When it happens, it happens, and no emotions from the past can prevent it.

There were no tears, and no big scenes, because neither of us admitted what was really going on. I loved Raymond, but he was always an emotional coward. Rae was no different in that respect.

"Let's go back," she said impetuously one night, when we were sitting in front of the television.

It was such an oblique remark that it shouldn't have made sense. But it did. Instantly.

"Go back where?" I said, not taking my eyes from the screen. Rae smiled.

"Saint Estelle!" she said with a flourish, as if it was an idea that had only just occurred to her rather than the well thought-out plan that I knew it was.

"No."

"Don't be so quick to make a decision, Marianne," she pleaded, taking hold of my hand. "It could work."

"For you, not for me."

"I need to… go back. I need to finally be there as me."

Maybe it was a kind of pilgrimage. Maybe it was a spiritual – or sentimental, depending on how you look at it – impulse to visit Patrice's grave and show that she had finally completed the journey they had embarked on together. For me, it was just an unnecessary return to the scene of the crime.

"I won't go," I said calmly. "I don't want to be there."

Rae was silent, but I knew she was not surprised. It was all planned. She knew she asked me to do the one thing, the only thing, I would not do for her. Could not do for her. When I refused, it would liberate her. I resented the cleverness of the trap she laid for me.

"It is too risky to go back. What if Charpentier calls on you?"

"Charpentier!" she exclaimed scathingly. "The man will be retired by now. In fact, he may be dead. I hardly think he's going to come calling on an unknown woman."

"Yes, Rae," I said. "It is different for you. You are no longer who you were. But I am not an unknown woman, am I? And what if the police come knocking on my door asking about 'Raymond'?"

She said nothing.

This was the moment she could have pushed things, engineered an argument, flounced out. She behaved more subtly.

"Maybe," she said, "I could go over for a while. See how things are, and if we could make a life there. And if being there for a few weeks is enough, then at least I will have got it out of my system."

"You mean we should split up?"

"No, of course not. Just temporarily. A holiday. A break. Then we can talk again. I will find out what possibilities there are for jobs for both of us."

"I see."

She stroked my hand.

"I want your permission, Marianne. I want you to support me in this."

"Do I have a choice?"

"Of course you have a choice."

Even the day she left we continued with the pretence that she was coming back. I put a Chanel suit on to go to the office that morning. A pair of black patent kitten heels. A string of smooth, creamy pearls that I asked Rae to fasten for me. I remember the touch of her fingers on the back of my neck, the way she lightly put both her hands on my shoulders for a second when she had closed the clasp.

She left most of her things behind, all part of the elaborate fantasy that we conspired to concoct. Her suitcase, a small black case with a white double stripe down the centre, sat in the hall waiting for the arrival of her taxi. A horn blasted outside.

"Take care," I whispered, hugging her.

Even in that last hug I sensed her desire to be gone.

"I will phone you this evening," she said, gathering up her things.

"Safe journey."

She opened the door and a burst of wind and rain blew in. She stepped out and then turned back to me.

"There is a bit of me that will always be yours, Marianne."

It was her parting gift, my consolation present.

"I know."

Her eyes filled.

"Whatever happens."

"Whatever happens."

Then she stepped back over the threshold and kissed me gently on the lips.

The last glimpse I caught was of her hurrying down the path, bracing herself against the wind and rain; a tall elegant figure in jeans and a tailored white jacket that was quite unsuitable for the British weather. Rae was no more practical than Raymond had been.

The reverse lights of the taxi lit up, the black cab manoeuvred into the driveway, windscreen wipers flying furiously, and turned to go back in the direction it had come from. And then she was gone. After all those years, all those fears, all those agonies, it really was that simple. Just jump on the bus, Gus. Drop off the key, Lee. And set yourself free.

CHAPTER TWENTY-ONE

Zac

"Who is this little friend you keep sneaking out to see?" demanded Jasmine, slapping Zac playfully with a pair of black kid gloves. "Why are you not coming with us to lunch?"

Zac felt the heat flush through his cheeks to the roots of his hair. He was uncomfortable around Jasmine. If he were honest, he was actually a little afraid of her.

"Leave Zac alone," said Rae reprovingly. He smiled indulgently and patted Zac briefly on the shoulder as he passed. "We will take care of Marianne."

"But I dare say he will come with us this evening!" said Jasmine archly.

I dare say, Zac mimicked in his head. I dare say! Why did she talk like that? Why did she constantly make herself sound like an actress in an Oscar Wilde play?

"Why? Where are we going this evening?" asked Marianne, looking up with bright eyes.

There was something very alive about Marianne in the last few days Zac thought, watching her carefully. Very alert, like a death rattle almost, a last burst of fervent activity before everything began shutting down for good.

"Just Patrice's," said Jasmine. "But I rather think our Zac has a little playmate behind the bar there. Don't you Zac?"

Zac looked at her warily, following her almost sullenly with his eyes, and Jasmine laughed lightly.

Bitch, Zac thought.

"Although, I think he is a little old for you, Zac. A father figure, perhaps?"

"Oh shut up, Jas," said Rae impatiently. "Take no notice, Zac."

Zac shut himself away inside his own head. The last two days had been the most amazing of his life. Every spare minute he'd had, while Marianne was with Rae and Jasmine, had been spent in the dingy bar or in Alain's flat above. Was he in love? No, he thought, with a level of self-awareness and honesty that surprised himself. Yet this relationship was the most intense and satisfying of experiences because it involved an awakening, a submission to something deep inside, and Alain would always be the person who awakened him, whatever happened afterwards.

Perhaps it was different for Alain. He insisted that he was unlike his father, Patrice, in every way, that as a rule he did not have relationships with people in the bar. This was different. Zac was special. And Zac, who was used to being ridiculed for being different, gloried in being celebrated for his uniqueness for once. It was a kind of fantasy and he melted into it, into Alain, with a passion that he had never felt before. But he did not kid himself the passion was for Alain.

Zac's eyelids flickered as he remembered the moment Alain's lips had finally fluttered over his, the sensation of his hand on his back, the heat of him close to him. He blocked out everyone in the room and thought about that moment, when all the vague longing he carried inside had abated and his soul had stilled. Zac had been dressed in a dark purple velvet dress and Alain had run his hand over the soft fabric causing a ripple to run through Zac's entire body. He had never had such a physically satisfying experience in his life. Did he mean sexually satisfying? No, he decided, physically satisfying. Emotionally satisfying. He felt whole and desirable and cherished.

Abbie. He tried to shut out the guilt but every so often, it clutched at his heart, flooded him with panic. He was a bad person, such a bad person. In his mind's eye, he could see Abbie, silently watching him, her blue eyes blinking with pain. But it was Alain's voice he heard.

"I like you…" Alain had said haltingly, "like this."

It was the full extent of his English, but it didn't matter. Zac had smiled shyly, pleased at Alain's attempt to speak in his language. They spoke in French normally and there was something touching about the effort. Like this… like a woman. He meant he liked him as a woman. Since that conversation, Zac had dressed every day in women's clothes, not just in the evenings when he went to Patrice's.

"I like you too," Zac had whispered. Alain smiled. Zac wondered fleetingly if the attraction was partly that there was no need for words, difficult, messy words and hard to express feelings. Everything was in a look, a gesture, an expression, a touch. It was a kind of liberation.

"Zac!"

Zac looked up sharply at the sound of Marianne's voice.

"Who is she talking about?" Marianne demanded, jerking her head towards Jasmine. "This person that you are seeing?"

Jasmine looked on with interest.

"Alain," mumbled Zac, flushing.

"Who is Alain?" asked Marianne.

"I think we knew his father, Marianne," Jasmine said. Her voice sounded almost malicious to Zac.

Marianne did not look at her.

"What is his name?" Marianne asked Zac.

"Alain. He owns the bar," said Zac.

"No, his surname."

"Moreau. Alain Moreau."

He wondered why Marianne gasped.

"What did you mean," he asked, turning to Jasmine, "about knowing his father? Alain did not know his own father. He was murdered."

"Yes, we know," said Jasmine, "we were all there."

"When he was murdered?" asked Zac incredulously.

"No, of course not," snapped Rae. "Jasmine means that we were here, in town, when it happened."

"Do I?" said Jasmine.

Rae followed her with her eyes as she walked over to a cabinet and calmly took out a bottle of gin.

"Drink anyone?"

"I thought we were going to lunch?" said Rae. Her voice sounded edgy and slightly querulous to Zac.

"There's always time for a drink," said Jasmine.

"What happened to Alain's father?" asked Zac.

"Yes," said Jasmine, unscrewing the cap of the bottle and pouring a generous measure for herself. "What happened to Patrice, Rae?"

The question hung in the air. Zac looked on silently, uneasy at the sudden change in atmosphere. What a strange feeling had descended on the room, as unexpected as a sudden flurry of snow in spring. He glanced at Marianne, but though her eyes glittered feverishly, she did not seem to be taking much notice of the conversation. At least, as far as he could tell.

"Well?" said Jasmine.

"What's got into you, Jas?" demanded Rae.

"You have never said.... either of you," said Jasmine.

"Said *what,* for God's sake?" said Rae.

"What happened to Patrice that night."

"How would we know? We know no more than you. Poor Patrice was stabbed by some, some... lunatic."

"I met Marianne that night," said Jasmine.

Zac noticed that her hand shook slightly as she raised her glass to her lips. The little display of vulnerability surprised him.

"You met Marianne a lot of nights," said Rae impatiently.

"I saw you in Patrice's," said Marianne, her voice breaking through the conversation. Everyone turned to her.

"Yes," said Jasmine, her voice softening. "We danced."

"No," said Marianne crisply. "YOU danced."

Jasmine's mask returned and she looked at Marianne with disdain.

"Yes of course, Marianne. You were always much too stuck up to dance with the likes of me."

"Oh God," muttered Rae, crossing over to the cabinet and taking out the bottle of gin.

"I saw you in the lane," said Jasmine suddenly. "Afterwards. Later that evening."

"Oh no," said Marianne calmly. "I don't think so."

"You know I did," said Jasmine. "You were upset."

Marianne's eyes fixed on Jasmine like two hard, black stones.

"You were crying. Why were you crying so hard simply because you could not find Raymond?" demanded Jasmine. "You had lost control. What did you think had happened? And where did you go?"

"For God's sake stop over-dramatising, Jasmine!" said Rae, screwing the top back on the gin bottle. Zac noticed he drank half her glass in one. "Everyone had been drinking that night. It's hardly surprising if things got a bit emotional and out of hand. They usually do when alcohol's involved!"

"She was trembling," Jasmine said accusingly, gesticulating at Rae's back. "Why would she tremble like that?"

"Because she was cold!"

"It was summer!"

"It was the end of summer. And anyway, Marianne feels the cold."

"Stop talking like I am not here!" Marianne snapped.

Zac looked between the three of them. Marianne looked a little confused but he recognised that mutinous look. Such a wave of emotion rolling between them about an event from so long ago…Zac did not understand. What was going on here?

"We met in the lane," repeated Jasmine. "You were upset. You had been looking for Raymond all night, you said."

"No," said Marianne. "It was earlier in the evening that I was in the lane. Then I went into the bar to buy cigarettes and then I went home. I was not in the lane again."

"Yes!" retorted Jasmine. Yes, yes, yes! Why are you lying, Marianne?"

"Stop it!" snapped Rae. "Leave her alone, Jasmine. You can see how she is… you cannot expect her to remember everything from so long ago."

"I remember perfectly," said Marianne flatly, and Rae and Jasmine stopped shouting and turned at the sound of her voice.

"If you remember everything," said Jasmine, her voice trembling, "who was the blonde woman who you told the police you saw with Patrice that night?

"Perhaps," Marianne said evenly, "it was *you*, Jasmine. I am beginning to wonder, with all these lies, if it was you."

"Don't be ridiculous!"

"Yes," continued Marianne. "You are trying to make up a story, to cause confusion."

"My hair has always been black, for God's sake!"

"It could have been a wig."

"Are you serious?"

"What is going on?" asked Zac, his stomach twisting anxiously.

"Nothing," said Rae soothingly. "It's just Jasmine causing mischief."

Jasmine looked at him bitterly and Zac had a sudden flash of insight. Jasmine had felt sorry for Marianne when she first saw her again. She saw the physical disintegration and pitied her. But the strength of the bond between Marianne and Raymond was too strong to be pitied. Zac could see the edge of envy in the way Jasmine's eyes flashed between them. She was the outsider, the one to be pitied, not Marianne.

"Patrice's wife had blonde hair," said Marianne suddenly. "Perhaps it was her. I would have killed him had I been married to him."

"She had auburn hair!" said Jasmine.

"Are we going for lunch?"

Jasmine looked at Marianne with incredulity, rattled by the sudden change in direction.

"You are mad!"

"I may be but I still need to eat."

"You still have an appetite after all that has been said?"

"Well Zac must be hungry," said Rae. "We are keeping him from his lunch date. Go on Zac."

"No, I…"

"Well I, for one, am no longer hungry," said Jasmine. She looked over her glass at Rae with an anger that was laced with contempt.

"Liquid lunch again?" said Rae. Her eyes flashed coldly in a way Zac had never seen. Rae always seemed gentle, ineffectual almost. A bit like me, Zac thought uncomfortably. It was like he did not exist in this room.

"What is this all about?" Zac asked. "Who was this blonde woman you are talking about?"

"Well it wasn't me," said Jasmine.

"What blonde woman?" asked Marianne.

Silence cut through the room like a scythe. Zac looked at Marianne curiously. Was she serious? Had she already wiped out the conversation they had just had? Or was she deliberately "forgetting" as Marianne sometimes could? Marianne glanced up at him, but her expression was impassive, and he could tell nothing from her eyes.

"I have to insist that we talk about this later," said Rae. "This is not doing Marianne any good."

"How convenient," said Jasmine, and she lifted her glass and drained it.

Maurice, Zac thought, was one of the kindest men he had ever met. They had taken to having coffee each morning when Zac left Marianne with Rae, and sometimes Jasmine. He felt enormously fond of him already. Maurice felt like his French soul mate, someone who understood without much explanation ever being necessary. He was old enough to be his father, Zac realised suddenly. He wished he could be. How good it would feel to have a father who understood you, loved you for who you were, unconditionally.

Yet there was also something contradictory about Maurice, a quality that seemed simultaneously simple but unfathomable. Something that made him seem alone even when he was with other people. A two-week friendship, Maurice had said, but Zac suspected it would take a lot longer to know this man. He was an enigma.

Maurice had a letter on the table in front of him when Zac found him in a dark corner of Patrice's one morning. It must be from a woman Zac thought; at least, it was written on lilac paper. Maurice was holding it as if he were reading it, but the edges of the pages were crumpled in his hands and Zac suspected that his mind was somewhere else entirely.

"Ah, my new friend," said Maurice brightly when he looked up to see Zac standing over him. "My two week best friend!" He stuffed the letter into the inside pocket of a suit jacket that looked like a limp rag.

"Is everything all right, Maurice?"

"God is in his heaven and all is well with the world!"

Zac smiled faintly.

"No really, Zac. When you have God on your side, what else do you need? Everyone else may desert you but He does not. But I see you have something on your mind. Come and sit down. I'll get some coffee."

He looked over his shoulder.

"Alain is on the bar, but I am not sure where he has disappeared to.

"It doesn't matter. Leave him for now. I want to talk to you alone."

"What's wrong?"

Zac hesitated.

"I want to talk to you about Alain's father."

Zac could see that Maurice was still fingering the letter in his pocket but he became very still, his eyebrows arching in surprise.

"Yes?"

"Jasmine was talking to Rae and Marianne earlier, and they said that they were here when Alain's father was murdered."

Maurice frowned.

"I think I knew that about Jasmine… but I had forgotten. A few of the old timers in the bar remember it. Anyway, what's the problem?"

"I don't know. Nothing probably. But Jasmine reminded Marianne that she had told the police that Patrice Moreau was with a blonde woman the night she died."

Maurice shrugged.

"It is no secret that Alain's father was… an adventurer."

"So it is known already? About the blonde woman?"

"I don't know."

"It is probably nothing but…."

"What?"

"I think Marianne knew who she was. The blonde woman."

"Really? Perhaps you should tell Alain, then. But it was thirty years ago. I doubt…" He left the sentence unfinished.

It doesn't matter, Zac thought as he turned away. It doesn't matter how long ago it was. A man had died. Wasn't that always important? And it would matter to Alain. It was his father and fathers were… fathers were what, he wondered? Perhaps this trip to France, his conversations with Maurice, were as much about coming to terms with his relationship with his father as coming to terms with his gender and his sexuality.

Maurice had certainly helped him to see that relationships, even with fathers, were not one-way streets. His father needed his approval as much he needed his father's. Nonetheless, he *did* need it, Zac recognised. Whether he liked him or not, whether he had him in his life or not, there could not simply be a gaping hole where his father should be. In the worst scenario, the space might be filled with sadness, or pain, or even an acknowledgement that things could never be fixed, but it had to be filled with *something*.

"Marianne said perhaps it was Jasmine," Zac told Maurice.

"Jasmine! I cannot imagine her blonde."

"Or Patrice's wife. Was she blonde?"

Maurice shrugged.

"You know women and hair," he said.

"It was very confusing." Zac hesitated. "There was something about the way Marianne was talking. I think she was only telling part of the truth. I could not help wondering if... if perhaps the blonde woman existed, but she was actually Marianne." He looked at Maurice seeking reassurance. "I don't know. Jasmine insists Marianne was in the lane below the flat just before the murder."

Maurice glanced down, fixing his gaze on the table.

"Speak to Alain," he said finally. "We will speak to him tonight."

Zac nodded. He stood up to go to the men's' room but at the door turned back instinctively. He saw that Maurice had pulled the letter out of his pocket again already.

"Maurice," he said, returning to the table. "Your letter... is everything okay?"

"My partner Francine," he smiled. "My EX partner... she's getting married. But not to me, obviously!"

"I'm sorry, Maurice." Zac didn't know what else to say. He felt very close to him but he had no past with Maurice, no points of reference to help him. He had only this strange fortnight in which they were being thrown together.

"Oh it's fine," replied Maurice, standing up and stuffing the letter in his pocket. "Come Zac and we will prop up the bar together. God is in his heaven and all is well with the world."

———

Zac was not sure that the others would turn up that evening but when they did, it was obvious that Rae and Jasmine were still snapping at one another.

"Oh I wouldn't miss it *for the world*," said Jasmine, enunciating carefully. She undid a scarf at her neck and retied it, carefully placing the trailing ends elegantly over her shoulders.

"Do you ever stop thinking about the way you look?" demanded Rae, watching her. "At your age!"

"I am younger than you, my dear,"

"You are a foolish old woman."

Maurice was drunk, so drunk he could barely stand.

"Don't serve him anymore," Zac pleaded.

Alain shrugged.

"He's used to it," Alain said in English.

"Have you asked him?" Maurice asked, feeling in his pocket for a cigarette pack. He took one out and placed it between his lips. He looked at Zac through screwed-up eyes. "Have you asked Alain?"

"Yes," answered Zac, but Maurice was not listening.

"A match," said Maurice, almost falling from his stool. "Who has a match?" He straightened up, banging into a stranger at his side. The man steadied him, helping him back onto the stool.

"Here," he said, taking a lighter from his pocket.

"Gitânes," murmured Marianne, breathing in deeply. "May I have one?"

"Marianne, you have not smoked for thirty years!" protested Rae.

"What difference does it make now?" asked Marianne, taking a cigarette from the packet Maurice proffered.

"Marianne," said Zac. "I am meant to be looking after you."

"Ohh!" said Marianne, waving a dismissive hand at him, as if shooing a child. "Just one."

"May I speak to you?"

The voice came from behind Zac, speaking in English but heavily accented. It was Alain. He had moved out from behind the bar and was standing beside them, looking directly at Marianne. She looked at him with black eyed interest.

"Are you…?"

"Alain Moreau," he said, holding out his hand. Marianne did not seem to see it.

"So you are Patrice's son." She exhaled, choking slightly on the smoke. "Patrice…" She turned to Rae. "About the eyes."

"Yes," said Rae.

"My friend," said Alain, nodding at Zac, "tells me you saw a blonde woman with my father the night he died."

"And the mouth," murmured Marianne. "Rae, you see the way the mouth…"

"Yes," said Rae interrupting sharply. "I see."

"It was you?" Alain said to Marianne politely. "You who saw the woman? The blonde woman? I always knew there was a woman but I did not know where this information came from. Perhaps you can tell me more?"

"It was a long time ago," said Marianne vaguely.

Zac grasped her hand.

"Marianne!" he said. "You have just told us all… you said…"

"I know what I said."

Marianne's voice was so cold, so flat, that Zac was silenced. She had never spoken to him in quite that way before.

211

Alain sat down beside Marianne and picked up her hand, engulfing it in his.

"It does not matter," he soothed her.

Marianne stared at her hand in his.

"You have your father's charm."

Alain smiled.

"My mother would say this is not a good thing."

If he expected Marianne to smile back, she did not.

"I agree. I did not like your father," she said, removing her hand.

"Marianne!"

"Yes, Zac?"

"That was very rude! Why are you…?"

"It is fine," said Alain. "Marianne is of an age where she can say whatever she feels."

"Does that seem fair to you?" asked Marianne. She took another small little puff of the cigarette. "I suppose it is in a way," she added vaguely.

"The only thing I want to know," continued Alain, "is if you knew this woman, if she was significant."

"I imagine she was significant." She turned, the cigarette dangling in her hand like a foreign object she no longer knew what to do with. "Pass me that ashtray, Rae." She stubbed the cigarette out lightly and left it propped as if she might re-light it. She glanced up at Alain. "He certainly seemed… intimate with her."

"She was my father's lover?"

"I would have said so. But your father had so many lovers. He was not capable of being loyal to those he loved."

Zac noticed the look that passed between Marianne and Rae at that moment but could not interpret the pain that it held.

"Is it possible that she was his… meurtrier?" He looked round the company for help. "Meurtrier?"

"Murderer," said Maurice drunkenly, before placing his head on the bar.

"His murderer?" said Marianne.

The company fell awkwardly quiet.

"No, I don't think she was his murderer."

"How do you know?"

Marianne shrugged.

"It is an opinion."

Rae drained her glass.

"You are lying!" Zac's words came out in an impulsive burst. Marianne turned to him and he flushed. "I am sorry. I have no idea why you would be lying about this but I know you, Marianne!"

"They were very intimate," said Marianne. "Very loving. The way he was holding her, it did not look as if she was about to murder anyone."

"How was he holding her?" asked Alain.

"As if his life depended on her. As if hers depended on him."

Zac caught another look flash between Marianne and Rae. There was the conversation in the room, he decided, and then the secret, silent conversation between them. Mind to mind, heart to heart.

"You know who she was," said Jasmine flatly.

Marianne shrugged.

"Of course she doesn't," said Rae. "She would have said."

Jasmine was staring at Rae.

"How stupid," murmured Jasmine. "It is so clear now."

"Did you tell the police?" asked Alain.

"I told them I saw her."

"But her name. Did you tell them her name?" asked Alain.

"No."

"Why not?"

"Isn't it obvious?" said Jasmine.

"No," said Zac. "Why?"

"Because the blonde woman was Raymond."

"Ah Jasmine," said Marianne sarcastically, "you were always so clever."

—◆—

"Alain!"

Zac caught up and grasped Alain's arm as he walked through to the office behind the bar.

"Are you okay?"

Alain looked suddenly greyer, older. For a second, Zac caught sight of a slackness in his facial skin, the way his top lip seemed slightly thinner than it should be, as if the tiny lines around his mouth were pulling it inwards into itself. Strange that he had not noticed it before.

The thought unnerved him, made him aware of the difference in their ages in a more acute way for the first time. Alain's age had made him seem so confident, sophisticated. Now Zac had a glimpse of something else. He pushed down the unease and ran his hand comfortingly up Alain's arm.

"I think that she… the woman Rae… Did they say…they think she murdered my father?"

"Don't."

Alain shook his head gently. "It is not that I feel…" He seemed at a loss to explain, his eyes full of an appeal that he could not voice. "I did not know my father. It is so long ago. And yet…" There was a rickety old chair and a desk in the office and Alain sat down suddenly, as if he might fall if he did not sit, the chair wobbling unstably to one side.

There was so much Zac wanted to say as he watched him but for the first time with Alain, he regretted being alone and wished he had some other support to help with this. Someone who knew Alain better. If only Maurice wasn't snoring over the bar in a drunken stupor, he thought in frustration, glancing through the open doorway at the slumped figure.

"I do not understand," Zac began. "All the talk of Jasmine and black hair and blonde wigs and Rae, it was all so confusing and I do not know which of them is mo…" Zac broke off suddenly, realising he was talking in English and Alain was lost.

"What will you do?" he asked in French.

Alain shrugged disconsolately.

"My mother is so old."

Zac nodded.

"She cannot."

"It may be nothing," said Zac. "Marianne said…"

"But you said she lied," interrupted Alain.

"Perhaps not lied," Zac stopped abruptly. What was it he had sensed with Marianne? Perhaps that she knew more than she said.

"I do not know what to think," said Alain.

Neither did Zac. He reached out and ran his hand comfortingly down Alain's arm. It was strange to no longer fear being demonstrative, to touch naturally, without anxiety.

"I know."

"I need you to find out more, Zac."

"I will try. Of course I will try."

"I will not say to my mother," Alain said quietly, almost to himself.

"Will she be upset?"

"She was always upset when it came to my father. Upset when he was alive. Upset when he died. This… brings it all back."

"I will do my best to find out discreetly."

"Thank you. Because there is something I feel very much."

"What? What is it that you feel?"

"I have never known my father," said Alain haltingly. "This is the closest I have got to him in my life."

"Does he matter to you?"

"Of course he matters. He is my father. Was my father."

Yes, Zac thought sadly. Fathers – and the absence of them – were important.

"It is hard to say you love someone you have never met," continued Alain. "And yet I do feel a love of sorts. Abstract, certainly but… but a bond for the man who should have been my dad. Should have been."

"You feel his loss?"

"I feel the loss of a father. When I felt sad as a boy, I did not feel sad for him, for Patrice. I felt sad for the father I had never known. Perhaps I cried for me, for my loss, not his, if that makes sense."

"Yes. Yes it makes sense."

"This is the first time there has ever been anything I can do for him rather than for me. The first and the last thing. For him. For justice."

—⁓—

Zac woke with a start, staring into the darkness. He rolled against a ridge of bedding that had twisted beneath him where he had kicked it, felt the coldness on his bare shoulder. Shivering, he pulled the blanket up round him, nestling in, searching for warmth and physical comfort.

A sudden memory had assaulted him so fiercely that his head pounded as if it would explode and he turned his face into the pillow. Greenfield Nursing Home felt like another life, an eternity away from France, but he had a clear vision of Shona, her pasty face rigid with shock and twisted into a grimace of concern. Marianne had linked her husband, Raymond, to a murder, she said. Was such a shocking thing possible? Did Zac know?

At the time, Zac had thought two things: firstly, that Marianne was goading Shona as only she knew how, and secondly, that she was talking about a dead man. Both those things had made him reassure Shona and then ultimately forget all about it. But something had dragged that memory out of his subconscious. Now he suspected that Marianne was indeed telling the truth. And Raymond was very much alive.

It all seemed so unlikely. Certainly he had seen Rae angry at times in the last week, especially with Jasmine, but it was not an uncontrolled anger. It did not strike him as in any way explosive and Rae had, at heart, a deferential quality that Zac recognised. But when it came to love, who knew how another's heart worked? Zac turned over to face the other way in bed, wishing he could simply drift back to sleep. The bed felt big, lonely. He realised, with some surprise that he wished he could speak to Abbie about this, lie in the darkness and hear her voice as they worked out what should be done.

Another pang of guilt stabbed him, and his stomach flipped instantly into a tight knot. He had betrayed her. It was as if, for most of the time, he protected himself from that admission but every so often, the truth broke through the shell of his carefully constructed psychological protection and pierced his heart. Each time it happened, he felt physically sick with himself. Betrayal was ugly. He was ugly. And yet, he reasoned, it was a betrayal that he felt was a necessity to gauge the truth of his own heart. By the time he went home, would he not know how he felt? Where his future lay?

The bed felt warm now after so recently feeling cold. He kicked the blanket down leaving only the sheet, then turned again to face the other direction. What were his responsibilities in this? Was justice possible after all this time? Did it even matter anymore? Zac had felt so much unfairness in his life that justice meant something to him. Justice for Patrice. Justice for Alain.

And then there was Marianne, with her sad wreck of a body, just waiting to die. Marianne with her overwhelming, unflinching devotion to Rae. Or rather to Raymond. Was he to be taken from her as a murderer, just as she had found him again?

Chapter Twenty-Two

Zac

I can hear Zac being sick in the mornings. He seemed so relaxed in our first days here, but he is in the bathroom now, retching and coughing and spluttering. He emerges, white-faced and wan.

"Why are you so anxious, Zac?"

I pat the covers and he comes and sits on my bed, one hand absently rubbing his stomach.

"Marianne, did Rae murder Alain's father?"

Poor Zac. So innocent, so well intentioned.

"No, Zac. He did not."

Zac breathes out deeply and I look for his long, thin hand in the rumpled bed covers.

"You told Shona he did."

"Oh, Shona!"

Zac looks tense.

"Zac, does Rae strike you as someone who could murder another human being?"

He shakes his head.

"But he was the last person to be seen…"

"That's true. And of course, how do you tell a murderer from an ordinary person? What does a murderer look like, Zac?"

His eyes seem darker than ever with confusion. It affects me, his confusion. For a moment, I forget what I want to say to him and concentrate only on his pain, stroking his fingers gently on the bed cover.

"Do you know that the majority of murderers offend once and never again?" I ask eventually. After Patrice died, I read a lot about murder. And then, of course, there was my job. "Unless, of course," I continue, "they are a career criminal or a member of the mafia. For most, the circumstances that lead to their actions occur in an explosion only once in their lives. An alignment of stars. Imagine that, Zac!"

"An alignment of stars? You make it sound almost poetic! What are you saying?"

"That lots of murders might never have happened if only there had been one little detail different. A chance meeting that did not occur. Some piece of knowledge that never came a person's way. A turn down one street - literal or metaphorical - instead of another."

"But it was not Rae? You are sure it was not Rae?"

"I have already told you that!"

"Please don't get angry with me, Marianne. I don't know what you are saying anymore!"

"It was not Rae."

"Why did you split up then?"

"Oh. Oh I see. Oh no, Zac you are going in quite the wrong direction with that!"

"Am I?"

"Well…"

Well actually, is it the wrong direction? Perhaps Zac is at least partly right. We *did* split up because of Patrice, in a way. Though perhaps he also held us together for longer than we would otherwise have been. Terrible events do that, bind you in secret unexplained ways. Until they destroy you, of course. Before that happened, I wanted to replace that terrible binding event with a wonderful one: a child. Of course it never happened. But yes…

"Yes, I suppose it was a factor."

"Are you trying to confuse me?" asks Zac.

"Now it is you who is getting angry!"

"I'm sorry."

"Come here."

He is like Raymond was, so needy. His cheek feels soft to the touch. It is like petting a small, trembling bird; the years turn back.

"After Raymond had his surgery, he needed to spread his wings. He came here, to Saint Estelle."

"And you never joined him?"

"It never happened as we planned."

"Why?"

"Because I did the one unselfish thing of my life."

I can feel Zac's body still and he looks up at me expectantly.

"What?"

"I kept delaying. I told myself that if he came back – if she came back – if he begged me to join him and told me his life would not be complete without me… well, then I would go. I would risk coming back here to join him."

"And he did not."

It is not a question. Zac's eyes are full of compassion.

"No, he did not."

"I didn't mean to upset you, Marianne."

"Love is almost always unequal. That is why it so rarely lasts."

221

"That's depressing."

"It is also true."

"Perhaps."

"Yes, perhaps," I interrupt with a smile. "You are young, Zac. Perhaps you will find your equal love."

Zac smiles at me like a child.

Come on," he says. "Let's get you up now. Jasmine and Rae will be here to help you soon. Shall we use some of that French lavender spray this morning – the stuff that I got you in the market?" Zac is rummaging around in the drawers of the chest next to my bed. "Look, here it is."

"Lavender Blue, dilly dilly…" I sing as he produces the bottle.

"Lavender Green…" sings Zac.

"When I am king, dilly dilly…"

"You shall be queen!"

We both smile and it melts my heart a little. Sometimes, it feels so easy with Zac, so natural.

"He wrote sometimes, at first. Raymond, I mean."

"Did he? Perhaps that should have been enough Marianne. To tell you that you should have followed him here. I am sure he loved you. You can tell."

"Do you think so?"

"It's obvious."

Zac's hand pats mine reassuringly.

"Smell!" he says, taking the top off the bottle.

"I can't really smell it," I say. "I have no sense of smell."

"Yes, of course," says Zac, stricken at his thoughtlessness. "Sorry. But I will put a little on your wrists, shall I?"

I do not tell him that I have never liked lavender. When I was young, I thought it an old woman's smell. Now that I am old, I am certain that if I could smell it, I still would not like it.

"And then I was diagnosed."

"Did you tell him?"

"No."

"Oh Marianne! You should have told him. You should have given him the chance…"

"He had stayed with me long enough. I was not going to trap him inside this grotesque illness, watching as my body grew rigid and my limbs shook. It revolted me, let alone him."

"You are not revolting."

"My body is."

"It is just a body. He would have wanted to look after you… the essence of you."

"I am not sure about that, Zac. Perhaps. But I did not want it. He was my lover once. I did not want him to be my nursemaid."

"You coped all alone?"

"For a while. And when I could no longer cope, I went into a home."

"You are very brave, Marianne. You are! Why are you laughing?"

"Because bravery makes it sound like I had a choice. I had none."

"Did you tell him where you were?"

"Absolutely not!"

"But…"

"In any case, he had fallen in love and moved to Paris by then."

"With Jasmine?"

"Don't be ridiculous!"

"Who?"

"Someone who didn't last."

There is a noise out in the hall, the sounds of a key in the lock and voices.

"That must be Jasmine and Rae," says Zac. He opens the door and then turns back.

"Marianne, you said something earlier…"

"Yes?"

"You said that if Raymond had come back for you, you would have risked coming here. Why would it have been a 'risk'?"

For a moment, I am baffled.

"I don't think I said risk."

"Yes, you did."

"Really? It's just a word. I suppose because I would have had to give up my job and my life."

"I see."

"Yoo-hoo!"

Jasmine's voice is full of insouciance, but when she and Rae come into the room it is obvious immediately that the atmosphere of last night is hanging over them still. I know how vulnerable Rae will be feeling. If this exposure had happened thirty years ago, I am sure I would have felt the same way, too. But other people knowing holds no threat for me anymore. I am entering the kind of territory where the past can't follow me.

———

The window is open in the sitting room and the curtains are shimmering gently in the breeze in the way they used to do. The light is beautiful: soft and muted and full of promise of heat to come. The house has lost its pristine, just-opened-up feel and is alive, breathing again with the signs of living. A few days of discarded newspapers lie on the table, an overlooked coffee cup left discarded on the floor beside one of the chairs, the tell-tale flurry of biscuit crumbs from afternoon tea. A bar of chocolate is lying on the table, a broken piece nestling in a shower of almond and chocolate flakes.

"Can I have it?" I ask.

"Chocolate first thing in the morning? Goodness me, your appetite has improved since getting here!" teases Rae.

"It is delicious."

"Of course you can have it."

"Are you two going to talk about nothing all morning?" demands Jasmine.

The door is ajar and I can see Zac out in the hall. He is alert to Jasmine's aggression and is pretending to occupy himself with something outside the door.

"Well?" demands Jasmine. "Don't you think it is time to get our stories straight?"

Zac moves closer to the open door.

"Don't be silly, Jasmine," I say swiftly. "There is nothing to get straight. Zac!"

Zac's head appears round the door.

"Yes?"

"Would it be possible to go downstairs to the boulangerie for bread?"

"Yes, of course."

He cannot hide his reluctance.

"Do not speak in front of him again!" I tell Jasmine as the outside door bangs.

Jasmine does not care.

"There will be a lot more people than Zac who want to know what happened."

"Nothing happened," says Rae.

"So you were with Patrice that night, Rae, but you did not kill him?"

"Correct."

Jasmine looks at each of us in turn and then walks from the room. The outside door closes for a second time.

Rae comes over to my seat and grasps my hand.

"Oh Marianne," he whispers. "How complicated things get when we are together! There was always that strange energy round us, but I would not have believed that time could roll back in this way."

"It cannot."

"No?"

"I wish it could. Oh Raymond, what would you give to have even just a year of it back? A year of being young. "

"It's going to catch up with us, Marianne."

I have called him Raymond but he does not correct me. He *is* my Raymond again: needy, vulnerable, reliant on my strength. It makes this frail shell that traps me seem like an imposter. I rise up from inside it with a kind of euphoria, reaching out to him, transcending my physical limitations one last time.

"Haven't I always kept you safe, Raymond?" My hands rub lightly over his arms. "Have I ever let you down?"

"I abandoned you."

"Shh!" I put my finger to his lips, and he grasps my hand. "I made you abandon me."

"I should have been stronger."

"Did you love any of them?"

"Who?"

"The ones who came after me."

"You have no need to be jealous. I have never loved any woman the way I have loved you."

"No, it is the men I had reason to be jealous of!"

"I have never loved any person in quite the way I have loved you, Marianne."

"Not even…"

He puts his fingers to my lips.

"Not even."

For the first time in many years, I feel a surge of pure happiness. Not just contentment, real happiness. People expect too much in life. Perfect happiness can only ever be a moment, budding, blooming, fading in a self-contained cycle. I suppose there was a similar feeling of happiness when Raymond and I married but there was too much fear for that emotion to be true happiness. Life was starting out and everything I had was there to be lost. Now it is ending, I have the unexpected joy of hearing Raymond say no one surpassed me.

I am obsessed. I was always obsessed.

"What if the police come? What do I say?" whispers Rae.

"They won't come."

The outside door bangs. Zac is back. When he comes into the room carrying bread, it is obvious he realises he is interrupting. He looks at both of us uncertainly.

"Everything okay?"

"Fine," *I* say. "Is it nice out?"

"Beautiful."

He goes into the kitchen and switches on the kettle, then begins to cut the bread.

"I saw Maurice," he calls. "He looked awful."

"He would. I am surprised he was out of bed," says Rae. "He will kill himself if he continues to drink in that way."

"He was going to the chemist for painkillers. Well, so he said. The last I saw him as I came out of the boulangerie, he was going into the wine shop."

Zac emerges from the kitchen with a plate for me.

"It was strange," he says, laying a clean cloth over a tray for me, "but he called to me from a distance."

"To say what?"

"Did I want to join him for lunch."

"What was strange about that?"

"Nothing. The way he said it… I don't know."

"Are you going?"

"No, I said I would stay with you."

"That was nice of you but you don't need to. Rae is here. She will look after me."

"I want to."

Zac pauses, smiling at me. He is a nice boy. Like my boy would have been.

"We can all have lunch together. Where's Jasmine?"

Rae waves her hand dismissively in response, but says nothing.

"After lunch, Zac," I say, "you must go and find Maurice. Be with him."

"But…"

"No buts. Rae and I have something to do."

"Do we?" Rae looks at me quizzically.

"We do."

"If you are sure…"says Zac.

"Perfectly."

I can tell Zac is happy to escape and I am happy for him to do so. He and Maurice will sit in Bar Patrice and drink coffee with Alain. He will pass the afternoon pleasantly and I can spend it alone with Raymond. I am glad that Jasmine has stormed off. This afternoon, Raymond and I have to complete what we started, finish the circle, lay it all to rest. There will only be him and me, the way it should be. The way it should always have been.

CHAPTER TWENTY-THREE

Zac

Maurice was nowhere to be found when Zac went looking for him after lunch: not at his office, nor his flat, nor at Bar Patrice. Zac felt uneasy for reasons he couldn't quite identify; something about the way Maurice had looked earlier. It was obvious something wasn't right. He paused as a hunched figure in a black coat scurried out of Sainte Maria church on the corner of Saint Estelle's main street, an old woman turning her collar up against the first giant splotches of warm rain beginning to fall from a sullen sky.

Out of the corner of his eye, Zac saw another movement, a flash of a retreating figure in a crumpled grey suit. He hesitated. Was that Maurice who just disappeared inside the church? He had been so busy watching the woman that he did not see a face, just a shapeless middle-aged man - who may, or may not, have been Maurice. The damp splotches fell onto Zac's white tee-shirt more insistently and the sky darkened. He ran, darting between cars that honked belligerently.

The swing doors of the church thudded behind him as he looked through the windows from the back porch into the interior. Zac always felt a bit frightened in churches. It was the coldness of them, the sterile beauty of soaring angles and hard stone, the feeling of being forced to face something he did not want to face. He always wanted to be back out into the streets, feel the brush of an arm in a crowd, see the flashing neon of a Coca Cola sign: the displacement activity of a life that seemed, in the moment, deep rooted enough to last forever.

The figure in the grey suit sat hunched in a pew. Was it Maurice? Yes, Zac thought uncertainly as he peered through the window at the back of the church, looking at the baldness on the back of the head, the tufts of hair round the barren patch. There was something about the way the figure was physically curled that made Zac uneasy. He recognised that position of the body, the way despair moved from something abstract in your mind into something physical and concrete that could be touched. He moved softly to the side door to enter the church, carefully closing it gently behind him to ensure there was no noise. As soon as he closed the door, he heard a wail, like the wail from an animal, and he stopped dead, hesitating to move forward into the light.

Zac stood motionless, concealed by a stone pillar at the back of the church that soared to a chorus of gold angels on the ceiling. The rain pattered on the stained glass above him, then turned into a relentless drumming, and he glanced up at the deep blue and purple hues of the figure of Christ with a lamb in his arms. The wail continued above the rain and Zac looked round, trying to see where it emanated from. Could it possibly be Maurice making that terrible noise, that unfettered, primal sound? He didn't know what to do. Then he heard a voice murmuring. Zac pressed himself close to the pillar and looked round the side. Maurice was not alone. A figure in black, a priest, had sat down beside Maurice.

"Francine," Maurice was saying, "Francine will marry. Here? Today?"

"Yes," the priest agreed. "She will marry here late this afternoon."

"But I love her."

The priest sighed.

"We have been through this, Maurice. So often. Francine is settled now. Let her go."

There was silence.

"Maurice, do not turn up here at the wedding," the priest said earnestly. "I absolutely forbid you to do so."

"You didn't tell me."

"How did you find out?"

"She wrote."

Maurice's voice broke. His sobs cut through Zac as he listened. That noise was so primitive, so deeply affecting. He tilted his head back onto the pillar and closed his eyes, thinking of Abbie. The day he tried to… He lifted his head from the cold stone, opening his eyes again quickly. He could not think of that.

"Maurice," said the priest gently, "This perversion. You will never be happy while you indulge this perversion."

Zac gasped silently for breath, as though someone had punched his stomach.

Perversion. This was what he, too, suffered from. Perversion. But his was worse than Maurice's. He and Abbie could have coped with Maurice's perversion. The voices dropped and he turned round, placing his hands against the pillar.

And still Maurice sobbed.

"But I can't…"

"Yes, Maurice. Yes, you can – or you will never be happy. God never intended for you to live this way. You must be prepared to live as God wants you to live. You must love God."

"I do love God, Fr Michel," Maurice protested. "I do!"

Fr Michel said nothing in response. Zac felt that silence as Maurice must: as a rejection. Was the priest holding him, Zac wondered? Was he touching? He peered round the side of the pillar but the priest sat upright while Maurice was bent forward, his head on the pew in front. Only a few inches between them, Zac thought, but a gulf, a gulf of pain and experience. That gulf could never be crossed with righteousness and judgement. It could only be filled with acceptance and love.

The stone felt rough and cold against his fingers. What did any person in the world want but to be loved as they were? For who they were. He could not see his friend but he could feel Maurice's spirit reaching out of his body in the stillness, hovering in the air above them, somewhere between the floor and the stained glass arches above, pleading to be rescued.

It was hopeless, Zac thought suddenly. Acceptance would never be his, or Maurice's or Rae's or Jasmine's. They didn't fit anywhere. Maurice was rocking now, rocking back and forth, back and forth. The priest sat motionless beside him.

"I do love God," Maurice repeated in a voice Zac scarcely recognised.

"Well show it," urged the priest. "Maurice, do you see now how much this… this… confusion has cost you? Why you must call a halt?"

"I want her back. I want Francine. I WANT FRANCINE."

Zac felt overcome by nausea. His back was to the pillar now and he slid down onto his heels. Such despair. Why did this man in black not comfort Maurice? Rescue him? Could he not hear the pain of those wails? Was he unaffected by them?

"Francine is gone, Maurice. You must use this, use it to force change in your life. No more of this… madness. Stay away from Bar Patrice. No good will come of you mixing with those people."

"They are my friends."

"False friends! They lead you into ways you must resist. With the grace of God you can resist."

"It is who I am."

Then change who you are."

"Did God not make me this way?"

"Do not blame God for your choices, Maurice!"

There was silence with only muffled sobs from Maurice. His voice when he spoke was clearer, but anguished.

"How Father? How? How do I change?"

Zac, resting on his heels, tilted his head and held his breath. What was the answer? How did a person change? How did he become someone else and leave behind what he was inside, right inside in the core of him. This was Maurice's question but it was Zac's too.

"You pray, Maurice," said the priest earnestly. "You pray to God for grace and for strength. You turn from temptation. You live like the man you were made by God to be. You offer the sacrifice on God's altar."

Pray, Zac mouthed to himself in repetition. Pray? A sense of anti-climax washed over him.

He felt as if he were standing outside his own body, looking down at himself crouching behind the pillar like an outcast. Pray and hide, he thought. Pray and hide. His legs were becoming painfully stiff with crouching.

"Let us say a prayer together Maurice," said the priest. "Our Father…"

"Who art in heaven," Maurice said, his voice barely above a whisper.

"Hallowed by thy name," continued the priest.

"They will be done," said Maurice but his voice broke again and he began to sob.

"On earth as it is in heaven." The priest raised his voice above Maurice's sobs.

Behind the pillar, Zac straightened up stiffly.

There was nothing here for him, he thought. Nothing. And there was nothing for Maurice either. He moved from the pillar to the door and let himself out noiselessly. Perhaps, he thought, he should call Abbie.

Chapter Twenty-Four

Marianne

The grave was in the shelter of a tree, its branches weeping over the small neat stone protectively. A calm spot, dimly cool and shaded, that seemed too safe somehow for Patrice's final resting place. A good place, perhaps, for the village schoolteacher, or the registrar of births marriages and deaths. But Patrice?

Rae is so upset she seems oblivious to the irony.

"Have you been before?" I ask.

She shakes her head.

"I needed you. I could not come alone."

I reach up from my chair to take her hand.

"I am here now. It has taken a long time."

"Our whole life has been lived in here," Rae says suddenly. "In the confines of this cemetery. We might as well have been buried in the grave with him."

"'Our life' has not been one life!" I retort, before I can think of the effect my words will have on her. But it is true. We have lived separately for so many years.

Rae's head drops slightly. She is wearing a scarf of vibrant blues and lavenders that normally suits her very well, but today she seems very pale, drained by the vivacity of the colour.

"I let you down. Both you and Patrice."

"No."

"Yes!"

"It was not your fault," I tell Rae.

"In a way, it was."

"You loved him."

"Yes." Her voice is like the whisper of a breeze, barely audible.

"Love makes you do strange things."

She looks at me with a kind of compassion.

"Just as it did you."

"Just as it did me."

"Shall we pray?" asks Rae doubtfully.

"Pray? Why would we pray?"

"For his soul. For ours."

It is a little late to start believing in redemption."

"Perhaps."

"It is not the next life I care about but this one. There is so little left."

"Perhaps redemption does not need God," whispers Rae. "Perhaps we need to redeem ourselves for ourselves."

She seems confused by the fact that I cannot answer, continues to look at me expectantly.

"It feels as if we should say something now we are here," she says. "It has taken so long to get to this moment."

"What? What can we say?"

"Sorry?"

"What good is that?"

"Well, why are we here?"

Questions, questions but no answers.

I push myself forward in the chair. I do not want to be confined in this place in front of Patrice. Perhaps I am just asserting the fact that I am still alive. Still claiming victory over the dead.

"I want to stand with you again."

"No Marianne, the ground is too uneven here."

"Yes! I insist I stand with you."

Reluctantly, Rae helps heave me to my feet where I sway a little until I gradually straighten and steady. Strangely, Zac has always reminded me of Raymond when he has helped me from the chair, but Rae seems uncertain of her strength. I feel vulnerable, as though I might fall.

"There." My arm is looped through hers now. For a moment, we stand together before Patrice. I wonder what Rae is thinking. For myself, I did not like Patrice enough to feel much sadness, but there is regret. Of course there is regret. I would not be human otherwise.

"Don't leave," says Rae suddenly.

Her words run through me like an electric volt.

"What do you mean?"

"Don't return with Zac. Stay here. I will look after you. I should never have left you."

A large splodge of rain drips onto my cheek and the branches of the weeping tree above, begin to rustle slightly as a wind whips up.

Guilt, I think. An attack of guilt. A shot at redemption. A small shower of leaves drifts down from the branches above onto my hair. I cannot remove my arm from Rae's to remove them and stay balanced. Can I live with Rae, knowing that she pities me? Almost immediately the question is formed, the answer comes. Old age is not a time for pride. There is no space left either for ego or for selflessness. Of course I can live with her pity.

The freshness of the breeze on my cheek makes me think again of the stuffiness of the home. To remain here... Not to return to Shona and her creeping, rubber-soled, pasty-faced intrusion... or Annie and her psychotic warblings. Not to be locked in timetables and uniform, or confined by the unchanging view from the bay window, the glorious, vibrant rhododendron bushes with their promise of another life that never materialises. I breathe deeply. Besides, it will be for such a short time. I will not be a burden for long.

I glance at Rae. I wonder if she hopes I will say no. But there is something else at work here. The same thing that kept us glued together after Patrice died. A glue of love and guilt and recrimination and one unanswered question: what had any of it been for - the pain, the jealousy, the desire, the violence, the guilt - if we did not stay together? But then other things, other desires, other needs had taken over. Life took over.

Here, in front of Patrice's grave, Rae is reminded that I am her last bond with him. How ironic!

"You cannot manage me, Rae."

"We will get a nurse."

"It would not be for long."

"Shh, Marianne. Stop!"

"Why? Why would you do this?"

The rain is dropping more insistently now.

"Why not?"

"Look at me!" The anguish is sudden, intense, and it feels as if it might kill me. "Look at me Raymond!" I cannot help that verbal slip. "Look at me! My wrecked body, these stupid... stupid... trembling limbs! What is uglier than this monstrosity?" I lift my arms to indicate my own body, turning awkwardly in Rae's arms. "I cannot move without help, cannot eat without drooling, cannot sleep without twitching, cannot control my bodily functions, cannot... cannot... cannot.... and inside I am that girl still. That girl you held. The one who wore high heels and perfume. She is in here, buried under plaster and rubble. She was never beautiful but she was me... ME!"

I can scarcely breathe for trembling. Raindrops are running with tears and I do not know the difference, my face wet in the wind, and all I can think is that I cannot wipe it myself. My twisting movement has unsteadied Rae. We rock slightly. In the confusion of the movement, I hear footsteps running towards us, a screaming cry for help. I twist further and see a tall, wiry dark figure flying through the graveyard.

"Zac!" I exclaim before losing balance completely.

Even in that moment I can recognise his distress, despite my own.

"Maurice, Maurice, Maurice," he is screaming before I hit the ground. "Maurice is dead!"

CHAPTER TWENTY-FIVE

Zac

Zac barely recognised Marianne. Her face seemed buried inside the pillow and it was hooded and angry, her eyes glittering feverishly like black lights. Something had changed, been lost in the fall. There was a feral quality to the way she assessed him, staring as if oblivious to the normal rules of convention, as if unaware that he was watching her back. Still, at least she was conscious now.

"Raymond," she hissed suddenly at him, and Zac started at the peculiar intonation of her voice. One wrist was strapped and immobile in a plaster cast, but her other hand snaked out of the bedclothes and she crooked a finger to beckon him. She was too frail to be menacing, he thought, and yet somehow the movement gave him the creeps.

"We have to get out of here."

"Marianne, it's Zac," he murmured.

Marianne stared.

"Not you too," she said. She looked at him suspiciously. "Have they got to you, too, Raymond?"

Zac wondered if he should tell her what had happened to Maurice.

"You remember Maurice, Marianne?"

Marianne's eyes seemed to be fixed somewhere beyond him.

"Marianne?"

She dragged her eyes to his.

"You remember Maurice?"

"Maurice who?"

Zac gave up. What was the point in trying to explain to her? As well as her broken wrist, she must be concussed. "It doesn't matter. Everything is fine, Marianne."

"No Raymond, it is not." She tried to push herself up.

"Shh, Marianne, stay still." Zac placed a hand on her arm, soothingly. "Stay still." He stroked her arm gently, tentatively, like he would pat a dog. She seemed different after the fall, but he supposed it was to be expected.

"Charpentier has been here."

"Who?"

"Charpentier," repeated Marianne exasperatedly. "Charpentier!"

"I see." Zac sat wearily down in a chair beside the hospital bed. Who was Charpentier? He smiled half-heartedly as a nurse bustled by. Marianne's eyes followed the nurse.

"She will kill me that one," she said in a low voice to Zac. "She tried to give me polluted water earlier. Thought I would not know. I was too clever for her."

"Good, Marianne," said Zac closing his eyes and seeing only Maurice's slumped figure again, face down, the grey wrists of his off-white shirt stained with fresh, red blood. So red, so vibrant, it was hard to believe such a colour seeped out of a dead man.

"Charpentier knows, Raymond."

"Knows what?"

"About Patrice of course! You... me... Patrice..."

Zac did not open his eyes. He wished he was home, even with his father. He wanted normality: to see Conchetta again, and Elicia, and the pecking wagtails in the garden, and the sight of washing pegged on the back green. He wanted to open the front door and smell his mother's Spanish fish stew, a smell he normally complained about. He wanted to speak to Abbie.

After hearing Fr Michel speak to Maurice, Zac had tiptoed out of the back of the church. He had used his mobile to try to phone Abbie but could not reach her. Huddled in the quiet of a back street, he listened to her voice on her answering machine and felt both disturbed and reassured by its familiarity. He had gone for a walk round town then, a long absorbed walk, trying to settle himself before going to look for Maurice. Poor Maurice. How would he be coping? He would no doubt be back home by now, Zac had thought, turning up past the delicatessen on the Rue de Cheval where Maurice lived. Drowning his sorrows in that wine he'd seen him buying. Perhaps he should call and check on him.

He rang the doorbell. No answer. Perhaps Maurice wasn't back. Just as he had turned away, he had noticed a narrow chink of light from the side of the door. It had seemed closed but instinctively, he reached out a hand and pushed. The door swung open.

"Maurice?" he called.

Nothing.

Tentatively, he had stepped into the narrow hallway. There was no natural light and it was made all the darker with a heavy, old fashioned, patterned wallpaper. The atmosphere felt oppressive to Zac. The place seemed eerily quiet and he found himself tiptoeing for a reason he could not understand. The unexpectedly open door made him anxious. Had someone broken in? Was someone still in the flat?

As he pushed open the door of the sitting room, he was aware of a crucifix on the wall, a wooden cross with a gold figure of Christ, before he saw Maurice crumpled on the floor beneath.

"Jesus!" Zac shouted, jumping back.

Maurice was lying in a pool of blood, one leg bent awkwardly beneath him. He wasn't moving. Should he touch him? Heart thumping, Zac moved hesitantly towards him, saw the pool of blood round his body, noticed the staining round his shirt cuffs, the pale, marbled look of his skin, and knew without question that he was dead. Who had been in here? Had Maurice been attacked?

Then he noticed an empty wine bottle, the painkillers Maurice had picked up from the chemist earlier in the day and a pack of razor blades. Maurice had removed any possibility of failure in his attempt. Zac turned in panic and ran, trembling, through the open door and fled to the next apartment, hammering on the door with his clenched fist and screaming, his legs threatening to give way beneath him. It could be him lying on that floor. Him or Raymond or Jasmine. But it was Maurice. Sweet Maurice.

By the time the ambulance arrived, a crowd of neighbours had gathered on the landing and Zac sat on a step forlornly, listening to the furore of French words that seemed to come from somewhere far away, the thump of footsteps on the stairs, a wail of another siren in the distance. He should never have let Maurice go earlier. He had let him down. It was when they brought Maurice out, a sheet covering his face, that Zac broke. The ignominy of it, a life reduced to this circus, a collection of gawpers and hangers-on, gossiping on the stairs about a pain they could only guess at.

"Raymond!"

Zac opened his eyes to see Marianne gazing at him with unnerving focus.

"Are you listening, Raymond? Charpentier knows!"

The evening air felt cold, the sky still grey streaked with rain, but Zac felt relieved to be out of the stale heat of the hospital. Out of Marianne's company, if he were being brutally honest. He breathed deeply, felt his lungs fill, wished he could inflate his spirits as easily. As he passed Sainte Maria church, Zac could see the flurries of confetti on the ground, pinks and yellows and purples that were trampled underfoot and smudged with mud and rain. A carnation head floated in a puddle. Through the railings, and the open door of the church, he could see extravagant vases of yellow and white chrysanthemums, and cascades of yellow ribbon fluttering in the breeze of the open door. The bride had been and gone, the remnants of her presence lingering like stale perfume.

Francine.

Zac wondered if she knew.

He put his hands on the iron railings and stared into the grounds. The light was fading fast. A flashing image of Maurice assaulted him, the pool of blood round his wrists, the waxy… no, he would not think of it. His fingers gripped the wet railings. From the church house at the side, a figure in a black soutane emerged. Fr Michel. Zac watched as he ran lightly down the front steps and headed for the church. The lights flicked off. He heard the thump of the wooden door closing over. The priest took a set of keys hooked to his waist and locked the door, then turned, catching sight suddenly of Zac.

Zac's hands remained on the railings as he met the priest's eye. Fr Michel smiled. Zac felt a thump of anger in his chest, a surge of adrenaline. He recognised something of that smile. It was coquettish.

"Puis-je vous aider?" asked Fr Michel, walking towards him.

Zac looked at him without replying, translating silently in his head. Can I help you? He doubted there was anyone in the world who could help. Fr Michel moved towards him. As he walked, Zac felt a sudden surge of awareness. Fr Michel transmitted something to him. It was in his walk, in his demeanour, but especially in his gaze. Zac knew that look. Whatever superficial piety it was hidden under, there was something worldly that he recognised: a suggestion; a silent proposal; an attraction; an invitation. He only had to respond to the possibility and it would become certainty.

"Quelque chose ne va pas? Je peux vous aider?" he repeated softly.

Something wrong? Zac shook his head.

"Non," he said. His hands dropped from the railings.

"Anglais?" Fr Michel said. His thin lips curved into a smile.

"Oui."

"You would like to see the church?" he said in English. His accent was accomplished, Zac thought.

"Non," he replied and he turned away before changing his mind.

The priest must know, surely, about Maurice.

"Maurice?"

The priest nodded. "Ah, yes," he said, shaking his head. "Very sad. Are you a friend? "

Zac looked at his black garments and his cold eyes and burned inside.

"Well if I can do anything for you while you are here…" said Fr Michel, filling the silence. "Anything?" Zac repeated. Another invitation. Another silent proposal. "You can do nothing for me," he muttered.

"God can always help you."

Zac walked a few feet and turned back. Fr Michel was still watching.

"YOU CAN DO NOTHING FOR ME!" he yelled.

CHAPTER TWENTY-SIX

Marianne

I can see Charpentier, smell him. The smell of garlic and tobacco. His hair is still cut into the wood like a military man and his face is impenetrably hard. I have never liked the French much. I have certainly never liked Charpentier.

Questions, questions, always asking questions. He stands by my bed with his notebook and a silver pen that catches the light and bombards me with queries about Patrice and Raymond and the blonde woman and my movements that night. He is sly, Charpentier. He always comes when I am alone, often late at night or first thing in the morning. He tries to trick me but I am a lawyer and therefore no fool.

I think he might be connected to that nurse who is trying to give me the poisoned water. They are doing a line, I'm sure. I think she is acting on Charpentier's instructions. They think they will get me so weak that I will crack and confess. I refuse to take anything she gives me.

I want out of here. It was only my wrist that I broke in the fall and it is set in plaster now. I keep asking Raymond to take me home but he says I must be patient. They have tests to do. They must make sure I am fit. But I don't think that Raymond realises that getting out of here is the only way to escape Charpentier.

"You know who killed him, Marianne, don't you?" Charpentier said last night, bringing his face so close to mine I could smell the Gitânes from his breath. "You know who killed Patrice Moreau?"

I watched him, cool as a cucumber, and said nothing.

"Admit it, Marianne."

"I have told you about the blonde woman. Why are you not questioning the blonde woman?"

"Oh I can question the blonde woman if you wish, Marianne. We both know who the blonde woman is. She is your Raymond, isn't she? That perversion of a man you call your 'husband'."

He spat the word 'husband' out with disgust. His face was so close I could see the coarseness of his skin, the pitted, uneven surface of his cheeks. His ridiculous moustache. I simply held his gaze and he stood up straight again.

"Raymond is transsexual. He was dressed as a woman that night when he was with Patrice Moreau. Isn't that so?" he continued. "You have used the blonde "woman" ever since as a decoy for us. We were looking for someone who did not exist. 'She' was really a he, playing in his perverted playground."

I was not going to accept that.

"Do not talk about Raymond that way," I told Charpentier sharply. "Raymond is not perverted."

"I suppose Moreau is the same," said Charpentier, ignoring me. "I don't know why I am bothering with him really. Why should I care who killed such a creature?" He took a pack of Gitânes from one pocket and a lighter from the other.

"You can't smoke those in here," I said.

He ignored me and lit up. It was further evidence that he is screwing that nurse. He would not have dared otherwise. The pungent smell of Gitânes filled my nostrils. I would have killed for one but I would not stoop to ask Charpentier for anything.

"The thing is," he said inhaling deeply, "I don't like loose ends. I don't like people like you who think they can break the rules, take things into their own hands. The clean middle classes who get away with crimes that people like me would not."

Hmm, he has a chip on his shoulder. A nasty, working-class chip. He has no idea where I came from. He could not possibly guess at the significance of a blue babygro, or understand the taste of abandonment that has always filled my mouth. What does he know? The nurse walked by my bed at that moment and totally ignored Charpentier. It was as if she simply did not see him. How could she do that?

"Is she your lover?" I asked. "Is that why she does what you want?"

Charpentier merely laughed.

"Never mind her," he said, though I noticed his eyes lingered on her retreating figure. "Just tell me one thing. It was Raymond, wasn't it? Raymond who killed Patrice Moreau. Admit it and then I can leave you."

"Why are you not questioning Jasmine? She was there. There in the lane. "

"As were you," said Charpentier in a flash.

I simply closed my eyes in response.

When I opened them again, Raymond was there but he kept insisting he was not Raymond and that his name was something else. I forget what.

"When did you arrive?" I asked him. "I have been waiting hard for you. Listen, Charpentier has been here."

I am not sure he believed me.

There was a strange conversation conducted round my bed tonight that I did not understand. I came round from a sleep and Raymond was there, and that woman Rae whom I do not entirely trust. There is something about her that does not convince me. I am not sure she is who she says she is.

Rae kept asking when I was going back to England. What business it was of hers, I do not know.

"Oh no," I said. "I am not going back to England. Raymond asked me to stay. I am going to stay here, in the south of France."

They had not realised I was awake until I spoke.

Rae looked agitated.

"No, it is impossible to stay here. Not now." She looked at Raymond. "Things have deteriorated too much. I do not know how to look after her now."

I do not like that woman. She meddles in things that do not concern her. This was about me and Raymond. About being together as we always should have been,

"Raymond will look after me, won't you Raymond? You said."

"Marianne, I am Zac, not Raymond," he said.

I just looked at him without responding. I knew there must be a reason why he was pretending to be someone else, so I kept quiet. Perhaps Charpentier was around somewhere, though the tell-tale aroma of his cigarette smoke was missing.

"Where is he?" I hissed.

"You see, Zac," Rae said urgently to Raymond. "There is no way that I can deal with this."

I do not know why she called him Zac. She is up to something that woman.

"I understand," said Raymond, putting a soothing hand on her arm. "There is no need to be upset. Marianne will be well looked after."

"We are staying here, then?" I said to Raymond.

"No, Marianne. We will go back to England."

I was surprised but delighted. I have no desire really to stay here in France. I just wanted Raymond. If he comes to England, it is even better. We can make a new life there. Just so long as I do not go back to the bay window and the rhododendrons and the buzzers and Annie and the creeping, pasty-faced Shona.

Chapter Twenty-Seven

Zac

Marianne's hospital consultant was a tall, elegant woman, kind enough in her way but with a certain briskness and a manner that Marianne, had she been more aware, would have dismissed as containing a certain *hauteur*. Much like Marianne herself, in fact. Zac had made an appointment with Madame Bertrand, but had taken Rae with him.

"She is not herself," Zac explained to the consultant. "And yet, we are told there is no evidence of concussion."

"This, I'm afraid, is not unusual in elderly people," explained Madame Bertrand, looking at Marianne's notes and toying with a gold crucifix around her neck. "A fall can sometimes prompt a distinct deterioration in dementia, especially in patients who already show some signs of the illness." She removed her glasses and looked at Zac.

"Marianne was already showing signs of forgetfulness prior to this fall?"

Zac hesitated.

"A few signs. But nothing like this. She was usually perfectly lucid."

Madame Bertrand nodded.

"It happens."

"She is hallucinating, getting us all mixed up. It is not like Marianne."

"There may be some improvement in that in a day or two as she gets back to normal, but I would not, if I were you, expect that to reverse completely. I see we have already tested Marianne for a urine infection which can also cause some of the symptoms we are discussing - particularly in the elderly. There were a few signs of minor infection there, so I have prescribed an antibiotic. That, too, may help."

Madame Bertrand sat back in her seat and looked at Zac and then at Rae.

"And your plans for her are…?"

"I will return with her to England when she is able," said Zac.

Rae said nothing but Zac, even without looking in her direction, could sense Rae lowering her head.

Madame Bertrand shrugged.

"There is no reason to delay particularly. Her wrist is set and we have done what we can. She will continue to take her antibiotics but the infection is mild. And the rest, well…" She threw her hands in the air in an expression of resignation.

Zac looked at her expectantly.

"The rest?"

"There is little likelihood that waiting will lead to much improvement." She closed the file in front of her. "I am sorry that I cannot be of more reassurance."

"No, that's…" Zac floundered and looked at Rae, who would not catch his eye. He looked up at Madame Bertrand. "Thank you for what you have done."

Madame Bertrand smiled thinly and stood up.

"You are welcome," she said, and stood up, holding out a well-manicured hand to alert them to the fact that the interview was over.

Zac lumbered awkwardly to his feet, caught off guard by the sudden termination of the conversation. He and Rae headed for the door but then Zac stopped and turned back. Madame Bertrand, who had already sat down again and begun writing, looked up at him expectantly.

"I wonder," he said, "how much of what Marianne says now about the past is true. Will her recall of events be sound? Is it only recent events that will be confused?"

Madame Bertrand looked nonplussed at Zac's question, then raised her hands in a gesture of supplication that said, 'who knows?'

"I cannot answer this question," she said. "After all, how much of what anyone says about the past is true? The best you can say is that it is true for them."

———

The hearse sat outside the funeral parlour in a side street close to Sainte Maria church, the coffin covered with an enormous bouquet of all-white daisies that spelled out Maurice's name. The simplicity of the blooms sparked a rush of emotion that caught in Zac's throat and he looked away.

The mourners began to gather behind the car, a white faced sister of Maurice, slightly crumpled as he had been, looking confused in the melee. A distressed middle-aged woman in a black dress came towards her, grabbed her shoulders and kissed both cheeks. Zac looked on curiously at the silent frisson that rippled through the crowd beside the car, the stolen glances where eyes met and immediately looked away again. Maurice's sister accepted the woman's gesture, but barely reacted. Her body was limp and she merely nodded, before turning away to speak to a man Zac assumed was her husband.

"Who is that woman in the black dress?" Zac whispered quietly to Rae. "The one who is crying."

"Francine," mumbled Rae.

Francine stood uncertainly for a minute and Zac noticed for the first time that she had a pink rose in her hand. The boot of the hearse was open still and Zac watched emotions flit like shadows across her face as the bouquets were brought from the parlour and placed inside the hearse. Francine waited for her moment, then quietly placed the rose on the coffin, her fingers trailing lightly over the wood. The intimacy made Zac look away and when he glanced back, she was gone.

The crowd shuffled into place. There was to be a procession behind the coffin from the funeral parlour to the church. Zac stood amongst them with Rae and Jasmine, wondering how this 'life' in France had taken hold of him so quickly. He and Marianne should be flying home today, he thought, looking at the vapour trail of a plane in the sky above them. Instead, she was in a hospital bed still and he was here, at the funeral of a man whom two weeks ago, he had not even known.

A two-week friendship, Maurice had said. He was right – more right than he could possibly have known. It had a beginning, a middle, and now it had an end. There were a few murmurs behind him from mourners talking sotto voce, a half-laugh, but he, Rae and Jasmine stood in silence. They had talked little in the last few days, taking over from one another methodically at the hospital so that there was always someone with Marianne.

The cortège was moving now. The mourners processed silently behind the hearse that snaked slowly and silently down the hill and round the corner to the church where Fr Michel stood at the doorway to receive them. He wore an old-fashioned, black, ceremonial cloak over his vestments.

"Ah, the Prince of the Church," murmured Rae as the priest came into view.

"Queen of the County, you mean," retorted Jasmine.

Zac stiffened and looked sideways at Jasmine. He had known, of course, from the priest's look that night, his come-to-bed eyes, but still… to hear it articulated.

"He's gay?"

"You think that cloak comes free with Trucker Weekly?"

"But what he said to Maurice. He said…" Zac broke off. What had Fr Michel said? It had been a call to celibacy, to obedience. "Turn from temptation," he had said, as if Maurice's inner being was a passing fad. "Live like the man you were made by God to be. Offer the sacrifice on God's altar. Pain brings you closer to the Lord."

Jasmine smiled acerbically when Zac recounted the words.

"The rules are for us, not for them, Zac."

It was Maurice himself who had been offered on the altar, Zac thought. The altar of orthodoxy.

The hearse pulled slowly into the church grounds. The mourners gathered each side of the church door as the coffin was carried past. Zac couldn't take his eyes off Fr Michel as he greeted the people filing past him into the church. He was loving the role, Zac thought suddenly, watching the swirl of the cloak and the dignified smile. He took the deference as his due.

Rae and Jasmine moved forward to the church door. Zac stayed still. Rae looked back at him.

"Coming?"

"In a moment," Zac said.

He watched the last of the mourners disappear inside. He was shaking, shaking with anger. He detested Fr Michel. A voice inside told him that it was not Fr Michel who had killed Maurice. Maurice himself had done that. But the argument raged with two voices inside his head. The priest might has well have killed Maurice, he thought. Words were the most dangerous, the most lethal weapon in the world. Zac knew that despite his anger with the priest over Maurice, part of the anger inside was about himself. Fr Michel's condemnatory words about deviancy applied to Zac, too. Once, other people's disapproval had oppressed him, made him spiral into silence and self-loathing. Now, he realised he was beginning to kick back.

Right this minute, he thought, feeling a tremble run through him, Fr Michel would be in there, poncing about on the altar. He would probably mention Maurice's kindness, his love of God, his love of others. Zac looked up at a thin sun breaking through the grey clouds in bands of watery light, like a grid in the sky. There would even be a pious exhortation not to condemn Maurice for talking his own life, because only God could judge. But he had judged Maurice in life, hadn't he? Zac thought. That priest in his fine robes. He drove Maurice to destruction with his judgement. Well, he wouldn't drive Zac to destruction.

The sound of singing drifted from the church. He looked up at the door, moved towards it, then stopped. For Maurice. He would go in for Maurice. But he couldn't. He couldn't for exactly the same reason. For Maurice. His two week friend.

Zac stood in the back porch and looked through the window, just as he had the day Maurice sat slumped in the back pew.

The church was full. People had turned out for him. In death if not in life, Zac thought bitterly. He looked through the window at the black clad figures in the pews but could not join them. His feet simply would not take him, whatever his brain willed them to do. He stayed where he was, shivering with a rage that kept erupting inside him like lava. What was it about, any of this? Not sex, that was for sure. Not sin. Identity, he thought. It was about identity.

From the depths of the church, a thin, high wave of tremulous voices reached out to where Zac stood.

> "Be still my soul, the Lord is on your side
> Bear patiently the cross of grief or pain
> Leave to your God to order and provide
> In every change, he faithful will remain."

Rae sat in silence as Zac stirred a teaspoon round a coffee cup in a bar across the road from the hospital.

"You think I am abandoning her again." Rae said flatly.

Zac looked up in surprise. "No, I don't."

Rae looked at him tearfully. "Well I am. I know I am," she said, burying her face suddenly in her hands. "I can't do it. I am not strong enough. Zac, I just don't know how to manage the fact that she does not know who we are. I had a chance to make amends but now it is gone. She came back and now she is lost again. I can't. I simply can't."

Zac laid a hand on Rae's arm.

"Rae, nobody is judging you. Certainly not me."

"You think I don't know what love is?" Rae demanded with an edge of defiance.

Zac looked bewildered. Who was he to judge? Who knew less than him about the nature of love?

"It would have been hard to look after Marianne. But I would have done it," continued Rae. "But this is not Marianne. It's just her shell. There is some imposter inhabiting her body and it feels as if she is dead. I wish she WAS dead." She took a shuddering breath inwards. "God forgive me." Zac touched her arm, but it made no difference. "God forgive me!"

"It's okay," Zac murmured.

"It feels like... like I shouldn't allow her to go, but I can't allow her to stay," said Rae.

"She thinks I am you, so she will go back with me willingly," said Zac soothingly, wishing it was all over now. All of it. He could not cope with any more emotional stress. His stomach burned permanently these days.

"I am weak... Marianne always said it."

"We are all weak."

"Not Marianne."

Zac watched a young couple at the next table scrape back their chairs and gather up their shopping bags, so engrossed in each other that they banged into Zac as they went.

"Pardon!"

Zac smiled absently then looked back at Rae. Perhaps he should tackle it now. There had been so little opportunity since Marianne's fall, what with Maurice's funeral and everything happening at once.

"Rae..."

"Zac..."

They spoke in unison. Both smiled.

"You first," said Zac.

"That question," said Rae curiously, "that you asked Madame Bertrand about Marianne's memory. Why did you ask it?"

"That's what I wanted to talk to you about."

Rae looked at him expectantly.

"The other night," said Zac carefully, avoiding eye contact, "I was alone with Marianne and she thought I was you."

There was silence.

"And she started talking about some guy called Charpentier or something."

Zac still did not look at Rae, but he could tell she was holding her breath.

"And then... then she started talking about what happened the night Patrice Moreau died."

"I see."

"Did you kill Patrice, Rae?"

"Is that what Marianne said?"

"No. But there is all this talk about you being 'the blonde woman'. Were you?"

There was silence. Zac watched Rae's face, waiting so long for the answer that he gave up.

"Yes."

Zac almost missed the word it was said so quietly. When he looked up, he saw a single tear running from the corner of Rae's eye. He watched it roll down her face, dripping from the cliff of her cheek onto the table. He waited a minute before speaking again. Rae quickly brushed her face with the heel of her hand but seemed composed.

"What happened?"

Rae shook her head, unable to speak.

"You killed him?"

"As good as," she said finally.

What did that mean, Zac wondered.

"Rae...?"

She did not answer.

"Rae, did you argue with Patrice?"

"I loved him."

"But did something…" Zac broke off.

Rae looked up at Zac

"Marianne was so jealous. I broke her, destroyed her. I should have protected her more."

"As you said yourself – Marianne is strong."

"As you said yourself – we are all weak."

Rae caught the arm of a passing waiter.

"Deux cafés, s'il vous plait."

"Madame."

"What is Marianne's weakness?"

"She fears rejection. She knows what it is to be abandoned. I never took account of it. I pushed her too far."

"Who rejected her?"

"Her mother, her contemporaries, life… and…."

"And…?"

"And me."

"How did her mother…?"

"Dumped at birth. On a doorstep."

"Poor Marianne."

Rae looked at Zac curiously.

"You are a nice person."

"Am I?"

"Not many people say that - 'poor Marianne'."

That was true, Zac thought, as the waiter put a coffee cup in front of him. People didn't like Marianne. He stirred a sugar into his coffee, thinking of Shona and her nervous distaste around the old woman.

"People never liked her much," said Rae, echoing Zac's thoughts. "I saw something different. I knew what lay beneath. Marianne never belonged. Not anywhere, really."

"Like you?"

"Like me."

Like me too, thought Zac, looking out of the window as a young man in a navy suit hurried by with a bag from a boulangerie. Office worker, he thought. Identikit. He wished he was him, that office worker, with his safe, dull life mapped out in front of him. What would it feel like, he wondered, to blend into a crowd? To have everything happen easily, naturally, instead of freefalling through the air, the sound of disaster whistling in your ears, and the ground constantly rushing to meet you.

"I knew all of that," Rae continued. "I knew it, and I still left."

"Marianne told me."

"What did she say?"

"She didn't blame you."

Rae looked as though she might crumble.

"The baby," said Zac. "It changed everything."

"Yes."

Zac could see the maelstrom in Rae's eyes.

"Why?"

"There was nothing left to keep me as Raymond."

"Just Marianne."

"And it wasn't enough. God forgive me, but she wasn't enough."

CHAPTER TWENTY-EIGHT

Marianne

I could never have imagined that I would feel like this on the way back to Britain. I was prepared for take-off feeling like the death of everything, the end of the last hurrah. Who would have believed that I would be returning with Raymond by my side? He is behaving strangely, insisting that I call him Zac, but I know it is something to do with Charpentier so I am playing along when I remember. I know he is simply trying to protect us both.

I have plaster on my arm. I cannot remember how that happened and when I asked Raymond, he told me something had happened, but I don't remember now what he said. I think he said I tripped in the street. It doesn't matter. He says it is nothing to worry about. He is very solicitous, tucking the blanket round my knees on the plane, ensuring my comfort. I am very lucky.

There is an air hostess who tries to give me a small pillow for my head but I will have none of it. I can tell the way she smiles at Raymond, licking those glossy lips in his presence and calling him Sir with naked flirtatiousness, that she is attracted to him. She does not look him directly in the eye, but glances upwards through black eyelashes heavy with mascara.

"I don't like her," I tell Raymond.

"Why ever not?"

"She is flirting with you."

"Don't be silly!"

"Men never see these things. They are foolish creatures sometimes."

"Yes... well..."

Outside the window, the cloud is drifting, white and free.

"Look, there is a dragon, Raymond."

"No, Marianne. No dragons."

"Yes, look. That part of the cloud is like the breath from his mouth."

"Oh, I see. The cloud... yes."

"Well what did you think I meant? I'm not stupid!"

The air hostess leans in to me, smiling in the way one smiles at a child. It annoys me.

"Would you like another drink, madam?"

"No."

"Marianne!" mutters Raymond. He looks up apologetically at the air hostess.

"No thank you," he smiles.

I ignore them both.

"Where are we going?" I ask Raymond.

"Home," he says. "We're going home."

Home. The word makes me feel so content. Home with Raymond at long last.

"What is going on? Raymond? What is going on?"

"Shh, Marianne." Raymond is rummaging in his pocket for change for the taxi driver. The blooms have all gone from the rhododendron bushes; the leaves carpet the lawns in the dusk. It is evening and there is only patchy light left in the sky, luminous strips radiating a ghostly light through the clouds in a blue velour sky.

"No! NO RAYMOND!"

"It's okay, Marianne. Please…" His hand is on my arm but I try to brush him off.

"Marianne, I will look after you," he says desperately. "Marianne, look at me. Look at me! It will be fine. I promise. I promise."

"Raymond, we cannot live here. I know this place! I know it."

"Marianne, your nails are digging into me."

"You're not listening! Raymond I have been here before. We cannot stay here. It is a terrible place. Listen to me. They will take me from you. They will keep me here. Raymond darling, listen. I have been here before! "

"Shh, Marianne, shhh." Raymond is trying to comfort me, stroking my arm, making soothing noises into my hair but I feel too angry with him to allow myself to be pacified.

Then I hear her, that voice, and I freeze.

"Come on, Marianne pet. Let's get you inside now."

Shona.

"No! NO!"

"There, there now sweetheart. You must be exhausted after the journey. Let's get you tucked up nice and snug."

I lash out at her, but I have no strength to fight her off.

Raymond looks on helplessly. Why is he doing nothing? I cannot believe this betrayal.

"Do not leave me here, Raymond!"

"Marianne…"

"Zac, hold her arms for me!"

"No, leave her Shona. I'll bring her in. No, please!"

A little gathering has assembled at the front door, a couple of the staff alerted by the commotion. The watched with folded arms

Shona turned her back to me then, murmuring to Raymond but I heard what she said. I heard her quite distinctly.

"Put her in the Blue Room. I have prepared the blue room for her."

"Mary…?"

"Died while you were away," Shona mouthed audibly. She thinks I am deaf now as well as senile.

"Perhaps she should have the familiarity of her old room," said Raymond. I could tell he was uneasy and so he should have been. Why did he not protest more strongly? Why did he not defend me? Why do those you love always let you down? Why do they never love you quite enough? I would have expected to know life's answers by now but I still have only questions.

"It's better this way," said Shona to Zac, walking towards the door. "Avoids another move in a few weeks."

If I could have killed her in that moment, I would have.

———

You do not come out of the Blue Room. I know that. The walls are a pale, thin, cold kind of blue, not the warm blue of a summer sky. The blue of the hospital where Raymond had his surgery. I do not like that colour, never have. It feels like a prison.

There is a terrible pain in my chest when I breathe, a sharp stabbing pain so intense it makes me want to hold my breath to avoid it, but eventually, I have to gasp for air. I have pneumonia, they say, and my body aches, every muscle grumbling when I turn in sweat soaked sheets. Perhaps the air conditioning on the plane, I heard Shona say. Or the bugs in those French hospitals. She is a ninny.

Despite the aches, it is betrayal that is the greatest pain. Raymond has abandoned me again, comes only to visit. My sense of loving him fills every thought and every minute. It is in the shaft of sunlight that hits my bed in the daytime and the rippled moonlight that tries to penetrate the wall of curtains in the Blue Room at night, creating silver waves across the floor. There is nowhere to go except inside myself, inside my own longing. I am trapped at the centre of my own physical grotesqueness, filled with beautiful thoughts of what love could have brought me in my final days. Even the whistle of my chest feels like a love song.

All of it for nothing. Unrequited love floods out like a living stream… and into nowhere. Unabsorbed. Pouring away like liquid gold into a dank drain. The lover and the loved. Raymond comes to visit and the pain becomes both a little sharper and a little sweeter. He does not explain the betrayal but a little part of me hopes that he has a plan that he will reveal in time. I replay the conversation in the graveyard in France over and over in my mind. Its sense of promise, of hope, of a new beginning. Surely it meant something. It had to mean something.

Raymond changes my sheets and helps me shower, but he is not here as often as I would like. It is lonely here in this pale blue prison. He does not talk as once he did. I blame her. That Shona one.

"She is so much worse," I hear her say to Raymond. She talks as if I hear nothing, comprehend nothing. "And she is totally confused by that fall. It is so often the way."

I hate her primness. I got my own back today, exerted the little power that I still have. She came into the room in that way she does, apparently vaporising in the middle of it rather than walking in the door. I watched her creeping round, refreshing water jugs and replacing towels, my eyes following her with hatred.

"Oh Marianne, pet!" she said with a start when she suddenly became aware that I was watching her every move. "You're awake! How are you feeling?"

I said nothing.

"Will I open the window just for a few minutes to air the room?" she said brightly, pulling back the blue floral curtains and opening the lock on the window that looked down over the gardens. "It's not a bad day out there, Marianne, though it started out a bit nippy this morning. Up at 5am, so I was, to come to work. Too early isn't it? Much nicer to be tucked up in a lovely cosy bed like yours."

She turned to me and smiled.

"Now can I get anything for you, sweetheart?"

"Come here," I whispered, beckoning her over.

I saw the smile freeze a little on her lips but she moved towards me.

"What is it, pet?"

"Sit down," I said, nodding at the chair beside the bed.

She sat, but I could see it was reluctantly.

"Is it a wee chat you're looking for Marianne?" she said. "That's nice, but I have to go and see to Mrs Leslie in a minute. Will I send Zac to see you when he gets in?"

"Remember I told you about Raymond?" I said, ignoring her question.

"About his painting?" Her voice held a false, brittle kind of enthusiasm.

She knows I don't mean his painting.

"No," I hissed. "About the murder. The blood dripping into the ceiling. The man who died like a pig with his throat slit…"

"Ah, come on now Marianne. Don't you be worrying about things like that, now." Her cool, pallid hand slid onto my brow. "You're a bit fevered. There's nothing to worry about."

"I'm not worried."

"Good, that's good."

She stood up. I knew she was desperate to be gone.

"Remember I said it was Raymond who was accused of murder?"

"Yes, yes I remember."

"Well it wasn't him who actually killed the man."

"No, of course it wasn't," she said, and I could hear the little glimmer of relief in her voice.

"It was me."

"No, no, pet, don't you be thinking that now. You've just got a wee bit confused."

"Not at all," I said, refusing to let my eyes fall from her face. "I know exactly what happened. I cut his throat with a carving knife. The knife that was on the plate with a noisette of lamb." Shona looks like she doesn't know where to run. "I cut his throat and I saw the blood drip from him like a pig."

I watched every flicker on her face - the surprise and the fear and the uncertainty - and I relished every emotion my words painted on her face. She had put me in the Blue Room but I was putting her somewhere she found just as frightening.

"Oh Marianne!" Her face contorted into a little grimace of concern.

"The police interviewed me but they never found out. I fooled them. It was the perfect murder."

Shona grabbed the water jug from beside my bed and headed for the sink.

"You've already done that."

"No, not this one."

"Yes! Yes you did!"

"Don't get excited now, Marianne. It's not good for you. Look, your face is going all red!"

"I told you that you have already changed it! Why don't you stop meddling?"

"I'll go and get Doctor Bell," she said, scurrying from the bedside.

I knew then that another dose of sedation was coming my way, that when I woke again there would be no more light streaming in the window and I would be facing evening. I considered it worth it.

When Doctor Bell arrived, hair slicked back with gel and his white coat flapping casually open, he looked at me indulgently, like one might look at a naughty child.

"Are you misbehaving, Marianne?" he said.

"No, I am not!"

"Well, what are these terrible stories you are telling Shona?"

"Was she frightened?" I couldn't disguise my relish at the prospect.

"They would frighten me! Why did you tell her you murdered someone?"

"I didn't."

"Oh really?"

"No. I told her my husband murdered someone."

"Did you?"

"Yes."

"Are you sure?"

"Yes."

"And did he?"

"Did he what?"

Dr Bell looked sideways at me. "Murder someone."

I am not sure there wasn't a glint of amusement in his eyes. He put a stethoscope into his ears and placed the end into the front of my nightdress to listen to my chest.

I lay back without answering.

"What is the truth of all these colourful stories, Marianne?" he asked, moving the stethoscope slightly and listening carefully. "Hmm?"

"I get confused."

He gave a small laugh. "Sometimes your confusion is very selective."

"I don't know what you mean."

Dr Bell smiled and gave me a surreptitious wink. "Be a good girl, Marianne," he said. "Or I'll have to put you to sleep."

CHAPTER TWENTY-NINE

Zac

Conchetta sat stiffly at one end of the sofa in her living room, her husband at the other, arms folded across his body. Conchetta studiously avoided looking at him. This was, Zac realised looking round with new eyes, very much *her* sitting room, with its extravagant baroque influences: gold cherubs on the mantelpiece and heavy gilt mirrors, ornate plaster roses on the coving and amber marble light stands. He looked across at her and smiled, an empathetic smile like she used to give him when he was growing up and in trouble. Her eyes softened as she looked at him.

Everything seemed different since his return, Zac thought, looking out the window at a sky that was grey with gathering storm clouds. So much had happened. Maurice, Marianne, Rae... He realised that something fundamental had shifted inside him. In a strange way all that tumult had left him calmer. Sadder in a resigned kind of way. He had stopped looking for perfect solutions. The first drops of rain splashed against the window panes. Maybe, he thought, he had grown up.

Grown up enough to know that Alain had been a conduit to a possible other life, but was not, in himself, that other life. The moment of take-off from France had been painful for Zac but he knew deep inside him that the feeling was temporary – for both of them. A few tears, a pang of regret, a wonder about how their relationship might have turned out in another time, another place, another life… but no, nothing that cut below skin level. Zac did not harbour notions that his future would revolve round a move to Saint Estelle where he and Alain would live happily ever after. Alain was already the past. He had a future to face.

Marianne had promised he would find himself in Saint Estelle. He could not honestly say that had happened but still… he knew that things had changed. That *he* had changed. Maurice's soft, podgy face flitted through his mind. His sad, kind eyes. Zac's own eyes welled up. In many ways, Maurice had been a more important part of the journey than Alain. That was the one thing he knew: whatever happened, he did not want to become a Maurice, a victim. A heavy sigh from the sofa cut into his thoughts.

"Where is Elicia?" demanded his father. "How long are we supposed to sit here and wait?"

"Here she is!" said Elicia, entering the room in a rush. She swept by her father planting a kiss on the top of his head. "Stop being an old grump!"

She threw herself in between Conchetta and her father and looked up quizzically at Zac.

"What's this about, bro?"

Where to begin, thought Zac. Three pairs of eyes watched him: his father's wary and hostile; Conchetta's dark and anxious; Elicia's full of careless insouciance.

"Is Abs coming?" asked Elicia, her voice sounding inappropriately bright in the room.

Her father tutted quietly.

"No," said Zac.

"Oh," said Elicia. She turned to her right to look at Conchetta and raised her eyes questioningly, bemused at the flatness of Zac's tone.

Zac took a deep breath. Despite his preparations, he did not know where to begin.

"Elicia," he said. "Do you remember when you were a teenager and you were a bridesmaid for Lizzie?"

Elicia looked at him and frowned.

"Remember, you wore a peach silk dress?" continued Zac, misinterpreting her silence.

"Well of course, I bloody remember, Zac!" said Elicia. "What are you on about? You gather us all here like somebody's died and then ask me about being a bridesmaid to Lizzie?"

"Give him a chance, Elicia," murmured Conchetta.

"Loved that peach dress, mind," said Elicia.

"So did I," said Zac.

"Did you?" Elicia sounded surprised.

"I wore it."

There was a second's uneasy silence, then Elicia giggled.

"This isn't funny," said her father.

"I think it's hilarious!"

She looked at Zac and something in his eyes made her smile freeze on her lips.

"Elicia..." said her father.

"Are you serious?" asked Elicia, looking at Zac and ignoring her father.

"Totally."

"When?"

"You were out. It was hanging in your room. On the door of the wardrobe." Zac caught sight of his father's face and swallowed. "I unzipped it and took it out and I... I tried it on."

"What?" said Elicia. She stood up and went over to Zac's chair, sitting on the arm. "Zac?" She took his hand. "Zac, why?"

"Because I wanted to know what it felt like. I wanted to see..."

"What you looked like?"

"Yes... no... I wanted to *feel* what I looked like. I know that doesn't make sense."

"Yes it does," said Conchetta quietly. She moved to the other arm of Zac's chair and sat down, taking her son's hand.

"Oh for God's sake! I've had enough of this," said her husband, beginning to ease himself up from the chair. "I told you, Conchetta. I've told you for years what I feared but you wouldn't listen."

"Stay where you are!" snapped Elicia.

"Go on, Zac," said Conchetta.

"It made me feel like... like..."

"Like WHAT?" said Elicia.

"Like me," said Zac.

"At peace?" said Conchetta.

"No, not at peace. I looked too ugly. It was too much a reminder of what I wasn't. But I felt like... I knew what I SHOULD be. I felt happy and unhappy at the same time. Euphoric. Distraught. I knew that if you came home and saw me you would be disgusted."

"No Zac," said Conchetta. "You could never disgust us."

"Yes, he could," snapped his father.

Conchetta's face contorted and she turned away. Elicia glared at him.

"Is that all you can say?" Zac asked quietly. His father held his gaze steadily but for once, Zac did not look away. "You've made me feel small all my life," continued Zac. "As I grew up, I just kept getting smaller and smaller and smaller. The more I tried to please you, the less good you made me feel about myself."

"Oh of course! I should have known it would all come to this. It's all my fault you're a freak!"

"That's enough!" said Conchetta.

Elicia laid a comforting hand on her arm.

"Ignore him."

"You think I can help what I am? That I can change it?" Zac's voice was even.

"Yes! Yes I do, actually!" His father's voice exploded in anger. "I think you could at least try. Look at you!" He waved an infuriated hand. "Look at you... that stupid floppy hair. Those ridiculous clothes... I have told you often enough what I felt about this... this unnatural behaviour."

"Calm down, dad," said Elicia.

"Walking about like some poofy hairdresser. Giving the neighbours something to talk about all these years. Making us all a laughing stock!"

"Oh for God's sake!" said Elicia. "Who cares about the bloody neighbours?"

"I do! I care about the bloody neighbours, Elicia, but obviously nothing I care about matters."

"I am sorry," said Zac, sitting down.

"Don't apologise to him, Zac!"

"It matters," said Zac. "What he feels." He turned to face his father.

"I am sorry I cannot be what you want me to be. I look like a man but I feel like a woman. I don't know why that has happened.

276

I don't know, dad. It is not a choice. I only know I can't change it."

His father's face, hard as granite, began to crumble. He sat down suddenly, hiding his face behind his hands.

"At least, not my mind," continued Zac calmly. He felt pity as he looked at the hunched figure in front of him. But how could he stop now? He had to finish this. "I can't change my mind, but it is possible I can change my body."

"I knew it! I knew it!" said his father into his hands.

"Oh stop it!" snapped Elicia to her father. "At least the façade has fallen at last. We have all tiptoed round for years pretending that nothing is wrong and I for one am sick of it. Sick of it! Why was nothing ever said openly? Why was the atmosphere in the house so awful?"

"It would have been even more awful if it hadn't been for you, Elicia," sad Zac. He smiled. "Bubbly, bright Elicia…"

Elicia turned to her brother.

"Zac," she said, taking his hand, "we would only ever want you to be happy. I'm glad you've told us."

Zac reached out his other hand and gently wiped a tear from her face.

"Don't cry," he said. "Please."

"What about me?" said Zac's father.

"Oh Zac," said Elicia. "What are you going to do?"

"I don't know, 'Licia. I just don't know."

"What about Abbie?"

Zac said nothing.

"Does she know?"

"Some of it."

"Do you love her?"

He shrugged, unable to answer.

"Will she stand by you?"

"I suppose it depends what I do…"

Outside, the wind had whipped up and there was a sudden rush of noise in the chimney. Zac looked out, watching the tree-tops wave with increasing ferocity. Conchetta had sat silently but stood up now and walked over to Zac. She put her hands on both cheeks. They felt slightly rough on the smoothness of his skin. He looked into her dark eyes and smiled faintly.

"Sometimes," she said, "it takes a lifetime to know yourself, Zac. Take your time."

He nodded.

Her voice dropped.

"Just know this," she whispered, "whoever you are, whatever you become, you will always be my Zac and I will always love you."

Zac put out his arms and pulled her to him. It was only when he looked over her shoulder that he realised his father had left the room.

Zac held Conchetta close, felt her arms squeeze him hard like they had when he was a little boy but somehow, he was now the comforter, Conchetta the comforted. He heard the outside door close, his father's footsteps on the gravel path outside. He had a sudden flash of memory. That day when Zac was barely con-scious in hospital. The sound of his father's crying. It was real that sound, just as real as the closing door. A feeling of calm descended on Zac. Perhaps some day, that particular door would open again.

Zac felt strangely peaceful as he waited for Abbie. He plugged in his laptop and waited for it to fire up. Perhaps Marianne had been right after all and he had found a part of himself in the south of France: a little steel. He still did not know what he wanted but he had taken a step closer. There were no neat answers in life.

What had he learned?. An image of Maurice's dishevelled figure sprang into his mind. Crumpled trousers and stubbled chin and the gentle, all-encompassing warmth of his eyes. Yes, he had learned from Maurice. He had learned about self-loathing and where it led you. He had learned about self-acceptance. Authenticity, Zac thought, as the screen of his laptop lit up. Authenticity led to true happiness. And yet you had to be careful about authenticity. Being authentic with the wrong people only led to rejection. The cursor whirled on his laptop as he clicked on the internet and he paused. Could he risk authenticity? He couldn't risk *not* being authentic, he told himself firmly.

The door banged. Abbie did not come in the room straight away. He had told her he needed to speak to her and he wondered if she was bracing herself out in the hall. He lifted his head and listened intently for movement. Poor Abbie.

"Hi."

She stood in the doorway, not entering the room. She was dressed in a steel grey coat that normally he liked against her blonde curls but today it made her look pale and washed-out. He felt guilty when he looked at the purple-tinged shadows beneath her eyes.

"Hi," Zac said. He held out a hand, palm towards her and she smiled faintly and moved to him, putting her hand palm to palm with his before entwining their fingers.

"Want anything?"

She shook her head.

"Just you."

"We need to talk."

"I know."

"Maybe some tea?"

She shook her head again. Zac could see the fear in her eyes but there was something else, something he did not normally recognise in her. A resolute quality. A determination to face what had to be faced.

"You are not sleeping properly," he chided, drawing a finger softly down her pale face.

"I missed you."

"I missed you too."

It was true, he realised, despite everything.

"When you phoned from France, you said there were things you needed to tell me. "

"Sit down here."

Abbie did not take her eyes from his face.

"You seem different," she said quietly.

"How?"

"I don't know. More… in control."

"Well…"

"Just tell me Zac!" she said quickly, with a rush of impatience. "You are leaving, is that it?"

"Not exactly. It's up to you."

"What do you mean?

"When you hear what I have to say, you have to decide if you want to stay.

Abbie sat perched on the edge of the seat next to him, her eyes scanning his face constantly.

"So tell me."

"You know about the dressing, Abbie…. the clothes… and you haven't wanted to talk about it, but now I must."

Her eyes dropped.

"I told you it began in my teens." Zac took a deep breath. "It was my awful secret and it was also my comfort. It was the only thing that made me feel real. It fulfilled something in me and I didn't know what it was or what it meant. I just knew that on a very basic, instinctive level, things felt right when I dressed that way."

Abbie did not look up, but Zac knew how intently she was listening. He had carefully prepared the first part of his speech but the rest of it suddenly deserted him.

"Abbie, I don't know if you can imagine what that feels like, to carry what people consider a sordid secret but which feels to you like the most natural thing in the world. It made me feel like a freak, a pervert. Every time my father looked at me I felt like he saw right through me."

Still she would not look at him.

"I longed to be normal, to be like everyone else. I wanted to be like the other boys, do as they did, feel as they did and…"

"And you couldn't?"

"I couldn't, no. I wanted to be a girl. I felt that was what I was meant to be."

"You liked boys?"

"Abbie, this is about gender, who you are, not just who you fancy."

Finally her eyes flicked up at him.

"You used me."

"No! I swear, I…"

"Yes, Zac. You did. "

Her blue eyes suddenly looked startlingly cold within the paleness of her small, pinched face.

"Tell me something," she said. "Was any of it real? Did you feel anything for me?"

"Oh Abbie, of course!"

"There's no 'of course' about it."

"I…"

"Did you love me?"

Zac felt his new-found sense of calm draining away.

"Well?"

Abbie seemed to be shrinking into something tight and small in front of him.

"Why can't you answer, Zac? It's a simple enough question."

"I don't know."

"You don't know why you can't answer? Or you don't know if you loved me?"

"Please!"

"Which?"

"I…"

"Which?"

She was relentless, Zac thought. He felt slightly in awe of her in this mood. But she had every reason to be relentless.

"Because you know what Zac? I loved you." She stood up, and her voice dropped as she turned from him, her last few words lost.

"Sorry?"

She turned back to face him.

"I said, I still do."

Her anger had suddenly distilled into a deep sadness. Zac could feel it snaking out to him in an umbilical cord of pain and suddenly, he didn't want to sever it. He didn't want to let go.

"Abbie, don't go. Not yet. Please."

"What's left to say?"

"There are things I want to tell you."

"What? You can't even tell me if you love me."

Zac hesitated. "I love you, but I don't know yet if it's enough."

"At least that's honest," Abbie said, but her hand went up to her face and she wiped one eye with the heel of her hand. "But if you don't know, then it's not enough. Not enough for me."

"Come here… please. Don't leave like this."

Abbie hesitated, but moved towards him and sat down again on the sofa and looked at him, waiting for him to speak.

"What do you want to say? What are the things you want to tell me?"

"Abbie, you are beautiful and sweet and any guy…"

"Don't, Zac!"

Abbie lay back on the chair, emotionally exhausted, then rolled her head to the side to face him.

"Don't," she whispered. "It's not enough."

Zac flinched. "When I said 'not enough', I meant that I don't know if it's enough to get us both through the next bit of this."

"Which is?"

"I need to be true to myself. Abbie, I need to tell people and not hide away. The secrecy is eating me up." Zac picked up her hand and took a deep breath. "I have to consider all my options and that includes surgery. I am not sure… but I need to examine the option."

He told her then about France, picking his way through his experiences. He hesitated when it came to Alain, but he had to be honest if there was to be any chance. There was silence when he finished. He heard a beep from his laptop as it went into sleep mode.

"I don't know if it's enough either," Abbie said eventually. Tears were running down her cheeks.

"If what's enough?"

"What I feel. Because your secret, Zac, is about to become my secret. Your confusion is going to be mine. Your exposure, my exposure. And I'm not sure I can do it. I love you, but I'm looking ahead and all I can see is pain and I just..." She broke off. "I'm sorry."

Zac shook his head.

"Don't be."

He rolled his head round from the back of his chair to face her, matching her movement, their faces just inches apart. He respected this new resolve in Abbie.

"Don't ever think I didn't care. I did. And I do. It's just…"

Abbie reached out and gently placed one finger on his lips.

"You don't need to say any more."

He smiled. "It's your choice now."

"You want me to be with you through this? Is that what you are asking?"

"I can't ask and I can't expect."

"And I can't promise."

"But we can try."

"One step at a time."

"And if it gets too much…"

"Yes, if it gets too much…"

He pushed her hair back from her face tenderly.

"You need a good night's sleep."

"Zac, we can be friends."

"Always."

"Maybe a good friend is better than a good lover."

"Maybe."

"Lasts longer."

"Yeah."

"Sex or intimacy – if you had to choose one, which would it be?"

"Intimacy," said Zac instantly. "Closeness."

Abbie smiled faintly.

"You?" asked Zac.

"Same."

"Although…" said Zac.

"What?"

"Sex is okay too." He grinned at her and she laughed, despite the internal pang. Did he mean with her or Alain?

"What's wrong?" asked Zac.

"Nothing."

"Abbs…"

"Yeah?"

"I'm going to put something on my Facebook account."

"Oh Jesus, Zac!"

"It's the easiest way."

He leaned forward and pulled the laptop round so that the screen faced her. He watched her face as she read.

"There will be no going back after this."

"I know."

"Can't you examine your options without going public?"

He shook his head.

"I don't think I am going to know what my options are, or how I feel, until I stop hiding. Only then will I know what I can live with – or live without."

"Have you told your family?"

He nodded. Abbie said nothing but he sensed a hurt that he hadn't considered before, and he wished that perhaps he had spoken to her first.

"It was my father that I had to confront before anyone else. Does that make sense?"

"I suppose so."

"I have to do this, Abbie"

"In that case," she said leaning forward, her finger hovering over the button. She looked at him and he nodded.

"You are sure?"

"Yes."

He couldn't watch.

"Done," she said quietly.

"Together," he said.

"Together."

———

"He knows I killed Patrice, Raymond."

Zac paused as he tucked the sheets into the bottom of the bed and looked up to the pillows.

"What?"

"I tell you, he knows everything. He came here to my bed. He is no fool, Charpentier."

Zac sat on the edge of the bed and looked at Marianne.

"You?"

"Yes, he knows about me. About both of us."

"You were the femme blonde?"

"What are you talking about? We may have burned the wig, but Charpentier knows you were the blonde woman. Believe me."

"What happened that night, the night Patrice died?"

"You were there!"

"Yes, but I wonder if my memory is the same as yours?"

"I have already been through this with Charpentier," said Marianne peevishly.

"Tell me."

"I watched you. I watched you from down below in the street. I saw you from the alley, the light in the window, the two of you…" Marianne's voice trailed away.

"And then…."

She looked up at him with hostility. "And then you closed the shutters. You shut me out and I had to imagine it… you with him."

Zac felt an intense stillness wash over him as he listened. Marianne's confusion between him and Raymond had often disturbed him, but at least this time he would get the truth about what had happened. The night Patrice Moreau died.

"You must have been angry," he said.

"I went into the bar. I thought perhaps the two of you would come down to the bar. But you did not. I waited."

"I am sorry."

"Yes, well…" said Marianne. "Sorry."

"Too late," said Zac.

Marianne fixed her glittering eyes to the floor.

"I waited and I waited. I knew. I knew what was happening with the two of you."

"And you met Jasmine in the lane."

"Cow," muttered Marianne.

"What did she say?"

"That I should come with her because you were not coming home to me."

"How did you feel?"

"You know how I felt," snapped Marianne. "Furious. I felt furious."

"Yes, I suppose you did."

"Murderous."

Zac looked up at the pastel walls of the ward and swallowed. He clenched his teeth together.

"As if you could be replaced by Jasmine," she continued. And what did she know of you and me, Raymond? What did anyone know? We were good, weren't we? When it was just us. Just you and me with nobody interfering."

Marianne's voice held a strange kind of pleading. Zac looked at her and nodded impotently.

"He should never have said it," she continued.

"Who?"

"Patrice. What he said."

"What did he say?"

Marianne sighed.

"Why are you being stupid tonight? Why are you pretending?"

"My memory," said Zac, "it is failing me tonight."

"You know that I am not violent, usually."

"No…"

"But to insult me that way, to say that a woman like me could never keep a man like you… who did he think he was? And coming after Jasmine's stupidity, well…"

"Yes," said Zac helplessly.

"He thought he was going to topple us. He would never have done that, would he Raymond?"

Marianne's white hair sat like an electrocuted halo round her head, making her eyes seem darker than ever.

"No."

"And that table…"

"What table?"

"What table! Your intimate little dinner à deux. The flickering candles and crystal glasses, the posy of pink freesias, the noisette of lamb and duchesse potatoes and whole baby carrots in that white tureen and… "

"My God, Marianne!"

Marianne narrowed her eyes.

"My God what?"

"Your memory is extraordinary."

"You think I could forget? I could draw that room, every inch of it."

"What happened then?"

"You know what happened."

"We need to get our stories straight for Charpentier. Every detail."

Marianne's eyes darted wildly.

"Yes. Yes, he will come back. He said so."

"So Patrice and R… Patrice and I were having dinner."

Marianne made a little explosion of irritation against the pillow.

"You were satisfying an altogether different appetite!"

"And you…"

"The carving knife… the noisette of lamb."

"You picked up the knife?"

"I don't remember picking it up but I remember it in my hand. The soft handle of it, the crumbs of lamb on the blade that mixed with his blood… Do you know the strange thing? I never told you this. The effort of pulling the knife out was much greater than putting it in."

Zac stood up unsteadily.

"Where are you going?"

"Nowhere. Nowhere."

He walked to the table at the foot of the bed and poured a glass of water. It was so warm in here. His hand shook as he poured some into the glass. He needed to get out of here.

"Do you want some Marianne?"

She did not answer and he turned his head to view her. She was watching him in that detached way again. She was crazy, he thought suddenly. Crazy. Something had happened here… the fall…. who could ever know now when she was telling the truth?"

"Do you want some?"

She shook her head.

"You cannot trick me."

"I am not trying to trick you!"

"You must not drink it. I warn you. That nurse… she is working with Charpentier."

"I see."

"Don't drink it, Raymond."

Zac put the glass down.

"No."

He watched Marianne for a moment. Her eyelids were drooping. He took a step and her eyes shot open.

"Are you going?"

"In a moment."

"Don't leave me. Charpentier will come back."

"Not tonight."

"How do you know?"

"It's late."

"Is it?"

"Look at the darkness outside the window."

"I don't want to see him."

"He won't come."

"What are we going to tell him?"

It was useless, thought Zac. She was lost in her own version of reality and all he could do now was humour her.

"I'll think of something," he said.

For the first time, a glimmer of a smile crossed Marianne's face and her eyes closed again.

"Yes, of course you will. You will think of something," she murmured.

The effort required to pull a knife out is greater than to plunge it in, Zac thought nauseously, watching her drift into sleep. A river of blood ran like a torrent in his head. He did not know if it was Patrice's blood or Maurice's. He only knew he needed out of here.

He tiptoed to the door. It squeaked as he opened it and he paused, but Marianne did not stir. He closed it quietly behind him and leant against it. The truth, he thought. Was she telling the truth?

CHAPTER THIRTY

Rae and Marianne

RAE

The flat seems full of ghosts, thinks Rae, as she watches the curtains waft gently in the breeze of the open window. She can still hear the faint squeak of Marianne's wheelchair, the scent of the lavender Zac had used to mask the unmistakeable odour of old age and illness. But it is the force of her presence that lingers most strongly, the sense that she fills every room and every corner. Rae misses her. Not for any reasons of guilt, she realises with a sense of wonder. For her, for Marianne.

What a marvellous thought that is. Marianne's body is wrecked and yet she endures; whatever it was that had touched Raymond's spirit all those years ago touches Rae still. She is in there, in a potent, distilled form: the essence of Marianne. For years he thought they were bound only by guilt and fear and recrimination but perhaps it had not been that way at all.

Marianne knew how to love, Rae thought wistfully, looking down into the street. It was the most important lesson Rae had learned after she left. She had disappeared in that taxi in the rain with the yearning of another life and a love that was beyond her fingertips.

She had never managed to grasp it and maybe that was because it was not beyond her at all, but behind her. She had left it behind when she left Marianne. A love that surpassed gender.

She looked down into the street. Maybe Marianne had been right all those years ago. There was no place for her to truly fit. She had lost much to learn it.

A police car turns into the end of the road. Rae watches carelessly as it crawls slowly past the dry cleaner, past the drug store, down towards the pâtisserie. Inching now, it halts at the striped awning, and a figure in the passenger seat looks up towards the window where she stands. The driver bumps the car up on a tiny end of pavement so that one wheel is half on and half off the edge. Both driver and passenger emerge casually, one in uniform, the other a slight man in a neat suit and polished shoes. The one in uniform says something that Rae cannot catch through the open window and throws a packet of mints to the other. The recipient grins. Rae shifts position, peering down to see what they might be interested in down below but she cannot see.

A knock at the door. Crisp. Confident. Rata-tat-tat. She opens it.

"Emile Pascal," says a man holding out ID. "Police."

She does not say come in, but stands back to let them pass, a sudden dryness in her throat. Emile Pascal. The years roll back. So often she has imagined this, but the reality is not what she had guessed. Perhaps, she thinks, leading the way into the sitting room, it is not what it seems. She is conscious of her heels on the wooden floor. They seem thunderous in comparison to the silence inside her head.

There is a glance between the two men as she invites them to sit down. She knows that look. Pascal is slight but there is something aggressively masculine about him. She knows what men think. There is respect in their voices, but contempt in their eyes. She is used to that. The voice lies. She believes their eyes, always the eyes.

This is a cold case review, she hears. They are here to discuss the murder of Patrice Moreau. Pascal's voice, thin and nasal, informs her that he was one of two investigating officers at the time, but his colleague is now retired. Still, it would be nice to clear the matter up.

Rae nods.

Can she confirm that she knew Moreau?

"Yes," says Rae, her voice giving out treacherously. She clears her throat. "Yes," she says clearly.

There is new evidence, says Pascal. Alain Moreau has suggested an identity for "la femme blonde". Pascal speaks softly enough, but his grey blue eyes are hard as pebbles. Rae has heard of la femme blonde?

"Of course."

"We have reason to believe that the blonde woman is you."

Rae says nothing.

"Can you confirm that?" asks Pascal. His companion stays silent, but Rae feels him watching her. She fixes her eyes on a vase on a shelf, yellow and pink tulips, stems twisting curiously with the first breath of decay.

"Madame...?" says Pascal. The word is heavier than it should be. Rae hears the trill of sarcasm in his intonation. *Madame.* What is there to say? What use is denial? The petals have begun to open and when that happens there is no going back. Before long, they will be floating downwards, exposing the core of the bloom.

"Yes," she says finally. "La femme blonde was me. Patrice and I were lovers."

"Did you kill Patrice Moreau?"

Rae looked at him and shook her head.

"I loved him," she says.

"Madame, I am going to ask you that question again. Did you murder Patrice Moreau?"

"Monsieur, you have asked the question twice. My answer is the same twice. I did not."

"Then who did?"

The images flash through Rae's mind. A distraught Marianne, the crash of crockery, light glinting off steel, blood and gravy and tears and trembling. And Marianne now, a pathetic heap of uncontrolled limbs and impulses. It is not possible to bring this to her door. It is time to love, as Marianne loved. In any case, Rae has always known deep down that she carried a heavy burden of responsibility whether she held the knife or not. To be careless with another's emotions… perhaps that, too, was a crime.

"Who did, Madame?"

"I do not know."

Pascal stood. In the ensuing jumble of words he spoke about her arrest on the suspicion of murder, Rae heard little. However long it had taken, coming back to Saint Estelle had, after all, been her downfall. She sat suddenly, her knees buckling beneath her, overcome suddenly by a weight that had been thirty years in the making.

———

MARIANNE

I see you, Raymond. I see you by my bed; in the shadows by the window as the moonlight falls soft and silvery when my eyes close in sleep; in the breaking of the red stained dawn when they open again. You flit in and out, a constant presence, a reassurance, a source of meaning.

I do not have long. I have heard Shona say as much, in that stupid, hoarse, stage-whisper. A day or two, she says to you, adding that pneumonia is the friend of the old. Stupid platitudes. I will last a month just to prove her wrong. Then dissolve, dissolve into the evening dew, glistening on the petals of the rhododendrons in the garden, evaporating into nothing in the heat of the morning sun. And if I am wrong? If something remains... well, I will haunt the stupid cow.

But not you. I will not haunt you. I will blow round you softly, like a warm summer breeze, soothing you until you join me. You will hear me whispering your name when the wind whips the dry autumn leaves; taste me in the tang of crashing waves when they pound against the rocks and spray fine, salt tears on your cheeks and lips. I will run with those tears.

I regret the things that lie between us. I regret Patrice. The heat of the moment, the purple cloud of jealousy that exploded into toxic, jewelled atoms around me, filling everything. Is it the strongest emotion of all jealousy? Stronger even than love? Why do people say jealousy is yellow? Yellow is too clean a colour. In my mind it is purple: deep, solid, opaque, staining everything it spills onto. Purple blood.

But there is one thing I do not regret. For all the violence and the pain and the trauma, I knew love in all its extremes. I lived, I loved, I felt. My love was complete in the way a full, bright moon is complete, a solitaire in the darkness. It was like a field of crops where the excess withers and rots amid groaning abundance. It overflowed like a river bursting its banks in the high spring tide, flooding everything within its reach. But Raymond, I felt, didn't I? I loved? It was not a half love, a crescent moon, a neat yield, a trim river flowing primly within its own confines.

What else is there? What else is life for but to experience that full connection finally being made, the heat and light exploding inside you, and in the ensuing brightness reaching out to another human being and saying this is me, this is everything. Take me, own me, heal me as I am. I loved you as you were, Raymond. You can never say that I did not. But I did not heal you. The more unconditionally I offered myself to you, the more conditional your acceptance became. But that is life. That is risk. That is love. The lover and the loved. The giver and the receiver.

I do not feel that it is over. It is true that I must go and you must stay. You have freedom and I do not. But what existed between us was done and cannot be undone. It remains in the history of the world, the dictionary of events. The energy of it remains in the atmosphere for eternity. When it is time to go, when the star finally shoots into oblivion in the night sky, the end computer finally crashes, the shutdown will be full of flashing disparate memories of life. The heat, the haze, the smoky nightclub blues; the scent of almond croissant, the curl of lilac ribbon... and you. Always you.